"A poignant portrait of a town where fate's kind and unkind blows are dealt out amid the Blue Moon Cafe, Myers' Hardware, Wilkaby's Five-and-Dime—all on the banks of the fictional Bright River. . . . The well-crafted prose of Greene makes it flow as smoothly as her Bright River. . . . These characters are complex and strong."

The Detroit Free Press

"This is a book that startles and grips the heart, a first novel written with such sureness and sensitivity that it will appeal to a wide readership. . . . Mundane on the surface, but tumultuous within, the lives of these and other residents of Hooke's Crossing, a small rural community bounded by Bright River, will change in surprising and heartbreaking ways. Greene has a marvelous command of language; images vividly transform the prosaic world and let us see with her characters' eyes. . . . Her gift is to illuminate the nuances of human relationships in unsparing but compassionate clarity."

Publishers Weekly

Please turn the page for more glittering reviews of
BRIGHT RIVER TRILOGY

BRIGHT RIVER TRILOGY

"Greene makes you ache for her characters: their ambitions, though small and simple, are never realized. The best they can do is to wake up and make it through another day. It's courage at its most basic that gives *Bright River Trilogy* its rousing dignity."

Glamour

ANNIE GREENE

"Greene has a feel for the emotional undercurrents of middle-class American life that is too rarely encountered in what passes for serious fiction in this country these days. . . . How Darcy matters most, Greene seems to be saying, is not as himself but as a man who changed the lives of others. And those others are beautifully portrayed."

Jonathan Yardley
Washington Post Book World

Bright River Trilogy

Annie Greene

BALLANTINE BOOKS • NEW YORK

To
MY HUSBAND

Library of Congress Catalog Card Number: 84-13876

ISBN 0-345-32902-3

This edition published by arrangement with Simon & Schuster

Manufactured in the United States of America

First Ballantine Books Edition: March 1986

The author gratefully acknowledges permission to reprint lines from the following:

"Canzone" in *W.H. Auden: Collected Poems*, edited by Edward Mendelson. Copyright © 1976. Reprinted by permission of Random House, Inc.

"East Coker" in *Four Quartets*, copyright 1943 by T.S. Eliot; renewed 1971 by Esme Valerie Eliot. Reprinted by permission of Harcourt Brace Jovanovich, Inc.

"Unharvested" from *The Poetry of Robert Frost*, edited by Edward Connery Lathem. Copyright 1936 by Robert Frost; copyright © 1964 by Lesley Frost Ballantine; copyright © 1969 by Holt, Rinehart and Winston. Reprinted by permission of Holt, Rinehart and Winston.

"Know Deeply, Know Thyself More Deeply" from *The Complete Poems of D. H. Lawrence*. Collected and edited by Vivian de Sola Pinta and F. Warren Roberts. Copyright © 1964, 1971 by Angelo Ravagli and C.M. Weekley, Executors of the Estate of Frieda Lawrence Ravagli. Reprinted by permission of Viking Penguin, Inc.

Lilly

OVER the rise there you can see Bright River. I live on Broad Street now and I can't see it, but I still feel it as if its waters flow in my veins. I suppose it was growing up in sight of the water that makes me feel kin to it. Even now on this cold morning, I imagine that my body, chilled and stiff in the joints, moves with the same icy dawdle as the winter river.

Our furnace hasn't decided whether it will heat this morning or not. And until that cantankerous contrivance shakes itself awake, my knees will bend like rusty hinges. I pull my sweater tighter around me, folding my arms and tucking my hands close to my sides. The last stair creaks under my foot. As I walk down the dawn-lit hall I can hear Jingles, our dog, padding toward me across the kitchen floor. Click, click, click, his nails meet the worn linoleum. His pace is lazy and slow. He is barely awake.

As I pass my son Darcy's room, I see the door is wide open. The shade is raised at a window that glows an uncertain gray and the bed is neatly made and empty. Damn that boy! Thirty-five years old and can't find his way home. A tiny wave of fear passes over me but I put it quickly behind me. God knows it's not the first time he hasn't come home and he's no boy, for crying out loud.

I flick the light switch in the kitchen and the yellow light gives the room a false look of warmth. Jingles nudges his wet nose into my hand. "Oh, go lie down, you old beggar," I say entering the kitchen. He wags his tail halfheartedly. The furnace lets out a tentative bleat and roars to life. Ah.

The sink spigots hold the cold as only metal can. When I was a child we had to pump our water outside. In the winter you had to be careful that your hand didn't freeze to the iron of the handle. Once we had a maid who let my sister Ivy and me bundle up and pump the water into buckets from the house. When the water gushed from the spout, slivers of ice swam in its flow like bright fish.

I fill the coffeepot and put water into a pan for oatmeal for my grandson, Tim. For a moment, I warm my hands over the two ragged rings of blue flame on top of the stove. The faint odor of gas hangs like a teasing hint of heat in the air, then vanishes.

Suddenly the telephone shrills in the silence. Both Jingles and I jump. Fear traces a sharp pattern over my heart. Darcy. The kitchen clock says 6:30. I walk as quickly as my creaky joints allow to the telephone in the hall.

"Hello."

"Hello, Lilly."

"For crying out loud, Evelyn, you scared me to death."

"Oh? Why?"

"It's six thirty in the morning here!"

Ivy says Evelyn probably doesn't even know what time it is where she is, much less here in Hooke's Crossing. She'll call at most any time and I can see where Ivy might be right. To tell the truth, I can't imagine the sun just rising here when it's high in the sky in whatever far place Evelyn happens to be in. It's as if she is calling us across time rather than distance, as if we could unravel her strange life for her with the jump we have on her at our end of the telephone.

"I suppose you heard the news," says Evelyn.

"What news, dear?"

"Why, our vigil, of course. You must be busting to say, 'I told you so.' "

4

"I haven't heard anything."

"Well, Lilly, I must say, you're as provincial as ever. I don't suppose the end of the world would be news in Hooke's Crossing."

"Really, Evelyn, I don't know what you're talking about."

"The vigil, Lilly, the vigil! There were hundreds of us. All the papers here were full of it."

"Where are you?"

I ask this idly, knowing she won't answer. We only hear from Evelyn over the phone, and she will never tell us exactly where she is, not even Tim. Perhaps she fancies we will come after her. I could tell her there's little enough chance of that.

"Wouldn't you just like to know," she says.

"Not really," I say, "and whatever it was in the papers, I missed it."

"I warned Tim, you know, that the end of the world was at hand. I suppose he never mentioned *that*."

"I don't want you talking to him about things like that. He worries enough as it is."

"Oh, I knew you couldn't help gloating," she says. "It must make you very happy to think of us all standing there waiting last Tuesday as the moment came and went."

"For heaven's sake, Evelyn."

" 'No end of the world,' you can say. It must give you great satisfaction."

"That the world didn't end?" I laugh. "Yes, that does give me satisfaction. Good Lord, girl." Oh, I don't have Tim's patience.

"I want to speak to Tim," Evelyn says icily.

"He's not awake yet. Why don't you call him after school?"

"You always keep him from me."

It's not true. I don't keep him from her. It's not that I'm above doing it, but he insists on talking to her and she is his mother after all. This is all he has of her, these strange phone calls. None of us has seen her since she left when Tim was a baby. I wonder what she could do

5

that would make Tim turn away. It's strange how we always seem to return in some way to our parents. I suppose they are the only stars we know to steer by and it doesn't matter how haphazardly they are placed in our sky.

"Call back when he's awake, Evelyn," I say.

"There's no way to beat the harm the eagle brings, Lilly," she says ominously and hangs up.

Good riddance. Maybe she will forget to call him back. Her phone calls eat at him for days, nibble his heart and mind in tiny bites. "Gran, how do we know the world isn't going to end? What if it did and we weren't prepared like Mama says, would we go to hell?" "I wonder what burns in hell if your body is here." And that's just the latest tangent she's been on. Before that it was flying saucers. It is such an intrusion to me! Tim's phone calls from his mother run through our lives like the work of some mad seamstress whose helter-skelter stitches bind us against our will in designs only she can see.

The coffee has begun to perk while I am on the phone. Its warm, dark odor fills the air. Overhead, I can hear Tim beginning to stir. I pour oatmeal into the boiling water in the pan. Tim's footsteps above are hesitant and shuffling like a ghost dragging chains. He's a slow waker. The sun has begun to rise and the window over the sink glitters a frosty gold.

When the coffee is ready, I take a cup to the table. As I sip, the ache begins to go out of my fingers. I half listen for Darcy coming in and again a small fear pricks the quiet morning. It's no premonition. I feel it every time Darcy stays away. Likely as not, he's passed out somewhere, at Jeff Maynes's little cabin or even at Ellen Gibbs's. I can picture my son lying in a rumpled bed while Ellen tries to wake him before her father catches them. Although what Melvin Gibbs would do, I can't imagine, fool that he is. I see Melvin often at Myers' Hardware where he works. He tells me nearly every time I see him that he is the first manager of the store in four generations whose name is not Myers. He tells it like the Myers family have passed over their own to have him run their business. The truth is Tom Myers, who was to have the store from his father, has gone into medicine and left town. Maybe I don't give the man the credit he deserves but it looks to me as if Darcy and Ellen are pretty safe from Melvin. But look at me, thinking the worst of poor Ellen just on what they say about her in town. Lord knows Darcy's never said a word. And Ellen is a delicate bird of a girl, soft-spoken, even prim, and I hear she's engaged to some fellow over in Glen Green. Yet, they say terrible things about her in town. But then the people in Hooke's Crossing can surely talk about this and that and everything that's nobody's business. Don't I know all about that!

I hear Tim's step on the stair and rise to stir the oatmeal bubbling on the stove. The dog moves against my leg, his tail wagging gently.

"Good morning, Tim," I say as my grandson comes through the kitchen door.

"Morning, Gran," he says kissing my cheek. He turns toward the table, nearly tripping over the dog.

Tim is tall, almost six feet. At fourteen, he's strong and long-limbed like my late husband's people. But as much as he looks like my husband, he doesn't derive the confidence from his size that his grandfather did. Tim seems buried in his big body as if someone had hung too much flesh on too small a frame.

"Did the phone ring this morning?" Tim asks as he takes down a bowl for his cereal.

"Yes. Your mother."

"Oh. How was she?"

"Same as ever," I say, "crazy as a loon." I turn from the stove and dish oatmeal into his bowl. The color rises in his cheeks. From the steamy pot or my remark, I can't tell.

"Sometimes she's like everybody else," he says sitting down at the table.

"If you say so," I say.

He eats in silence for a while. His hair, lank and blond, hides his eyes. "Dad's not home?" he asks.

"No."

"Did he come home at all last night?"

"No."

I carry a glass of milk for him to the table. "Can we go look for him?" he asks me.

"Tim, I want you to go to school."

"I will, I promise, after."

"No, you go to school first thing, and don't worry about your father."

"I'm not worried."

"Yes, you are."

"I just like to know, that's all."

"Remember the time he went to New York and came back with gifts for everybody?" I say.

"Yeah, he called the second day and said he didn't remember how he got there."

"All right. Don't worry then."

"I could just walk to town with you when you go to work. I could do that before school and catch the bus up by Ames's."

"Oh, all right, if you promise to go to school."

"I promise," he says and begins to eat more hurriedly.

Tim doesn't always go to school. Even when I see him on the bus I may still get a call at the stationery store where I work. "Mrs. Blunt, this is John Welles at county high. Is Tim sick this morning?"

No, no, I must tell him, Tim is not sick. He's a big, healthy boy who hardly ever gets a cold. "Why doesn't he come to school?" asks Mr. Welles.

"Why don't you go to school?" I ask Tim.

"I don't know," he says, "I just don't like it there."

Tim has no friends. He's not a fractious boy, looking to get into trouble. That would be like his father as a boy. Tim is hiding. One time, Sheriff Jim Atherton found him in the woods north of town. Jim said he had a little campsite as if he'd spent a lot of time there. I'd like to think of him in the open air, shouting, rousing the birds and scattering them to the sky. But probably he is quiet, alone and dreamy, scuffling through the moist musty leaves, inhaling the loamy wet odor of the woods and trailing his hand along the convolutions of the trees.

He is alone. Mostly there's no one up there but Owen Coulter who lives somewhere in those woods. Owen went away to World War II and when he came back to Hooke's Crossing, he built himself a shack in the hills. No one but his brother, Slade, has talked to him since. The last thing he ever said to anyone in town was to Sam Dudley. "People are no damned good," he said, and I guess he hasn't changed his mind since. People stumble across Owen from time to time, but they don't stay to talk. He's tall with a long beard and hair that looks like something chewed it off short. Earl Begley said when he came across him, Owen was kneeling by a stream drinking water from his hands. He said his eyes were like something wild caught at bay and that he turned when he saw Earl and ran off through the trees as if he were running for his life. I suppose he's scared now thinking all those years on the evil of human beings and nothing to prove him otherwise. He and Tim would surely make a pair, the two of them up there alone with only their own thoughts to try to make sense out of the world.

Later, when Tim and I walk out onto the porch, our heads are wreathed in steam from our breath. Tim chains Jingles to the side of the porch. The dog prances in the cold air, barking excitedly. "Ssshh," hisses Tim but Jingles barks until he spies someone advancing from the end of the block. I know without looking that it is no one we know because the dog subsides with a whimper and slinks under the porch. Jingles only barks at people he knows. Strangers are another story; he hides under the porch. He's not much of a watchdog but his barking is a joyful noise . . . all is well.

The sky is clear, and the wind from the river is sharp despite the sun. The snow piled along the street sparkles with a sugary glitter that doesn't bear looking at for too long. Tim walks beside me, his feet sliding in and out of his unbuckled galoshes with a windy whoosh. His arms swing awkwardly as if they are alien and inconvenient to him. His feet always seem to be several steps ahead of the rest of him with perverse minds of their own. As we walk along this morning, he puts his hands in his pockets, takes them out again, and then clasps them behind his back.

Broad Street, where we walk, runs parallel to the river. Because the air is crisp and clear this morning, we can hear the ferry clanging into its moorings at this side of the river. It's early yet but later in the morning cars bound for the city will begin to line up. There are more cars every year what with the new houses going up outside town. Those houses seem to spring up quick as toadstools after a rain. I guess there are new ways of building nowadays.

The houses on Broad Street weren't built so easily in their time. They are big houses, venerable and serene on their neat squares of lawn. The trees around them soar like cathedrals into the sky. The river even at its highest mark has only dared to lap at the farthest curb of this street. The houses are old and so are the families who live here. On this street then are the doctors, the lawyers, the small-town elite. Many of their ancestors settled this town before it was even Hooke's Crossing. My family is from Philadelphia on my mother's side and with only three generations of my father's family in Hooke's Crossing, we have been interlopers. My father was clerk of wills at the courthouse for most of his life. He retired before the county seat was moved out of Hooke's Crossing. My family was respectable but certainly the people on Broad Street, including Aaron's parents, considered that I had married above myself when I married Aaron. My mother, Philadelphian that she was, sniffed at such small-town arrogance. But my husband's family rested their pride on the fact that their family was older here than anyone could remember. There had always been Blunts in Hooke's Crossing. All that's left of the family bloodline now in town are Darcy, Tim and old Hannah, Aaron's mother, who doesn't speak to any of the rest of us. And much as it must pain Hannah to think of it, my little family are still the Blunts of Broad Street, our house, grayer and shabbier than all the rest, standing among the others in the same stately shade of old trees.

As we pass these houses, there will be people raising a shade or pulling back a curtain to see us. There are lights on at Irma Carey's. She is probably looking out at us from the respectable comfort of her warm house this very minute and saying to her brother, Joe, "There go Lilly Blunt and that grandson of hers. Going to collect Darcy, I imagine." Then they will both shake their heads and say, "Tut, tut, poor Lilly," as if they are truly aggrieved. Irma and I went all through school together. And even when we were little girls in the school yard, you could always find her whispering behind her hand about somebody. Some things never change. I'm glad I made Tim comb his hair before we came out.

We turn a corner and walk through two blocks of houses that are not so grand as the houses on Broad Street. Soon we are downtown and passing the long stone wall that runs around the old county courthouse. Hooke's Crossing hasn't been the county seat for years, not since the first big highways came through the state and bypassed our town. The courthouse serves as the sheriff's office and houses the town government.

Across the street, the sun strikes the marquee on the movie theater. The same movie is playing that was playing last week and the week before that. Tim and I have seen it twice. The streets are nearly empty and in the early-morning light the plate-glass windows of the Dairy Maid Luncheonette and Wilkaby's five-and-dime stare at us blankly. The Dairy Maid is open for business, its window steamy in the cold. Wilkaby's will open at nine. Farther up the street, the big clock at the top of the bank says 7:30. A man is opening the door. I don't recognize him. He is young and his clothes have an odd arrow-thin

11

cut to them. There was a time when my husband, Aaron, was with the bank, that I knew everyone there.

At the next corner, we can see Jeff Maynes's filling station. Above it on a long pole there is a sign that revolves when the station is open. The sign spells out the name of the station over a red, winged horse. It turns, the red horse glinting and galloping in an endless round above the town. As we approach the station this morning, we can see Darcy's car parked near the air pump. Darcy bought the car years ago with a veterans' loan. It was a flashy car then, long with a convertible top. But now it's old and battered, its night-sky blue paint an undistinguished gray.

Jeff Maynes who owns the station stands out front, a steaming cup in his hands. Jeff and Darcy have been friends since grammar school. They joined the army together and went to Laos to fight. That was before Vietnam. There are people now who say that is a bad war. I don't know. All I do know is that when Darcy and Jeff went, people were still proud to see a man in uniform.

"Morning, Mrs. Blunt," says Jeff. "Morning, Tim." Jeff has the kind of smile that makes you feel as though he's been waiting just for you. His hair is as fair as Darcy's is dark. "Salt and Pepper" I used to call them when they were children.

"Morning, Jeff," I say. "How are you?"

"I'm fine, ma'am. And you?"

"Have you seen Daddy, Mr. Maynes?" asks Tim quickly. I suppose he is impatient with our grown-up way of conducting business.

"We're looking for Darcy, Jeff," I say. "Have you seen him?"

"No, ma'am. I ain't seen Darcy since he left his car here and that would be two days ago. Saturday morning. It's all fixed now," he says, patting the car's dull fender tenderly.

"He didn't come home last night," I say.

"Well, you know Darcy, Mrs. Blunt."

"Yes, we just like to know he's all right."

"We just like to know is all," says Tim.

"Hey, I know that, ace," Jeff says punching Tim lightly in the arm. Tim is pleased and squares his shoulders, pulling his too short coat farther up his wrists.

"Have you tried the jail?" Jeff asks softly, staring up toward the turning horse.

"Not yet," I say. "Thank you, Jeff, we'll head over that way. If you do see Darcy, tell him we're looking for him, will you please."

"Yes, ma'am, I sure will." Jeff waves as we move off.

We turn back toward the courthouse. Crossing the street we pass under the statue of Colonel Harmon Hooke that stands on the grassy strip that divides Hooke Avenue, our main street. Colonel Hooke was a Confederate officer who led his men across Bright River at just the path the ferry plies. Hooke's Hellions later fought at Manassas. Colonel Hooke now stands erect and stalwart, his hat raised toward the river in a salute. He casts a shadow, blue and brave, across our path. I shiver in the shade and as we pass the courthouse again, Tim and I both glance toward its high arched doorway. One spring morning we found Darcy there passed out, his cheek against the cool white stone. We carried him home that day. Tim wasn't as big as he is now. What a sight we must have made . . . a rumpled old woman and a grim-faced boy supporting Darcy, rubber-legged, between us.

I knew how hard Tim took it because he never asked a single question. He spent even more time alone. I suppose he had to bend and turn that day in his mind, press it through the fine, pale colors of his daydreams until he could live with it. Darcy was pained to see the boy brood so and even quit drinking for a while.

Up ahead at the corner is the stop for the bus for Gatonsville, the new county seat forty-five miles away. Ellen Gibbs is waiting there. "Hurry, I want to talk to Ellen Gibbs," I say to Tim and we pick up our step. He says, "Slow down, Gran." He worries I'll fall.

"Ellen," I call as we get closer. She turns toward us. She is small and trim with the glowing good looks of her German mother. Greta Gibbs is a Schumacher, one of a scattering of German families who settled on small farms around Hooke's Crossing when my father was a boy. Ellen wears white gloves, small banners of defiance to the town gossips. That's right, Ellen, let them talk, as though you had to earn the right to wear white gloves.

"Ellen, how are you, dear?" I say as we reach the bus stop.

"I'm fine. How are you, Mrs. Blunt."

"Fine."

"Tim?" says Ellen with a smile and Tim blushes, his hair fairly standing on end.

An awkward silence falls and then Ellen says, "And Darcy, how is he?" Her eyes are anxious despite her even tone and again I feel my heart give way a little in my chest.

"We haven't seen him since yesterday morning," I say.

"Oh," says Ellen. Her voice is very small and she bites her lip.

We all look away up the street, watching for the bus.

"So you're off to work, Ellen."

"Yes, ma'am."

"Where do you work?"

"It's an import-export firm that ships out of Baltimore."

"That sounds very interesting."

"It isn't really. Mostly what I do is type invoices." She shrugs. "But it's a job."

"Well, a pretty girl like you will be married before long, I'm sure," I say smiling.

"Oh, no," she says flustered. "Well, yes. I'm engaged actually."

"Yes, I believe I heard something about that. Anyone I know?" I ask. Tim stirs restlessly at my elbow.

"No," she says absently, "someone from work. He's from Glen Green. And you say Darcy didn't come home last night at all?"

14

"No."

"Well, one time when I was getting gas at Jeff Maynes's he said Darcy sometimes had business in Baltimore." Her eyes were grave and her cheeks were red from the cold.

"Baltimore?" I say. "Well, yes, he did have a job in a bar there once, I believe. Was it Baltimore, Tim?"

"I don't know if it was right in Baltimore but someplace close by there, I think," says Tim.

"Oh, well, whatever," I say, "I'm sure he's just fine. Just fine."

Tim nods vigorously and Ellen says as the bus pulls to the curb, "Oh, yes, ma'am. He's fine, I just know it."

She steps onto the bus. The driver greets her with an eager smile. "Good-bye," she calls over her shoulder in her high sweet voice.

"She's nice," says Tim as the bus pulls away.

"Yes. How do you know Miss Gibbs?" I ask him.

"Sometimes when I'm uptown with Daddy we see her and he always stops to talk."

I glance at the bank clock and say to him, "Honey, it's time to go to school. Go on up to Ames's and catch the bus."

"Aw, Gran, come on," he begs, "I just want to find Daddy, then I'll go."

"It'll be too late by then for the bus. Go on now. You promised me. So do what I say. Your daddy is fine."

"What if he's not?"

"Tim," I say sternly.

"Most of the time he calls if he's not coming home."

"Sometimes he doesn't."

"When he doesn't, Gran, do you think we never cross his mind at all?"

"I don't think that's it, honey. I suspect he just passes out before he gets around to it."

"I guess."

"Sure. Now you go on. Bye-bye."

Reluctantly he turns and starts up the street toward the school bus stop.

"You better go to school," I call after him. "You promised."

"I know," he says but I can barely hear him. His fine hair waves like winter yellow grass in a sudden swirl of cold air.

When Tim disappears around the corner, I walk toward the courthouse. Its big metal doors clank shut behind me and I take the familiar route to the sheriff's office. "Morning, Mrs. Blunt," the three clerks greet me as I walk in. Sheriff Jim Atherton steps out of the open door of his office. He is a large man with graying hair. His eyes always seem full of regret as if someone had just told him something he didn't want to know. "My, my, Mrs. Blunt," he says, "its awful nice to see you. What can I do for you today?" Jim is gallant. He acts as if each visit I make to his office is my first.

"Darcy didn't come home last night. I'd like you to keep an eye out for him."

"Oh?" says Jim. "Well now, you hurt my feelings, Mrs. Blunt. You know I always look after Darcy. Darcy and I are old buddies. I don't want you to worry about a thing. He'll turn up and I'm going to give him the devil for worrying you."

As I start for the door Jim takes my arm. His touch feels foreign, too large, too warm. It's been a long time since any man but Darcy has touched me.

"Well, thank you, Jim," I say moving away from him. "It's not that I'm seriously worried. I just wanted you to know."

"And I appreciate that."

"All right then, good-bye. I'll call you if I see him first," I say going out into the hall. "He's probably home right now."

"I'll bet that's exactly where he is. Don't you worry now." Jim's hearty voice booms in the empty hallway.

My heart feels lighter as I step out of the stuffy courthouse into the clear cold air. Our conversation, Jim's and mine, is a litany we have repeated so many times I'm soothed by the very sound of it. All this walking

16

through town, seeing Jeff, seeing Ellen, seeing Jim, is a ritual I perform to appease some vengeful god. And if each step is taken with care, if every sacrifice and incantation receives its proper due, this god will yield up my son unharmed to me.

I look at the clock once again. It's too early yet to go to the shop. Mr. Enderly, my boss, will still be at the Dairy Maid having one last cup of coffee. I turn away from the center of town and head down a side street. After two blocks I come to my sister Ivy's house. I hesitate at the sight of her husband Otis' car in the driveway. His watch must be broken. I don't believe he's ever been a minute late in his life. I approach the door knowing Otis will be gone soon. I raise my hand to knock but the door flies open suddenly. Otis is poised in the doorway to rush out. He lets out a yelp of surprise.

"Morning, Otis," I say laughing.

"Morning, Lilly," says Otis straightening his hat. He makes no pretense of being glad to see me. "Ivy's in the back. I'm off to work."

"Tell Ida I said hello," I say as he hurtles past me.

"Ida?" he says stopping short and turning to face me.

"Ida Henson. The secretary at the plant."

"Is that her name, with the black hair?" He looks astonished.

"Yes, Otis."

He turns and walks to his car, shaking his head. That's just like Otis not to know. For crying out loud, Ida's worked out at the electric plant as long as he has.

When I step into Ivy's house I call, "Ivy!" Her house is small and warm. She calls back from the kitchen, "Lilly, honey, come on back."

In the kitchen, Ivy greets me with a kiss. "Well, hi, honey," she smiles, her cheeks rising round and red as tiny suns beneath her eyes. The sun outside lights the gold rims of two coffee cups on the table. One cup bears the mark of Ivy's bright red lipstick. Through the window where the snow has drifted, there are pieces of toast strewn for the birds. "Here," says Ivy bustling over to me, "take your coat off."

The small shiny kitchen trembles under her weight. Ivy is enormous and seems to be in a perpetual flow like the sea heaving under her clothes. I'm still amazed by her size after all these years. I remember her wrists, frail as bird bones, when she was a girl. All the young men in Hooke's Crossing wanted to marry her.

"How are the boys?" she asks bringing coffee cake to the table.

"Darcy hasn't been home since yesterday morning."

"Well, he's probably just fine, don't you think?" Ivy settles across from me and cuts herself a piece of cake.

"Oh, I suppose."

"Of course he is, honey," she says.

"You know, Ivy," I say, "it's occurred to me that I have failed all the men I love. Even Aaron. And look at Darcy, worthless as a bent penny. . . ."

"Lilly!"

"I don't fool myself, Ivy. And Tim . . . my Lord, I sure don't know any way to mend him."

Ivy cocks her head, her red hair is fiery in the sunlight. "Lilly, I'm surprised to hear you talk like that. Aaron was a fine man who made a mistake, that's all. And Darcy, why, honey, he could charm the birds right out of the trees. And you know little Tim couldn't be a sweeter boy." Ivy takes my hand across the table and smiles.

"You're right," I say. "I guess I just got up on the wrong side of the bed this morning."

"Sure, that's all it is. You'll go home tonight and there'll be Darcy big as life."

But in the evening as I walk home from work, I still haven't heard from my son. Worry has gathered like storm clouds in my mind. I imagine seeing him tonight and saying to him, "Darcy, for Lord's sake, what are you thinking about to worry Tim so?" As I turn onto our block, I can see Tim and Jingles in the front yard. The dog chases the boy while Tim holds a stick out of his reach. It really is too cold to be playing outside and I know that Tim would be in the house if Darcy were there. Darcy doesn't work steadily. Often when I come home in the winter, he and Tim will be there together, listening to the radio, playing cards or making a mess of my kitchen trying to get dinner.

"Tim," I call approaching him, and his face brightens at the sight of me.

Jessie

In my beginning is my end. In succession
Houses rise and fall, crumble, are extended,
Are removed, destroyed, restored. . . .

—T.S. ELIOT

I haven't seen Darcy in days. Not long ago I wouldn't have worried. Darcy, I would have thought, tomcatting, no doubt. But now it's not so easy. With all I've had on my mind, I'd only begun to miss him today. No, that's not true. I've missed him every day but it's only today that it seems odd not to have heard from him. I think of calling his mother but it seems too awkward. Does he talk about my father and me to her? Would she know who I am? I realize that although Darcy talks often of his mother and son, I never think of him with any connections but the ones he's made for himself. Maybe if I had lived all my life in Hooke's Crossing, if I had seen Darcy in mischief as a boy or seen him at a high-school dance, he wouldn't seem to me such an improbable citizen of Hooke's Crossing. What a terrible little town! All the streets slide down to Bright River where the dank smell of the tomb floats in the shallows with the trash. All the buildings of the town seem to lean toward the water as though seeking its power for their small pretensions. I can only be glad Dad chose to live here on Willow Creek Road three miles from town.

My father dreamed of this place, this farm, all his days as an army barber. He had grown up on a farm that was sold for taxes when he was eighteen. He spent the next thirty years of his life working his way back to the country. "Must have cut a million heads," he often said, "and sometimes I'd get to dreaming and the hair coming off them clippers seemed like nothing so much as threshed wheat." We didn't come here when he would have liked. My mother was long dead, and I was nearly grown. Our unsettled life in the service has left me always feeling a stranger to Hooke's Crossing, but it seemed not to mark him. He took up life here as if he'd never spent a day away from a farm.

I could use some of my father's stubborn rootedness, especially tonight without Darcy's good-hearted consolation when my life seems unfurled, unwound to some desperate extreme. I stand by the wide window in the dining room, thinking of Darcy and Dad. The room is the hard blue of a cold sunset. Outside, I can see the dog kennels and the runs. Snow is piled around the fencing where I've cleared the runs. Only Queenie's pup, Ginger, is outside. She paces behind the kennel fence. Beyond the kennels, the cornstalks in the field poke spiky fingers through the snow. A small mountain, no more than a swell in the earth, rises black in the distance.

I sigh, cradling my protruding belly. I'm never prepared for winter, no matter how many I begin. It's such a closed-in time and old ghosts walk with a heavier tread and new ones dog your every step. And as I stand here in the winter gloom, time and memory all travel forward from a day last fall.

It was late autumn, that time when the slide into winter is swift. One week walking the garden finds the cabbage heads split open across the tops oozing the juices of their ripeness and the next week may find their leaves thin and dry as paper from the cold. That evening I was standing at the stove. The chicken frying in the pan before me spit and jumped as though it still held some protesting nerve. When I turned I could see my father through the window. He squatted by the kennels, his fingers curled through the wire of the fence. He was smiling at the pups lunging and barking in their tin-whistle yips.

I pushed the chicken around in the pan, aware that I

was holding a protective hand over my stomach. I had been to Baltimore that morning. The doctor there said there is a gradual thickening of my uterine wall that nothing can reverse. There would have to be a hysterectomy. I'm twenty-six years old. I pressed my hand into the soft flesh of my belly. Traitor body! growing lumpy shapes out of sight, below the surface like a potato!

I jumped as the screen door slammed behind my father. "Smells good in here, Jess," he called, kicking off his muddy boots in the pantry. He padded across the kitchen in his socks. There was a hole in the toe of one of them. He lifted the pot lids on the stove, sniffing.

"Fried chicken, lima beans, stewed tomatoes and I smell biscuits," he said as if he'd discovered gold. Every meal is a celebration to my tall, spare father. He marks off his days by mealtimes and he can tell you what he had for lunch a week ago Tuesday.

He reached out to pick a piece of skin from the chicken in the pan. I clutched my stomach, suddenly furious. I said, "Dad, you have a hole in your sock." I might have caught him stealing the way my voice accused him.

"Yeah, you're right, Jess. Noticed that this morning, in fact." I swear there was a note of pride in his tone.

"Then why did you put it on? There are other socks in the drawer."

"I don't mind wearing it," he said.

"It makes the hole bigger, for heaven's sake," I shouted.

He edged away from my anger. "Didn't look at it that way, Jess. I'll sure remember it, though." He retreated into the bathroom to wash up for dinner. I knew I'd been mean and took extra care over turning the neck of the chicken because that's his favorite part.

I should tell him about today, I thought. But I cringed at the idea. I could see him listening, listening, his long ears red with embarrassment. There were huge areas of bodily function that my father and I never discussed. When I was twelve, he'd had the nurse at school call me in one day and tell me what he thought a girl my age should know. I had always wondered how, in his fear-some shyness, he'd gotten across to her what he wanted.

At the dinner table he gave the food a regretful glance and then looked at me. "Uh, Jess," he said, "seems to me you been awful cooped up here of late, what with canning and all. Why don't you go to town for a movie or to buy a new hat or something?"

"Dad," I laughed, "nobody wears hats anymore."

"Is that so?" he said shaking his head. "No hats. Well, think of that."

He was truly perplexed and that made me laugh again. He laughed too, forking three pieces of chicken onto his plate.

It was later that night when I was awakened by sounds from the yard. It was hours before dawn. But when I looked from my bedroom window, I could see Dad down in the kennels. I put my coat on over my night-gown and walked outside. Dad knelt in one of the runs. There was a lantern by his side. Our prize dam, Queenie, lay on the ground in front of him. "Ummm, ummm," Dad crooned to her. The dog's eyes were white-rimmed and she panted rapidly.

When I came into the run, Dad said quietly, "She can't whelp." I nodded and knelt down beside him. Queenie's chest heaved. She didn't whimper. Animals can suffer pain in such awesome resignation. The sounds she made before Dad came would have been soft, yet he heard her. I've known him to sleep through thunder-storms that shook the house but he heard Queenie the same way he always seemed to hear me if I cried out at night as a child.

Dad gently fingered Queenie's swollen belly. "It's a breech. Can feel the head right here."

He rolled the dog over. Beneath her tail two tiny, slickly furred legs protruded. Dad kneaded Queenie and gave a tentative tug on the legs. "All right, now, here we go. Here we go," he whispered. He gave another light tug and the pup's body and head popped out like a cork out of a bottle. Queenie put her head down. Dad

26

tapped the puppy's narrow ribbed chest. The pup began to wriggle inside the clear membrane of its birth sac. Queenie tried to move toward the pup to clean it.

"Easy, Queenie," Dad said, "I'll take care of it."

He pierced the sac with his finger and pulled the sticky membrane away. He held the pup close to the lantern. "A nice little girl, Jess. Look here at the markings. Spunky, too, I guess, hard as she had to fight to be born. Look here," he said running his finger between the tight blind eyes. He looked as wonderstruck as if he hadn't seen hundreds of puppies born.

"She's beautiful, Dad," I said, and I loved him so much as he knelt there in the smoky lantern light with the pup cradled in his big, rawboned hand.

Dad set the pup down next to Queenie and Queenie began to clean her. The pup nuzzled into her mother. The next two puppies were born easily and the dogs were all asleep when we walked back up to the house. Dad put his arm around my shoulder. "Thanks for helping."

"I like to."

"Sometimes I wonder how your mama would have taken to farm life. She was a city girl to the day she died."

"Was she?"

"Yeah, maybe she would've hated it."

"Do you think about it very often?"

"Well, it crosses my mind from time to time."

I go back to bed thinking of my mother. I was only eight when she died. My memories of her are dim and happy. I wish I could picture her as a young wife with my father. If I could imagine her full and fleshed with a heart and a mind of her own, maybe I could take the measure of whatever love may have been between my parents. As it is my mother is distant as an echo. I only know that I loved the sooty splendor of Baltimore for the few years I lived there and my father said my mother was a city girl. I wonder if my mother ever talked to me about her childhood. I like to think that somewhere in me there are memories of her that I can't call to mind but nevertheless have sustained and formed me since her death.

Sometime during the rest of the night . . . it must have been toward morning because it was light when I woke from it . . . I dreamed that Queenie's pups were dead. In the dream, they weren't the strong, handsome little animals of the night before. They were half formed and shriveled, strewn about the kennel in ragged heaps. As soon as my eyes were open, I ran outside. The first frost rimed the grass in shady places in the yard. The sun where it struck, like the last stand of summer, had melted the frost to dew. Queenie lay serenely within her kennel door. All three pups squirmed hungrily against her.

Ellen

... in the orchard, it was hot and the trees were already bending down with so many apples. The air smelled as sweet as the wine. Kenny put his arm around me so we could share the bottle and after we drank it, it was like our bodies were the same temperature as the air and either we had disappeared or we were just air and were everywhere. Kenny was the kind of guy who would talk about stuff like that. That's probably what made me love him ...

IN The List, this is my first love, my first lover. It was a boy I hardly knew and my love was as wide as the apple-sweet orchard. Or maybe I was just too drunk to conjure up the blessedness of my hymen one more time. In The List it says I loved him, this boy who carried away the prize of my chastity and disappeared. "I love him," says that page in The List, written when I was sixteen years old. I wrote it in big block letters as if my love were an indictment of his treachery, as if I wouldn't be poised to love every man in The List from the first to the last. The last. Darcy. Gone, too. Probably not gone for long but gone without saying, my love incidental to his life, no matter what he says.

All day at work I thought he would call. But now in my bedroom it is evening and I haven't heard from him. But he's so strongly in my mind, I almost think I could turn quickly and see him lying in my narrow bed. He's slept there often enough through the dark hours before dawn. He lies still as a dead man sleeping off whatever he's had to drink. Darcy is my last lover, the forty-ninth on The List, and I will write on his page too that I love him. Maybe he's the only one I ever loved at all.

When I marry David in three weeks I won't see Darcy anymore. I may meet him on the streets of Hooke's Crossing or see him down by the river on a hot Saturday afternoon but I'll never see his face on my pillow anymore. It will be over in three weeks, final and finished. It sounds like the end of my life.

The floor of my room protests sharply as I walk to my bed to sit down. Our house is old and the floor in my room slopes in toward the middle like a long-slept-in bed. I turn on a lamp against the early darkness of winter. The shadows are long in the room and the sky is still red through the window. I can see the top floor of the sleek office building behind our house. The last of the sunlight reflects in golden smears on its glassed front. On a clear day, Bright River itself reflects from a distance in its panes. A year ago, a field, a stream, and a small stand of trees were where the office building stands now. It is, at five stories, Hooke's Crossing's first skyscraper.

My father says that if the people who have built it turned their backs long enough, the woods and meadow would reclaim the ground for their own. And I can picture the grass and vines and brambles advancing silently and inexorably over the parking lot and building until the view from my window was the same as when I was a child.

With a sigh I rise from the bed and get ready to go downstairs. David and I are going to see a photographer tonight about the wedding. David hasn't liked any of the others we've gone to see. He's a particular man, an exacting and precise man who will make a fine husband. After we see the photographer, we are to have dinner in Baltimore with his parents. They are well-to-do and although they are always gracious, they must wonder if David has made the best choice in me. A small headache beats just at my temples as I turn out the light.

Downstairs, my father sits in front of the television watching the news. There are no lights on in the living room and the light from the screen wavers in a ghostly blue over the walls. " . . . in Vietnam," the newscaster finishes as I step from the last stair. The daily televised films are as relentless as the war itself. "Daddy," I say softly.

"Just a minute," he says, his eyes never leaving the screen. My father is attuned to Vietnam, an exposed nerve electrified by all the details and grief of the war. "Good, brave boys," my father says and sometimes weeps. His interest in the news is new . . . only since last fall. Now there is a man on the television selling new cars. Daddy turns to me. "You and David going out?"

"Yes."

"He's a fine boy, Ellen." He says it sternly as if I might not believe it.

"Yes. We're going to see the photographer tonight."

"Oh, I thought that was all taken care of."

"No, not yet."

A silence falls as it often does between me and my father. "Hmmm," he says after a while and returns his attention to the television. Now there are pictures of a crowd of long-haired people running from the police. My father shakes his head. I stand watching for a moment and then turn to leave.

"Good-bye, Daddy."

"Good-bye," he says smiling fondly at me. "That wedding's going to be some big party, huh?"

"Yes."

"You know David's parents said we could have the reception at their country club. Did Mama tell you?"

"She said you decided not to."

"No, sir. Nobody can say Melvin Gibbs is putting on airs. You'll just have to settle for the best *I* can afford," he says as if I've protested.

"It's fine with me, Daddy. Really."

"That's all I need to know, sweetheart," he says and then a smile crosses his face. "Still I wouldn't mind being invited out there once you're married. Just to see the inside of a place like that, you know."

"Next thing I know you'll be learning to play golf," I tease.

"You think I'd make a good duffer? That's what they call golfers . . . duffers."

"Is it?"

"Yes," he says. "What time are you meeting David?"

"Seven."

"Oh, oh, you better get a move on," he says looking at his watch.

"Yes," I say and soon he's watching television again, his chin sunk on his chest.

My father watches the news from the fortification of his armchair as though it were a test for his tolerance of pain. I think he feels insulted and betrayed by the changes in the world. He doesn't like change and the news is all about change and nothing about staying the same. Maybe he thinks if he dedicates himself to a vigilance of the world's troubles he will never again be ambushed by some terrible truth as he was by my brother, Bip.

I hate to leave him, I'm telling myself in an absent-minded way as I go out the front door. Oh, but I *don't* hate to leave him and I mean for good. I try to imagine myself disconnected from my father, bound only by my own expectations, but the future is vague, too far out of focus to catch hold of. And now on this winter evening with my lover gone and my fiancé waiting for me, I am breathless, choked with loss to think of leaving home. The umbilical cord is cut at birth. It's an enforced separation that sets you off from the agent of your creation without so much as a by-your-leave. You're an angel flung from the face of God. Tears well in my eyes as I stand clutching the porch rail with a shaking hand. Leaving home. A newborn couldn't have a greater sense of having a vital life supply cut or feel more terror at having to draw for itself the harsh sweet air of the world.

There is a rude roar in the street and I look quickly, expecting to see Bip rounding the corner on his motorcycle. But it is someone else and I shake my head to clear it. I begin walking toward the car, thinking of Bip. Last summer he and Daddy used to sit out in the backyard in the evenings. They would both sit, slightly turned toward each other, in straight-backed chairs set out on

34

the lawn. They looked like actors on the wide green stage of our yard. They would be faced off over the open red book on my father's knees, a volume of the set of encyclopedia that my mother bought book by book at the grocery store years ago.

When I think of last summer, it seems to me that I can remember every word spoken over that book. Yet that couldn't be true. My father and my brother had been reading the encyclopedia for too many years. I wouldn't have been listening to them any closer than I would have to the wind against the house or the soft clickings and swishings of my mother doing dishes. I can only say that I do know something about masonry and Midsummer Eve and Missouri and Montreal and mosaics. And volume 16—Map-to-Motio—was what they were reading all last summer when I was twenty-two and Bip was nineteen. Those memories roll on for me with the tender monotony of home movies.

"What? What's that you say, Bip? Marat wasn't even a Frenchman by birth. It says here he was born in Switzerland. But there are a lot of Frenchmen in Switzerland. Germans too. But we'll get to Switzerland in another volume."

It was after dinner on an evening last summer and I was in my bedroom dressing to go out on a date. My father and brother were sitting outside below my window, reading from the encyclopedia. Both of them read a certain number of pages a day before discussing them. My brother, Bip, would read those pages with the devotion of a penitent.

That evening they sat together, their heads inclined toward each other. The cultivated green of our lawn merged into the rough-and-tumble green of the field behind our house. The woods across the field hid the houses on the next street. Our house, with its hedges on either side, appeared to be isolated.

"Charlotte Corday," Daddy said, "remember her? Killed Marat. Murdered the man right in his bath. She was convent-educated, you know. I wonder what they teach them there.''

There was silence in the yard until Daddy hooted, ''Lord, Bip, what do you know about that? The treachery of women, indeed.''

In the mirror, my face was pale as the moon as I brushed my hair. I leaned into the mirror and drew a line of green over my eye. There was a square of light reflected in the eye. If the reflection were my mirror with my face in it, my image would echo into the mirror and back into my eye forever. I would be small as a speck of dust, small as an atom, then smaller than any sense could perceive. And would the image reverberate on in some world beyond retrieval? Ah, pretty girl, pretty girl, forever in a moment.

''Marcel Marceau,'' said Daddy. ''Yes, I knew you'd be looking forward to him. Hmmm . . . 'considered to have almost singlehandedly revived the ancient art of pantomime.' Says here he was in New York in 1955. A French fellow. Well, it makes me wish I'd gone to see him. I've always enjoyed the stage, you know. As a matter of fact, there are people who think I might have made a fine actor.'' I knew Daddy would be smiling ruefully and watching Bip for his reaction.

''What people?'' said Daddy. ''Well, my mother, for one. And several of the fellows at the Lions' said as much when I gave that speech there two years ago. Rudy Waller in particular.''

I walked to the window. My father's face looked just as I had imagined it. He regarded Bip warily as though my brother were someone who had often tricked him. And it's true that my brother did trick my father with ease, coming upon him from nowhere and escaping the conditions of my father's love as completely and mysteriously as a rabbit disappearing into a magician's hat.

When Bip was eight, Daddy took him out of the Chesapeake School for the Deaf. He had decided to see to my brother's education himself. ''They've allowed him to sign instead of speak. I've heard deaf people talk and some of them, you can hardly tell they're not normal. The signing is just a bad habit," Daddy declared.

My father began by having Bip read aloud from volume 1 of the encyclopedia. Through the cold gray months of that year Bip's strangled voice filled the house. It wasn't enough that he read lips better than any of his classmates or that he was quick and bright. Daddy would, by God, teach him to speak. The painful rhythm of his speech made my heart ache and I would swear Mama hid in those evenings. She said nothing but I know for sure that she allowed Bip to sign when Daddy wasn't there.

In the evenings, then, holding Bip's face to guarantee his attention, Daddy would shout, "No, no, watch me." Sometimes, Bip's hands would dart up quick and pale as doves flushed from cover.

"No signing!" Daddy would shout, covering his eyes. Bip's hands would drop defeated to his lap. There were times before Daddy uncovered his eyes that I saw a breathless rage in Bip's face. The anger was all the more terrible for being unutterable.

From my window, Bip's face only looked pensive in profile. He leaned toward my father pointing a finger at the book in his lap. "Yes, I saw that," Daddy said. "Marceau's most famous character's name is Bip."

Bip signed.

"No, no, we didn't know that. You're named for your uncle Ben. We always called him Bip as a child because he couldn't say Benjamin. But you know that."

Bip signed rapidly. His hands seemed disembodied in the evening air until he patted them emphatically on his chest. "Me," the hands said, "me, Bip."

I check my face one last time in the mirror. Daddy's voice is distant and sharp. "I certainly would not call what you do pantomime. Calling signing pantomime would be like calling running dancing. It's not the same thing at all. And you can show a little respect, buster."

I took the back stairs down through the kitchen where my mother sat darning socks at the table. Her hair was pulled sharply from her face and there was a light fringe of sweat at her hairline.

"Mama, I'm going to wait outside. It's too hot in here."

"Do you think that's nice, Ellen, waiting outside. A girl shouldn't look anxious," she said laying her mending aside.

"Oh, Mama, it's so hot inside and I just had a bath."

"Well . . ." said Mama and I walked out onto the small screened back porch. It was filled with Mama's ferociously healthy plants. Mama's stern care would allow for nothing less. I walked out onto the back-porch steps. The evening air was heated, heavy, purple as a veil dropped over the house. In the yard, Bip and Daddy sat silently. My father looked up at the sound of the back door. "Ellen," he called in his heartiest voice, "sit with us awhile." I sat down on the top step.

"We've just had a little disagreement, the old Bipper and me." Daddy put his hand out to ruffle Bip's hair but Bip pulled away.

Daddy sighed, then took some papers from his back pocket. "Listen to this, you two," he said, tapping Bip on the knee with the papers. Grudgingly, Bip looked up.

"You know Claude Barnes . . ." Bip shook his head.

"Sure you do," Daddy insisted. "The real-estate man who lives over on Adams, married that friend of Mama's from school. Well, anyway, he was in the store today for tenpenny nails and he told me the city has just sold this property behind us." We all stared out at the field. Daddy's parents had owned the house before him and he had spent his childhood, just as Bip and I had, running through the field and playing along the creek. The creek widens farther on and empties over by First Street into Bright River. Daddy tells about a time in 1944 when the creek rose nearly to the back steps.

"The worst of it is," Daddy went on, "they're going to build some kind of office building on the land there. Some fellow from Baltimore is going to build a sky-scraper, don't you see? Right in our backyard!"

"Oh, no, Daddy," I said and I remembered being in our backyard at evening as a child. It would have been some special day . . . the Fourth of July maybe . . . when Bip and I were allowed to stay up past our usual bedtime. The familiar backyard was transformed by the coming darkness. There was a new, grave majesty to the trees, the grass, the little thread of creek. Fireflies were fairy lights darting up like sparks where the sky struck the earth. Sounds were lucid, lingering, trapped by the dusky hush. The darkness held them longer than the daylight. And when I went to bed I was excited as if I had nearly grasped some secret important to know.

" 'Over my dead body,' was what I said to Claude and you can quote me. I've written a letter to the mayor and council," he said, waving the papers in his hand. "I hit the city fathers pretty hard but I think they deserve it. It's a sad day in Hooke's Crossing when money is more important than the peace and well-being of a citizen."

Daddy looked expectantly at Bip who crossed his arms over his chest and said nothing. Then Daddy turned to me.

"That's terrible, Daddy."

"Well, we'll see who has the last word. We'll see," he said, once again thumbing through the encyclopedia.

" 'March, the third month of the Gregorian year.' Ummm, Gregorian, Gregorian, it's right on the tip of my tongue."

Bip languidly made a tall hat with his hands.

"Of course," Daddy cried. "Pope Gregory something or other. But it says here, in Rome, March was the first month of the year. I wonder why old Gregory thought that needed changing."

Bip tapped his temple and I glanced at my watch. I had a date with Tom Drager. The only good thing about that was that I wasn't going out with poor dull David. I hoped that Tom and I would go to the Blue Moon Cafe and he would get drunk as usual. Then I might dance with Darcy Blunt. But then it was possible that Tom would stay sober enough to take me home and we would end up going parking in the backseat of his old Mercury. That backseat was big as a bed.

I sat on the back steps watching the sky darken. I knew if I could sit long enough, I would see the sun go down and I might decide to stay home. There are times in the pink and gold of a sunset when it seems as if there is nothing that couldn't be soothed by the light of the sky. And I might have that night, washed in the light of just such a sky, stayed far from the first drink that begins it all.

It's the drinking that catapults me into the long howl of night. After midnight, after hours of drinking, everything is all right, all the secrets of my days pouring into the night until morning jolts me upright, upright, the soul of rectitude by breakfast.

"March seems like the month Mother Nature had in mind to start things off. What is January anyway?" said Daddy, his indignation growing. "It's not even the first month of winter."

Bip signed and his hand swept the sky. My father said, "You're probably right, something to do with the sun. But I still think I prefer March."

Bip nodded.

"I guess that's the farmer in us, son." Daddy clapped Bip on the knee and smiled. When he turned back to the book, he said, "Ah, here's one, Rocky Marciano . . . one of the great ones."

Bip was in sudden motion.

"Clay?" Daddy was amazed. "Clay doesn't have the class in his whole body the Rock has in his little finger. What a fighter! It says here he had forty-three knockouts in his career."

Bip stood and shuffled, throwing punches into the air.

"Okay, okay," Daddy said. "Clay's good, I'll give you that. But Rocky was always a gentleman and you can't say that for Clay."

Shrugging, Bip sat down.

Daddy's face stiffened. "It matters a great deal, buster.

Being a gentleman has to do with honor and that's darned important in my book."

Bip raised his hands, palms out, in a conciliatory gesture. Daddy, his face still hard, said, "Well, all right, just so that's understood."

As Daddy bent back to the book, Bip turned and smiled at me. Sometimes Bip and I talked about Daddy. Bip always made me laugh because he could contort his face until he looked just like Daddy. Leafing through the book, Daddy looked vulnerable and foolish. Even being certain he was right couldn't dispel his air of foolishness. He never seemed to have a clear-cut sense of victory with Bip. On that evening, he glanced at Bip from the corner of his eye as though he suspected the smile that had just left Bip's face. Daddy turned a few more pages but his heart wasn't in it.

After a while, Bip rose and with the same unconscious grace as the shadows gliding over the lawn, moved off around the corner of the house. The last rays of the sun slanted over Daddy. His white shirt, rolled up at the sleeves, was luminous. The sweat on his face gleamed.

At the sound of a car in the driveway, I started down the steps. Daddy walked toward me. With the sun behind him, his face was featureless. "There's my good girl," he sighed. "So beautiful."

And in the fading sunlight, I knew I was framed in gold to his eyes, Tinker Bell, an angel. I smiled back at him. He put his arm around my shoulder and we began to walk. "Ellen, Ellen," he said, "you never worry your old man."

Lilly

"Mama, is that you? Yes, this is Tim."

"I can hardly hear you. Why are you whispering?"

"You should go to the police if someone's after you."

"Where is Berkeley?"

"If I were there, Mama, I would make them go away. I'm big as most men."

"Honest. I'm almost six feet tall right now."

"I don't look a bit like Daddy. Maybe I look like you."

"You could come and see."

DARCY was born in the blaze of August two years after my father died. There was a drought that year and the sun seared the trees and sucked the river up until it lay low in its bed. The riverbanks dropped off sharp as jagged teeth where the water had receded. The water itself ran brown and puddeny, little more than mud.

Darcy himself looked parched for water when he was born. A seven-month baby, he was fleshless and wizened, more monkey than boy. Yet I loved the look of him. He was born after four miscarriages, and every baby I had lost had seemed to me a soul betrayed, an entrusted spirit I couldn't give a proper anchor. I owed a debt to God and Darcy was my vindication.

I remember Darcy's being born. The cold, inviting ether in my lungs drew the minutes out in a strange darkness shot through with sudden bursts of light. The past met the present like comets colliding, and while my child was born, Ivy and I were children squatting on the riverbank. The mud that oozed through our toes was silken, cold. When I lifted my head up to peer up over the rise of the bank, I could see our house on the hill above the river. A screened porch ran the length of the house and Mother's hydrangeas with their blowsy balls of blue flanked the back steps. In the yard, there was a tiny table with four chairs painted red. Two dolls sat in chairs. Ivy and I were supposed to be having a tea party.

But on the riverbanks, everything bends toward the water. Trees live at angles you would swear must kill them and trail their limbs along the surface. Vines clamber down the banks looking for water. And Ivy and I, our bottoms wet and gritty from sitting in the mud, were drawn in the same irresistible way no matter how many times we were scolded. In the ether dream, our hands were in the water that slipped through our fingers with the rich flow of satin. I turned over a stone and sent a crayfish scuttling, his panicked ripples agitating the dragon flies hovering in the air above. Up these elegant creatures darted and beat their wings to rainbows.

I would have been the one to lead Ivy away from the tea set and dolls. She wouldn't have dared it alone. When Mother caught us, as she always did, Ivy would cover her eyes with her muddy hands and cry. But I never did. I was too happy at the river's edge to believe that I wouldn't go there again the first minute my mother's back was turned. I felt strong and free there by the water, at the very center of the business of the earth.

Ivy shrieked at the sight of the crayfish and leaped back from the water's edge. From the house, I could hear my mother calling, "Lilly! Lilly!" in a dream as long as my childhood. When I opened my eyes, a nurse was looking down into my face. My temples beat in a heated throb and I heard her say, "You have a son, Lilly." And then I rocked that baby, my little son, in my arms, held him to my heart before I even saw him. There was an expansion to my life as though my eyes could crack the blue of the sky all the way to heaven. Where was the space that opened up to contain my mother love? What vast reach had laid empty within me until that moment? The love lit on such welcome ground at the simple sound of the news. When Aaron and I first saw the baby, I was struck dumb by the sight of his head no bigger than a man's fist and fringed by downy black hair. And Aaron only said, "He's so small." He said, "I never saw a boy so small." It must have seemed an injustice to Aaron that he should have this tiny child when his brother's babies were round and solid as tug-boats. I knew how he had longed for a son. He and his brother Ben were the last of the long line of Blunts in Hooke's Crossing. When I was a girl it seemed as if half the town were Blunts. But over the years some of the younger ones had moved away and the older ones had died off. There was one whole branch of cousins who had had nothing but girls. So although there was still plenty of Blunt blood in town, the name rested with Ben and Aaron and their parents. Without ever saying, I think Aaron had thought that he and his brother would establish the old strength of the family in town once again.

"He's so small." Aaron's voice was filled with disappointment as if the baby's frailty made him unfit to carry the ponderous weight of the Blunts' reputation. I believe I left my husband in my heart at that moment and bound myself to the infant lying, remote and immediate, behind the hospital glass.

Darcy was too small to take home when I left the hospital, and I went to stay awhile with my mother and Ivy down by the river. Aaron came to visit in the evenings and it seemed exactly right, as if he had to woo me all over again.

While I was with my mother, Ivy fluttered around me, pampering and teasing but I had changed with the birth of my baby. I felt an importance to myself that made Ivy seem light and aimless as a leaf on the water. Her youth and innocence were burdens I thought she must be eager to shed. I didn't want to be with Ivy. I only wanted to sit on my mother's screened porch in the simmer of the summer air and watch the thirsty river stretching its sad brown arms toward the sea. I remember how the time like the river crept, stunned by the heat. And I remember how I missed my baby, my breasts aching for him long after the milk had dried. I must have been sullen and difficult. Ivy, I suppose, was puzzled, wanting the girlish closeness we had had before my marriage.

One evening, she and I were in my mother's bedroom.

Mother's old furniture, big and black, squatted like bears in the airless room. The windows were open and the frogs croaking and the whisper of the river made a fine summer chorus. Ivy stood in front of Mother's big mirror trying on a dress she would wear for her first date with a college boy. She was eighteen.

"Lilly, what do you think," she said, "should I wear it off the shoulder?" She tugged at the sleeves of the dress until her shoulders were bare.

"Mother won't let you," I said fanning myself with a magazine.

"Do I look daring?" she said, pulling her shoulders back until the curve of her breasts swelled above the round neckline of the dress.

"Mother will never allow you to wear it like that," I said, tiring of the subject.

Ivy pouted into the mirror, then collapsed into a dejected heap on the bed. "Oh, it doesn't matter. I'm an ugly old thing anyway."

The air in the room was still and Ivy's skin under a thin film of perspiration was pale and luminous like magnolia blossoms in evening light. Her hair was the rich red of mahogany. She was slender with a ripe roundness to her arms and face that made her seem as though she had been formed with more care than other girls.

"Ivy," I said, "you have more boyfriends than any other girl in Hooke's Crossing."

"Claire Atkins has lots more than I do."

"She does not. It's just that George McGrath has a crush on her, and you like him best."

"I used to," said Ivy softly.

"That's just like you, to want the one that doesn't want you."

"Well, I don't want him now."

"Oh, Ivy, really. The last time I talked to you, you said you were in love with him."

Ivy rose and walked to the window. She stood looking down at the river. "Do you remember Bertram Hale's parties, Lilly? The way you and I would climb out on the roof at night to watch?''

"Yes, I remember.''

"I wonder why he sold that place. It was bigger than any other house on the river. It was just a summer place to him, I guess. But it looked absolutely magical when they put out the Japanese lanterns. Do you remember that?''

"Yes," I said. There was an odd sadness in her voice and on the flow of that sadness I remembered the men in their white summer suits and the women in their pale light dresses glowing in the summer like fireflies on the broad sweep of the Hales's lawn. And Ivy was right, the lanterns did seem enchanted spilling soft and gold as moonlight on the river. By the time Darcy was born the Hale house had been torn down and the neon lights of Willard Maynes's Blue Moon Cafe, lurid-blue and blinking, rode the water there.

"I thought I'd never grow up then, never grow old and unhappy," said Ivy.

"Well, you're hardly old, for crying out loud.''

"Love ages you, don't you think?" she said regarding me seriously.

"You don't even know what love is," I said impatiently.

"I might," she said, coming again to look at herself in the mirror. She swept her hair up on top of her head. "Do you like my hair like this? Do I look older?''

"Who is it now, Ivy?''

"No one you know," she said with a little smile.

"Don't tell me if you don't want to," I said rising to leave.

"Lilly, wait," she pleaded and we stood facing each other. "How did you know you loved Aaron? Did you know all the time that you loved him?''

"Ivy," I said in exasperation, "I've known Aaron all my life, for heaven's sake. If you're talking about something like love at first sight, that only happens in the movies. There's so much more to true love than the color of somebody's eyes or the way they dance.''

49

"What do you mean? Tell me exactly."

"Well," I said, puffed up in the importance of my age and experience, "it should feel solid and steady."

Ivy made a face. "You make it sound awful," she said, "like eating spinach or saving money."

"It can be very satisfying," I said primly and even then I knew I was walking a thin line between truth and pride.

"Still, Lilly, don't you ever wish that Aaron were more exciting?"

"Exciting?"

"Oh, you know. It's just that he's so serious," she said apologetically.

"You're rude and impossible," I said moving toward the door.

"No, Lilly, listen." She caught my arm. "When I was little, I used to dream I could fly. And I think love should feel like that, free and dizzy," she said and flung her arms out wide.

"That's a good word for you, Ivy . . . dizzy. You're like a child."

When I snapped at her, Ivy's eyes filled quickly with tears and her mouth opened for a moment, then closed as if she had started to say something and had thought better of it.

A few weeks later, in the first days of September, just as I had brought Darcy home to Broad Street, just as the first few leaves showed yellow in the water of the river, Ivy disappeared from Hooke's Crossing. Mother had found a note on her dresser. In Ivy's careful, round hand, the note read, "Dear Mother, I have gone to marry the man I love. Please don't worry about me, he loves me too but you would say that I was too young and he was too old. I'm so happy. Please be happy for me. And tell Lilly, please, that it is just like flying."

I thought about the conversation we had had, Ivy and I, at Mother's. I marveled at my sister biting back the secret of this man. When we were children, Ivy never could keep anything to herself. Guilty secrets undid her.

They seemed to crouch inside of her, growing on her fertile conscience until they were too big to contain. And she always seemed as surprised as anyone when they popped unbidden out of her mouth. That summer night when Ivy and I talked about love, her lover's name must have quivered on her tongue with every breath.

For three days after my sister left, my mother wouldn't tell anyone but Aaron and me. Aaron made some discreet inquiries but we couldn't find anything of Ivy. At last without mentioning the note, Mother went to the sheriff to say that Ivy was gone. The sheriff at the time was Rufe Abert and the first thing he did was drag Bright River. My mother stood on the riverbank watching. She wore a black dress so stiff it barely stirred around her legs in the smart breeze off the water. From boats, the sheriff and his men hauled the long-jawed steel hooks back and forth. The silty bottom of the river roiled into murky clouds that followed along behind the boats. Nothing I could say to Mother would persuade her to tell the sheriff the truth and the whole town buzzed with the mystery.

No one could find her. She'd vanished quick as a whispered word in a high wind. She had left us and we hardly knew then who was gone. Ivy was like a person in a dream who suddenly changes face and disturbs the whole action of the dream. There were all the things we would have sworn to knowing about our Ivy, her obedience and the million little fears she harbored . . . and then there was her audacious absence.

Then three weeks to the day she left, Ivy came back to Hooke's Crossing. To my mother, it was worse even than the words uttered behind closed doors while Ivy had been gone. Worse than kidnapping, worse than murder, Ivy had traveled with a man she wasn't married to and she didn't deny that they had shared the same bed. "Shame!" screamed Mother. "Ivy Ann, shame!" and Ivy hung her head but still she didn't seem so much ashamed as half asleep, a dreamer caught with the tail end of a dream just beyond her grasp. The man she had been with had told her he was married and put her on a train for home. I believe he was a traveling man of some kind but Ivy never said. "He should be tarred and feathered," Aaron fumed. No one ever knew who he was because Ivy had learned to keep a secret at last. It burned in her, lighting her eyes like people who say they've seen angels. "I've known true love, Lilly," she would say as if that explained it all.

Mother had tried to protect her but things have a way of getting around a small town. The air itself has ears. After Ivy came home, my mother's porch that had greeted all of Ivy's suitors was empty and it stayed that way. Ivy was a leper in Hooke's Crossing, tarnished and unforgiven. Aaron never mentioned the incident, the same way he wouldn't have mentioned insanity in someone's family or a glass eye. And I . . . well, I told Aaron that blood was thicker than water and after all, Ivy was so young. But in some secret part of me that I couldn't quite place at the time, I loved her for the sheer boldness of what she had done. The gap I had imagined between us closed. But my mother never forgave her. She treated Ivy as if she were an unwanted guest whom Mother, too well-bred to be impolite, was forced to entertain. So Ivy, in those days after she had come back to town, spent nearly every day at my house on Broad Street helping me care for Darcy.

Darcy was an unlovely creature, gnomelike and wrinkled. He was piebald where the hair he had been born with had fallen out in patches. His pinched shanks could fit into the span of my hand. Ivy and I were mad with love. We wove him through our lives, this frail thread of our blood that reached into the future. In turn, we wove ourselves into the heart of him. And Darcy, like any other baby, was formed by the events in the lives of the people around him just as surely as he was by the messages carried in the blood that built his body cell by cell. Ivy and I were so ready to love him. My own love was honed on the wild ache in me for my lost children. And Ivy in her dreamy sadness took a mute comfort from the tiny frame of my infant son. All the first year of Darcy's life, until Ivy married Otis, she passed her time caring for the baby and talking about love.

I can still see us, young women, sitting with the baby one day on my front porch. We were leaning toward each other, talking, and the spice of fallen leaves was in the air. A radio was playing somewhere in the house, dance tunes I think, something our maid, Rachel, liked. Ivy held Darcy, his small body a question mark against her breast. She rocked the baby and I rocked with her, watching his silky dark hair ruffle under her breath. "Mr. Stanton sang to me," Ivy said of her lover. "He sang me love songs, Lilly." She always called him Mr. Stanton when she spoke of him. "Purely for convenience," she said. "Of course that's not his name."

"He couldn't have been much of a man to have treated you the way he did," I told her.

"He was an honorable man. He was brokenhearted by what happened."

"That's only what you wish he was, Ivy."

"No, Lilly, you're wrong. He was everything I wanted. I wouldn't have loved him if he wasn't."

"Those things were never there, don't you see?" I said in exasperation. "You made them up."

"Lilly, you can't make things true just by wishing," Ivy explained patiently.

"All right, Ivy, I give up," I said and sighed as if a young girl's dreams weren't strong enough to pin to a man like a flower on a ragged lapel, as if women when they fall in love don't dress their men up like heroes, gods, in the stuff of our dreams. It's only later that we cry to find them bound to earth. To Ivy, it was all the same, dreams and truth, truth and dreams. And that man, her lover, stayed just the way she'd last seen him through the eyes of an eighteen-year-old. He may as well have died or been cast in stone for all the difference time made to Ivy. I suppose that's how she could marry that mean-spirited Otis Webber. He was the only one to come courting her after she came back to town. All the other boys stayed away. Mother longed for renewed respectability for Ivy and she pressed her on Otis. I've thought perhaps my sister acquiesced to our mother's wishes believing that any marriage for her would be loveless since she was in love with one man for all time.

My love didn't wrap itself around my heart like Ivy's did. And sometimes I'll find myself wondering at some foolishness or another somebody has committed in the name of love. Whatever could have made them behave like that? I catch myself wondering. Oh, yes, I can recall that I was in love with Aaron when we married but I don't recall the feeling anymore. But I do know, though, that there is a density to love and that loyalty and habit are a thin thread next to it. I don't know how I fell out of love with my husband. I often think it wasn't even fair. The things I loved most about him at the beginning were the things I held against him later on . . . his certainty, his pride. It wasn't his fault; he didn't change or make mistakes, at least not by his reckoning. It was only that after choosing him to marry, I wished a different father for my son. And even now, I can barely say what I would have wanted from him.

I could blame him because he hardly seemed to believe in the existence of the baby before Darcy was born. But surely, it's too much to expect a man to believe in an unseen creature that tosses and turns and rolls like a wave down the inside of its mother's belly. How could he take on faith the tiny heart beating, the fingers unfurling like flowers, all the things a mother sees in some female inner eye.

I couldn't say he didn't love Darcy. Even though "love" may seem a strange word for what passed between them all those years, nothing else could explain the pain between them.

I remember their coming up against each other when Darcy was eleven. He had a dog who had caught the mange. The dog's name was Bo, I remember, and he was old and deaf too. But the dog, old and ill as he was, ambled everywhere after Darcy. The boy seemed to slow down just a bit to accommodate the dog's age-stiffened gait. But aside from that, he didn't seem to notice Bo's deterioration.

By the summer of that year, Bo had little coat left. What fur he did have stuck up stiff and gray between the scabrous patches of mange. In the close air of summer, he had an odor that drove me to banish him from the house. Aaron was horrified by the slowly dying Bo. The dog's age and deafness could be politely overlooked but the mange was a public weakness, an embarrassment to the family.

"Lilly," Aaron said, "something has to be done about that dog. He's a real eyesore and it can't be healthy for Darcy to be around him."

"Dr. Charles said the dog can't infect Darcy," I said.

"He ought to be put down."

"Oh, Aaron, he's so old. How much longer can he live? And Darcy's so attached to him. Couldn't we just let him be?"

"All right," he said, "but not for long."

A few weeks later when Aaron said the dog would be put down, I knew there would be no reprieve. I couldn't argue with him. There wasn't much to say to his hard-headed practicality.

It was early evening when he told Darcy. We were on the front porch after supper hoping for a cool breeze, but the trees were motionless and even the sky seemed dusty in the heat. Aaron and I sat on the white porch swing. Darcy sat on the steps scratching a mosquito bite on his leg. The clean shirt he had put on for dinner was already wilted in the collar. Below him, Bo lay cooling himself on the brick walk. The lawn, tended by our yardman, John, was a fastidious lush green and seemed to scold the dog for his naked degeneration.

"Darcy," Aaron said, "Bo has to be put out of his misery."

"What do you mean?" Darcy asked. He put his hand on the dog's knobby head.

"I mean he has to be put down."

"You're going to kill Bo?" The boy's face was full of disbelief. When he turned to me, I looked away.

"Yes," said Aaron, "it's a kindness to the dog."

"Killing, Daddy, it's not a kindness. He doesn't hurt anybody. He doesn't even go out of the yard anymore. Please, Daddy." Darcy walked down the steps and stood by Bo. The dog opened one eye.

"There's no discussion," said Aaron. "This is best for everyone. Do you see?" He didn't raise his voice.

Darcy hung his head. "Yes, sir."

"All right, I'll send John over tomorrow to take care of it." Aaron lifted the newspaper in his lap.

"How?" Darcy shouted, his face wet with perspiration and tears. "How will he kill him?"

Aaron looked up over the newspaper. "A gun," he said. "It's painless and it's quick. John will bury him too."

Darcy closed his eyes and clenched his fists. Then he startled us both by saying, "Daddy, could I do it? I mean kill him. He's my dog."

Aaron hesitated. I knew he was deciding between having the job done as well as possible and the opportunity for a lesson in responsibility for Darcy. I think he may even have felt some pride for the mysterious son of his who must have often appeared so untouched by his influence. Perhaps at the moment he may even have thought he saw a bit of himself in Darcy.

"All right," said Aaron at last, "I'll help you."

"No, sir," said Darcy, "I can do it myself."

Aaron smiled briefly at the boy and agreed.

The next day, Darcy talked to Aaron before he left for work. All that morning, Darcy and I could barely look each other in the eye. After lunch, I looked out the kitchen window and saw Darcy leading Bo on a chain into the woods across the road. He cradled a heavy gun in one thin brown arm. His shoulder blades under his T-shirt stuck out sharp and hard as flint. As the two of them disappeared into the extravagance of the summer woods, Bo's ragged tail lazily fanned the underbrush.

I went to the sink and began washing dishes and listening with the ends of every nerve for a shot. A short while later the gun's sharp report cracked through the heavy afternoon heat. All the rest of the day I kept going to the window to look for Darcy. But I was in the kitchen cooking supper before he came home. I heard the front screen door swing shut and then I heard him plod slowly upstairs to his room. I went to his bedroom door and knocked.

"Yes?" answered a muffled voice through the door.

"Darcy?"

"Yes, ma'am?"

"Dinner's ready soon."

"I don't want to eat with him."

"Don't talk that way about your father. Now, you wash up for dinner."

"Yes, ma'am."

That night at dinner, Darcy was silent. I thought of my small son shoveling the dark damp soil deep in the woods, and I thought he must be very tired and sad. But Aaron was expansive, even jovial. He clapped Darcy on the back and talked to us about Wilbur Payne at the bank who had saved enough money to buy a house for himself and his young wife. "It's knowing where your responsibilities lie that makes for success," he said, sending a solemn wink at Darcy. Darcy's face was bland. After supper, Aaron and Darcy walked into the woods to see Bo's grave. In bed that night Aaron said he thought everything had turned out well.

In the days that followed, Darcy was subdued but he wasn't brooding as I had expected. He disappeared for long hours at a time, but that was nothing unusual for a boy set loose for the long summer vacation.

One day a few weeks later when I was alone in the house, I heard a trash can clatter to the pavement behind the house. The crash was followed by a jingling like pennies being shaken. I opened the back door just in time to see Bo, dragging a chain, vanish around the side of the house. I ran down the steps and around the corner after him. There I saw the dog. He had caught his chain around a forsythia bush. He was tugging futilely to free himself. "Bo!" I said. When his eyes finally settled on me, he wagged his tail.

I didn't want to touch him. I thought about saints caring for the lepers and wondered at their strength. How could Darcy bear to care for him? A fetid odor shrieked in the quiet summer heat. There were leaves stuck to the sores on his legs. He looked as if he had risen, half-dead, from some rank hole in the earth and taken on the dressing of the woods. I took hold of the very end of the chain and unwound it. When I chained him to the clothes pole, he lay down in the shade. His breath was ragged and raspy. I went back in the house to wait for Darcy.

Around noon the front door slammed. You can trust a young boy to come home to eat. Darcy ran for the kitchen where I stood ironing. "Hi, Mama," he said pulling a bottle of milk from the refrigerator.

I said, "Darcy, go look out back." He walked to the back door and stood there staring as though the dog's appearance were a surprise to him too. The rain-sweet smell of ironing rose in the silence and a fly buzzed against the screen. "Well?" I said.

"Mama, I . . . " Darcy began. He turned and carefully put the bottle of milk down. He smiled.

"Darcy, I'm warning you . . ."

"Mama, please, I got him all fixed up in the woods and nobody knows but Jeff."

"What will happen when Daddy finds out?"

"He doesn't have to find out," he said and his eyes pleaded with me.

I laid a damp shirt on the ironing board and slid the iron over it with a hiss. No one could do Aaron's shirts to suit him except me. I didn't look at Darcy but I could feel the stillness of his small body. Outside, I could hear Bo moaning faintly in his sleep. I thought of all the secrets I had kept from my husband, small secrets of our daily life and other secrets, smaller still, of the soul.

Aaron commanded order and he got it even if we had to trim the truth now and then.

I ran the iron to the tip of the collar, holding the handle firmly so as not to crease the edge and pressed the white cotton down smooth as ice.

"It isn't going to work," I said; "what will happen when it gets cold?"

Darcy's face clouded. "I don't guess he'll live that long."

"Then why, honey? Why not let Daddy put him out of his misery?"

"Because he isn't in misery. You should see him, Mama. He lies in the creek to get cool. He likes to roll in the leaves. He likes to see me. He's just happy, that's all. Please Mama."

Through the door I could see the old dog lying in the shade. Flies buzzed around him, but he barely twitched. I suppose he didn't even know they were there. There should have been buzzards circling over him, for crying out loud, he was such a pitiful heap.

"Please, Mama."

"All right," I said. I never meant to set my son against his father. I only wanted peace between them. And once again I found myself like the little Dutch boy with his finger in the dike sealing up the latest breach in Aaron's notion of order.

Bo didn't live long after that. Darcy went to the woods one day, and although the dog only appeared to be sleeping, Darcy said he knew he was dead. He buried Bo and Aaron's will was done at last.

On the last days of that summer, Darcy got on his bike most mornings and took off, off with Jeff by the river, I imagine. If he went into the woods again that year, I don't remember. I do remember asking him if he ever visited Bo's grave. He seemed surprised by the question. "No," he shook his head, "Bo doesn't care now whether I come anymore or not."

One evening soon after the dog's death, Aaron and I were sitting on the front porch after supper. He sat on the steps in his shirtsleeves. He was whittling, his one idle occupation. Shavings, long and curled like apple peelings, collected at his feet. The porch swing creaked soothingly as I set it gently rocking. Caroline Saunders passed by in a new car and Aaron and I each lifted a hand in a wave.

"Now where would they get the money for a Buick?" I wondered aloud. Aaron shook his head and drew a smooth swath down the stick in his hand.

"Did they borrow at the bank?"

"Now, Lilly, you know I can't tell you. I'm no different than a doctor."

"Oh, I know. I'm just curious. She always talks so poor mouth at Altar Guild."

"Hmmm," said Aaron. "Where's Darcy?"

"He rode up the street to get a Popsicle."

"He's not going to the woods much these days, is he?"

"He doesn't go at all."

"Well, I'm glad he's over that morbid death business with the dog," he said pitching the skinned stick toward the street and closing his pocketknife with a click.

"Yes," I said.

And all my memories of them are the same . . . the two of them at odds. From the very beginning when I would hold the baby out to him, Aaron would draw away, his big hands explaining wordlessly how awkward he felt. He had a big man's fear of appearing clumsy. He never danced for that reason, afraid he did it badly. And handling Darcy must have seemed just as sure to make him look foolish. It seemed a small thing at the time. Babies were a woman's province anyway. When Darcy grew older, I told myself, he and Aaron would come together naturally in their maleness. But when Darcy was older and they were still at sixes and sevens with each other, I could see the rift for the wound it was. Lord knows I would have healed it if I'd known how. And Lord knows I've thought about it for the rest of my life, chewing it over like a meatless bone and puzzling over the same questions again and again.

Where did it begin? Was it when Aaron said he couldn't see Jeff Maynes anymore? "The boy's a roughneck," said Aaron. And Darcy went right on playing with Jeff, even bringing him to the house with my complicity when Aaron wasn't there. Did it begin there or was it earlier?

When Darcy was five, Aaron refused to allow him to kiss him good night. "Men don't kiss," he said and offered his hand. Darcy looked confused for a moment, then raised a small hand. Aaron, smiling, leaned toward his son. But Darcy quickly put both hands behind his back. "Aren't you going to shake my hand?" asked Aaron.

"No, sir," said Darcy and I don't believe he ever touched his father again.

However it began, it only got worse as Darcy grew older. By the time he was in his teens, Darcy's rebellion against Aaron was as open, as obvious, as old Bo's mange. Aaron was bewildered by his son's contempt. He was a steady man and he lived by his ideals with the unshakable faith of a mariner steering by the North Star. Yet Darcy fought him on every point.

His manner was crude, his speech rough, and his friends were the children of people who would only have met Aaron if they were making a loan at the bank. Broad Street society was distinct if not always distinguished. But I, not being a Blunt, didn't worry so much about Darcy's friends. His best friend, Jeff, was the son of Willard Maynes who kept the Blue Moon Cafe down by Bright River. He was a good child and I'd known him a long time. But I didn't know the other boys Darcy had chosen as companions. They drove strange-looking cars that growled and grumbled, trembling like tigers on leashes when they stopped for him in front of the house. Their radios blared along the quiet street, setting the polished windowpanes to shaking. The music was savage and guttural and seemed to me to be calling my young son back to the beginnings of the human race.

Oh, that music! I can still hear it when I think of Aaron and Darcy going up against each other in that time. It throbs in my memory, fast and urgent, like gunfire, like the heartbeat of someone running, running. It blasted out of Darcy's radio in his room, swelled his walls, invaded the hall as Aaron and I climbed the steps one day to speak to our son about being suspended from high school. "Now, Aaron," I said, "keep your temper." I said this to the great bulk of his back as we neared the top of the stairs.

"For god's sake, Lilly, the boy's been suspended from school." He loomed at the top of the steps. He seemed expanded by his outrage. "Darcy!" he shouted.

But the music was too loud for Darcy to hear him. And thus Aaron gained the first advantage in the battle by appearing suddenly in Darcy's doorway and surprising him into an undeniable start. The boy's fury was quick and instinctive. He extended his hand with great nonchalance and turned up the volume of the radio. The music screamed in my ears. Darcy tapped his foot, his face averted from us. Aaron spoke. His words were lost beneath the crash of the music. He walked to the radio and pulled the plug. The sound died quickly and then there was a silence in which Aaron and Darcy glowered at each other.

"So you have finally managed it," Aaron began. Darcy stared back at him insolently. "You have finally pressed those good people . . . who happen, whether you know it or not, to be very interested in your well-being . . . into suspending you from school."

When I had gotten the note from Martha Kemp, the principal, I had been surprised to see that she planned to call Aaron. She had been born and raised in Hooke's Crossing and had overlooked Darcy's mischief many times to avoid offending Aaron. She and I had made a silent pact to keep the worst from him. I had wondered at the time if there wasn't more to it than the simple cutting of class mentioned in the note.

"Is that what Kemp said?" asked Darcy.

"Mrs. Kemp to you, young man. And yes, that's what she told me."

"Well, it must be true, then."

"What could possibly have been so interesting that you couldn't attend class?" asked Aaron.

"She didn't tell you?" Darcy said with a laugh.

"No, maybe you better tell me."

Darcy looked to be considering telling his father but in the end he only said, "Nothing to tell."

I breathed a sigh of relief. Martha Kemp hadn't quite mustered the nerve to tell Aaron everything apparently. An hour after Darcy was home from school, Ivy had called to tell me what Otis had heard at work from a cousin of the Latin teacher at county high. When Darcy had been found out of class, he was caught in a store-room with a bottle of cheap wine and his hand up Susan Payne's skirt. It made me blush to hear Ivy tell it and I knew I'd never mention it to Aaron or Darcy.

"Very well, Darcy," said Aaron, "but you're going to pay for this transgression. You can bank on that, my friend."

"I'm not your friend," said Darcy, his hand inching toward the disconnected cord of the radio. Aaron spied him and kicked the cord beyond his reach. "You don't realize it," Aaron said, "but I'm the best friend you have right now."

"The hell you are," Darcy said.

Standing beside him, I could see Aaron's chest heaving shallowly beneath his suit coat, but his voice was even, reasonable. "All right, let's see what two months' confinement will do for that cockiness. And further-more, for every disrespectful outburst, I'll add another day."

"I don't care what you do to me," said Darcy. He rose to stand looking up at Aaron. "You're not ever buying my soul for your straitlaced shit."

"Darcy," I pleaded but he never even looked my way. Aaron raised his hand as though to strike the boy,

63

then lowered it slowly to his side like a cowboy reholstering his gun.

"I'm not playing your mug's game, Darcy. You will learn that you can't shame this family without paying for it. I will teach you what it means to be a Blunt in this town if it's my last act on earth!"

"I know what it means. It means being a hick in a hick town, you bloody, fucking Shylock."

"That's two months and a day," Aaron said and we left the room, Aaron holding my arm firmly as if to keep me from staying behind to comfort Darcy. Aaron closed the door quietly. As we paused in the hall, there was a cry of rage from inside the room and something landed against the door with an energetic thud.

"Two months and two days," Aaron called calmly through the door. "Two months and two days," he said under his breath as we descended the stairs.

Yes, yes, I told myself when the battles raged, it was only time that was needed. Time for Darcy to grow into a man, time for him to learn to understand his father, if not to agree with him. I had grown to love my mother more when I had a child of my own. I had come to understand her, even how she must have felt when Ivy left town or, more to the point, when she came back. I could see her pain. It's hard to believe that love is no good-luck charm, that a child, no matter how well loved, can break our hearts. It's an injustice that rocks us to the soul. We've made all the proper sacrifices to the little god of love and still he turns away.

But sometimes those children return to us just as I returned to forgive my mother for so many things, and just as I had hoped Darcy would come around to Aaron. It's time that brings us home again and for Aaron and Darcy there was little enough of that.

Sometimes I've thought their differences arose from their very souls, as if they would have clashed in any meeting and the chances of their coming together as father and son couldn't change that. For whatever bit of truth there is to that, I only think of it when I am tired and souls seem too tied to this earth. Then I can imagine for a moment that I don't hold any blame. But I'm getting too old to think in terms of fate. I can't arrange my memories for excuse so well anymore. After all, my own hand in what my life has become is the only power I have, the only face I own to offer up to God.

Jessie

May something go always unharvested,
May much stay out of our stated plan. . . .

—ROBERT FROST

OUTSIDE the window a coarse brown dust filled the air, and shot through with sunlight, it turned to gold. It settled in the grass and the trees that had just begun to turn in the shortening days of autumn. Big machines lumbered like elephants through the fields behind the house as Dad and the three men he had hired harvested our corn crop. The dogs, excited by the activity, ran back and forth in the kennel runs. Their sharp barks barely rose over the clamor of the harvesters. The windows of the house were closed against the dust but still it wavered in the inside air and lit down, powdering every surface.

Because the men were there for the harvesting I had spent all morning in the kitchen cooking a big midday meal. Steam rose from the pots on the stove and sweat ran down between my breasts. The dense smoky odor of ham baking filled the house. The bread cooling gave off the clean airy smell of yeast. It was a good time to cook. Although a lot of things in the garden had gone before the August heat, others were at their richest. Freshly dug potatoes parted under the knife with a crisp snap. Kale, blue-green and ruffled, floated in cold water in the sink like petticoats caught in the wind. And tomatoes were heaped up on the sink, so many, ripening in the garden too fast to get them all put up, ripening in a joyful explosion that had me picking twice a day. They were piled one atop the other and they were squat and red and big like smiles and they reminded me of happy summers.

I didn't mind the extra work. I was glad to have something besides the doctor's news to think of. I pride myself on my cooking. There is something about a busy kitchen that seems to attend to the heart of the matter of life. There is a suggestion for me of a quiet connection to the earth and even the stars. I get the same feeling plunging my hands into newly turned soil in the spring of the year. In these times I know how much my father's daughter I am and I understand what sent our ancestors out into their fields to dance.

On that day last fall, I was content to be cooking and looking forward to noon. I took care salting the potatoes and cleaning the kale. The din outside increased and I knew the men would be working closer to the house. When I walked to the window in the dining room, I could see them halfway across the nearest field. My father drove the harvester that snarled and shuttered over the rows of corn. He left a bald path behind him. Farther back one man drove a tractor with a cart attached. Two other men walked along behind, heaving cornstalks on the back of the cart. The dust stuck to the sweat of their naked backs and their skin looked rough as stone. One of the men was tall and spare. He looked like so many of the other field hands my father had hired over the years. Close-muscled men, nothing wasted, the veins and sinew in their arms naked as though they were missing a layer of skin.

But the other man walking with him was different. Even from the house I could see it. While the tall man, shoulders sloping, plodded up and down the rows, the other man strutted. He wasn't tall but there was a power of energy to his legs and shoulders as though they took their force from his good cheer. He wore a bandanna over his nose and mouth, yet I could tell by the set of his head that he was laughing and joking with the other man. It was Darcy Blunt. He was some kind of hero in the local bars or so I had heard, a bad boy never grown

70

up. I'd seen him in Hooke's Crossing and we had said hello. I liked the way he smiled, quick and brilliant, as though he'd been taken by surprise and couldn't help himself. "Hi, Miss Jessie," he would say when I saw him in town and that was all. But if I'd been honest with myself, I would have had to admit that Darcy was a lot of the reason I'd taken such pains with the meal.

Out in the field, my father stopped the harvester. The tractor came to a halt and the silence was loud as a sound. Puzzled, the dogs stood still and looked out toward my father. The men all turned toward the house. I wheeled quickly and ran up to my room to brush my hair. It would take them awhile to come into the house. They would stop first at the old pump outside to wash. By the time they came through the back door, I was back in the kitchen slicing ham.

The men Dad usually hires for harvesting are taut, quiet men who say only "Yes, ma'am" and "No, ma'am" to me. But I could hear Darcy's voice before they opened the back door.

"Hey, we're a team out there, aren't we? Whoever cut more corn for you, Cecil?" Darcy said as they all came in the back door. Dad's response was muffled as they came into the kitchen.

"This here's my daughter, Jessica Talbot. And Jess, this one here's John Stokes," said Dad. The man was red-faced from the sun. He held an old felt hat in his hands. "Ma'am," he said inclining his head.

"Harvey Wilkes," said Dad gesturing toward another man, "of the Glen Green Wilkeses. Jess, you remember Margaret from the bank."

"I sure do," I said. "How are you, Mr. Wilkes."

"I'm fine and dandy," the man said staring at the ceiling.

"And me, in case you're wondering. I'm Darcy Blunt." He stepped forward and held out his hand. I hardly knew what to make of him. There was an arrogance to him I should have hated but I didn't. His outstretched hand was a challenge I couldn't meet. Ignoring it, I stepped back and lifted a lid from a pot and stirred. "Everybody out of my kitchen now," I said, "if you want anything to eat." They left with a good-natured grumbling.

And later when they were all seated at the table eating, I could see them through the door. I felt silly and young at having let that man get the better of me with that small gesture. I was angry with myself. I could hear Darcy's voice from time to time. The other men ate, saying nothing, their knives and forks clacking with a steady rhythm. Dad smiled peacefully, passing the dishes around the table.

I ran water into a sticky pan and when I turned the tap off, I could hear Darcy saying, "There's this little gal down in Hodges and I can tell you boys . . ."

"Nothing dirty now, Darcy," said Dad.

Darcy laughed. "Cecil, I never say anything dirty. Not in mixed company. Jessie," he called, "come out here."

I felt as if I'd been caught with my ear to a keyhole and I could feel a flush creeping over my face. "Damn you," I said under my breath. I took my time drying my hands and walked slowly to the kitchen door. I leaned against the doorjamb and said, "Is there something I can do for you, Mr. Blunt?"

"I just wanted to tell you," Darcy said, his smile wide and impertinent, "that the only reason anybody ever works for your daddy is to eat your cooking."

I met his eyes with more boldness than I felt. "If I didn't know what a smart aleck you are, I might believe you."

"It's good to know my reputation is still intact. But I could be a changed man for all you know."

"I doubt it. You look entirely too pleased with playing the bad man to give it up."

"Bad isn't always disagreeable," Darcy said and winked at my father. The other men smiled down into their plates.

"Maybe so," I said, "but being bad is no guarantee it isn't disagreeable either."

"She's got you there, Darcy," Dad chuckled and I, fairly bursting with laughter, turned back into the kitchen.

"Don't count me out, Jessie," Darcy called after me.

I stayed busy in the kitchen cleaning up the pots and pans. But even with the water running, I could hear Darcy's voice from the dining room. I couldn't hear the words and there must have been times when they were eating in silence or someone else was speaking whose voice was too low to hear. When Darcy did speak he always seemed to make the other men laugh and there was a feeling of a party in the air. It had been a long time since I'd been to a party. I was glad to have Darcy there.

When the men finished eating I could hear their chairs scraping the floor. As they passed through the kitchen, I stayed turned to the sink, intent on scrubbing a pot. Behind me the screen door slammed and voices called, "Thank you, ma'am." "Thank you, ma'am." "Thanks, Jess."

After several minutes had passed, I turned to find Darcy standing in the doorway of the dining room. Startled, I screamed. Darcy jumped and looked behind him. "Was that for me?" he said laughing.

"God, you scared me to death," I said irritably.

"I just wanted to help." He held some plates. He offered them toward me.

"It's not necessary," I said taking the dishes and stacking them on the sink. He put his hands in his pockets and leaned back against the refrigerator. We faced each other across the quiet kitchen. His smile was slow and he shifted his weight as if he were preparing for a long wait, a wait that wouldn't disconcert him at all. He fixed me with a stare and I looked back at him, staring too, watching his face, the way his eyes never left my face. His skin was tawny, his nose sharp and straight like a knife blade down the center of his face. His hair was black as a crow's wing and I thought that he was like a crow, clever and disreputable. I concentrated on that thought until I mastered the flutter of fear in my stomach. Then I found myself grinning back at him. It seemed as if we had touched each other across the space between us, yet neither of us had moved. I felt a quick hot stab, nearly a pain, between my legs. It had been a long time since a man had flirted with me. Not since Stephan. I looked away and the moment passed.

Darcy shook his head and said, "You're a funny woman, Jessie. Pretty as you are and stay so much by yourself."

"There aren't many people's company I prefer to my own," I said.

"Why don't you give my company a try?"

I tied an apron on and turned away from him. I could feel the heat rising in my face again. "What'd you do, Darcy," I said, "run through all the rest of the women in the county?"

Darcy laughed. "That's right. You're the only one left. What about it? Meet me at the Blue Moon Saturday night and I'll dance your feet off."

I crossed my arms at the waist, pressing my belly. I was sure I could feel something there hard and unyielding as if I were made like the earth with iron at the core. Outside, the machines started up again, their clatter harsh between Darcy's question and my answer.

"Okay, Darcy," I said finally and was flooded by a warm rush of daring.

"Well, all right, then," he said with a little salute. "I'll see you Saturday about nine."

Too breathless to speak, I said nothing.

Ellen

. . . The worst part of the whole evening when I went to talk to Darcy at the gas station is I kept wondering what it would be like to kiss him. I mean he's an old guy and everything. Not really old but a man. Maybe I have turned into a nymphomaniac after being with Kenny, even though it was only one guy. I don't know. That would be really terrible because Darcy said I was still technically a virgin and I have decided that I am *never* going to do it again until I get married. I swear to God.

PS. You know, God, that I am really sorry.

IT was another summer evening and we were all in the yard, Daddy, Bip, Mama and me. Mama sat with me on the steps of the porch. The evening sun sent hard rays into the sun porch and cast a jungle of shadows through Mama's plants. Daddy and Bip hadn't opened the encyclopedia yet and Daddy sat turned in his chair to talk to Mama.

"What do you think, Gret? I met the mayor today and he thanked me for a 'beautiful letter.' "

"Yes," Mama nodded, "you told me."

"That's an exact quote, mind you, 'beautiful letter.' I guess people remember when they've heard from Melvin Gibbs."

"Melvin, there were men here today, measuring. In the field, I mean."

"I think the letter did the trick, you know. It should put a stop to this building. You'll see."

"Melvin," Mama said a little louder than before, "today there were men here. . . ."

"Men? Today? Where?" Daddy twisted all the way around in the chair.

"Men in the field," said Mama, "measuring."

"That's called 'surveying' when they do that," said Daddy, "not measuring, surveying, okay?"

"Yes," sighed Mama and rested her head against the railing behind her. A small breeze gathered speed as it moved across the lawn. It smelled of the river and was cool. Mama folded her skirt carefully around her legs and turned her face into the breeze. She closed her eyes.

Below, Daddy and Bip flipped through the book. "How about this, Bipper? Does it look interesting? No? This then," said Daddy. His voice rolled along steady as the wind off the river and Mama sat still as stone. Her cheekbones were broad beneath the deep shadows of her eyes. Her hair was the light dry yellow of the scrubbed oak floors of the house. My mother didn't speak but then that was her habit. She was wrapped in silence like the sky is wrapped in stars as though to prove that the simple matters of our life would never go unobserved. There is a furious concentration to her silence that forbids intrusion. And I didn't talk to her as she sat resting on the porch but I wondered, Are you listening, Mama? as Daddy talked on.

"Now, here, Bip. Here's one I think we ought to take up . . . marijuana. I read the other day where this is getting to be all the rage with the kids."

Bip spread his hands in innocence, questioning.

"Well, it's a drug, son. You smoke it like tobacco. Let's see what it says here. ' . . . the user may have dreamlike experiences, with a free flow of ideas and distortions of time and space; a minute may seem like an hour, nearby objects may appear to be far away.' "

Daddy was kindly and Bip listened solemnly. Bip, old Bipper, my dear brother, I thought, you're probably sitting on an ounce of marijuana this very minute. Bip loved to be high. Sometimes we would smoke it together when Mama and Daddy were gone. But I was a timid smoker, having come to it later than Bip and I didn't often do it. When my brother smoked marijuana, he smoked it in long gulps and he sniffed what was left in the air. He couldn't get enough. It wasn't only being high; the sweet musty odor was a bonus for him. Smells were important to him. His deafness made them sharper, I guess.

When Bip was high, his hands were joyful and articulate as puppets. "When I'm high, I can see better, smell better," his hands said, "I can hear." And he would roll on my bed in time to the music on the radio. I'm sure it was only the vibrations that he felt but sometimes I would forget and sing the words out loud expecting him to sing along.

The pages of the encyclopedia fluttered in the wind. Daddy admonished Bip, "I don't want you to even consider it. God knows you have troubles enough."

Bip's face darkened. He signed, pointing to the book.

"What?" said Daddy, his eyes wide. "Of course, I never tried marijuana. Don't even joke about a thing like that. What makes you ask a question like that?"

Bip signed tensely and pointed again at the book.

"What?" said Daddy. "Here? ' . . . may destroy or deform the offspring of laboratory animals . . .' "

Daddy stopped short and Bip glared spitefully. Daddy was always so wary with Bip and yet each time my brother landed a blow, Daddy never seemed to have seen it coming. Why did Bip have to push him face-to-face, take him to account for his every foolishness. I got angry with Daddy too but I never even came home late. I put the lie to my father's inventions of me in other ways. Since I was sixteen, boys and then men had climbed through my bedroom window. They were stealthy and driven as tomcats and they loved to climb to the porch roof and slip through my window. Rapunzel, Rapunzel, let down your long hair.

I could see the pain and confusion in Daddy's face. Mama seemed suddenly called to attention. She opened her eyes and turned toward my father and brother.

"It's not my fault you were born deaf," Daddy huffed. "It was God's will, that's all there is to it."

"Ach," said Mama. She said the German word with the same righteous energy she used to sweep disagreeable things from the porch. She trained a sharp stare at Bip who wouldn't look at her. Daddy brushed at the knees of his pants, trying to recover himself. He'd taken another beating from Bip and for what? A lecture to Bip on an accomplished fact. Drugs were everywhere by then. In Baltimore where Bip went to school, there were grass and acid available, whatever you wanted, red pills, green ones, black hash, Colombian. It was on the streets, in the schools, even the Chesapeake School for the Deaf or the Chesapeake School for the Criminally Deaf as Bip called it.

Daddy talked to me about the beauties of chastity when I was going away to college. It was roundabout, being Daddy, and again it was after the fact. I wish I could say I laughed at my father for what he didn't know, but I didn't. There were times in college when I felt nearly free, when I took lovers in a new heady defiance and loved them with a bravery I could scarcely believe. Yet when they left me, I was brought full circle each time to be haunted by my father's faraway faith. And then I would mourn again my lost virginity as if it were a limb torn from me. It's not so strange to have wanted it back. Didn't the men I knew love me best when I smiled out of some notion I had of saints and little children?

Daddy turned the pages of the encyclopedia. He shook his head, perplexed probably by Bip's attack. He flipped the pages idly, seeming to find nothing of interest there. Suddenly three brightly colored pictures darted up gaily from the book. Daddy spelled the heading out, "M-A-T-I-S-S-E."

"That's Matisse, Daddy," I called.

"Matisse, right. A French fellow. Well, I don't know what to make of these pictures he's painted here."

Bip signed.

"Well, yes, pretty colors. But I'm of the opinion that if you're going to paint a cow, it ought to look like a cow. Otherwise, what's the point? Did you ever see a woman who looked like that?" He jabbed a finger at Matisse's garishly complected woman in a white blouse. "If your mother looked like this, I'd take her to the hospital. What do you suppose this fellow was up to?"

Bip laughed silently and Mama closed her eyes again. If Daddy had asked me, I could have told him a little bit about Matisse. I had majored in art history in college after all. But he wouldn't have asked me for my opinions on the encyclopedia any more than he would ask my mother. He measured me by my mother and she was fearsome in a silence deeper than a preference or personal peculiarity. Yet there was no chilliness to my mother's silence because I believed, and perhaps my father did too, that that silence began in some femaleness that had to do with the bloody beginnings of life and all the mean secrets of the body that she knows from tending us. And the terse instructions she gave to Bip and me . . . . "Brush your teeth." "Drink your milk." "Don't touch cats, you'll get ringworm" . . . had seemed like constant conversation between us. My father laughed and joked with us and if we had dared to entertain the question, I think we would have said we loved him best. But it was my mother in her utter devotion to the details of our daily lives that ordered the world for us and provided our security.

Oh, I've felt the tug of her wisdom. Sometimes when I would help her wash dishes or bake or drag the rugs out to the line to air, I could nearly see by the sheer intensity of the care she took that her days had the single-minded purity of a monk's day. I've been shamed by a patience in her that could only be explained as love. I remember a day when my grandfather was still alive. He was very feeble by then but he had insisted on weeding the garden. My mother had set a small low stool outside for him. He was wearing one of Mama's floppy straw hats as he sat leaning as far from the stool as he could reach to tug up the weeds. He plucked at them with a great finality as if forbidding them from ever sprouting up in the garden again. I was in the kitchen with my mother helping her can tomatoes. The tomatoes bubbled on the stove and the odor mingling with the steam in the hot kitchen seemed red and pulpy as the tomatoes themselves. And all through the long busy afternoon, my grandfather called, "Greta, Greta. Greta, please." And while I only wanted to clap my hands over my ears at the sound of his old cracked voice, my mother would lay aside whatever she was doing with no sign of irritation and go to him. Then she would help him to his feet and set the stool down somewhere else. And when he was finally seated in his new place, each time she would set his hat aright again against the sun. "Greta, Greta. Greta, please." I can still hear him call and when I think of that day tenderness springs up in me and makes me think I will never not love her again. But there are other times when I would do anything to keep myself from sinking under the fleshy weight of her woman's wisdom, sinking out of my father's sight, any man's sight.

I looked at Mama on the porch. Wispy hairs at her temples caught the breeze and fanned her pale cheeks. Her hands were clasped in her lap. I wondered if my father felt the same about talking to Mama that I did, as if he had to prove the importance of whatever he wanted to talk about. Did my parents talk at all . . . heart to heart, I mean? Could it have been that they did their talking when no one else could hear? Was it part of their marriage more secret than sex? Maybe if I had walked by their bedroom door at night, I would have heard them. Mama telling Daddy what she thinks of when she stares out the kitchen window, Daddy speaking with an immediacy I've never heard.

I didn't suppose any of that to be true. It seemed to me men and women only came really face-to-face in extremes of desperation. And until those times we go on acting out of other people's ideas of us. Those ideas wrap us as we grow until we're like the little nest of dolls that rest one inside the other. And if we broke each one open like an egg to see the smaller one inside, would we at last find a core explaining all the rest or would we find, when every doll lay halved, nothing there at all?

I've wanted special words that would be used only to express the heart. I've wanted love to alchemize honesty from fear. And lately, there have been times at the Blue Moon Cafe when I've been talking to Darcy Blunt and it seemed as if we were speaking the best possible truths about ourselves and the world. But then Darcy and I began talking a long time ago.

When I was sixteen, I picked Darcy from all of Hooke's Crossing to talk to. I had a problem and I'd chosen him to take it to because my problem was exotic and so was Darcy. He had a flashy car that was almost new, a secret-keeping smile as if he knew more than he would ever tell. And he had cool-eyed out-of-town girlfriends. Everybody knew he'd been to a whorehouse in Baltimore. I don't know who was there to see him, but all the boys in town swore it was true.

When I went to see him, Darcy was twenty-nine. I knew he was divorced and had a young son. That first night I waited until late to go to see him where he worked. He was night man at the gas station Jeff Maynes had bought on the GI Bill. I had had to sneak out of the house and when I got to the station I could see Darcy sitting behind a desk inside. He was reading a newspaper. His hands, man's hands, hairy and large, were splayed out on the desk. The sight of those hands nearly sent me home again, but the enormity of my problem drove me inside. When I came through the door, Darcy said, "What are you doing out so late, Ellen?"

I shrugged and with a smile pulled up a chair by the desk. I'd seen my father do this when he came to the station. It was bright inside the station. An air conditioner whined and rattled in a window, yet as cool as it was, sweat rose under the hair on the back of my neck, traced a course down my spine.

"Hadn't you better go home?" asked Darcy.

"No, sir."

"You don't have to say 'sir' to me. You're not in the army."

"Okay, but could I stay a little while? Then I'll go, I promise."

"I suppose," he said and his smile suggested there were reasons for my being out I hadn't thought of. He reached into a drawer in the desk and pulled out a half-empty whiskey bottle. Without spilling a drop, he poured the whiskey into a Coke bottle. Slow, slow movements, all the time in the world. He had hours before closing and people stopped in at the station all the time.

"I sneaked out," I said. "I wanted a Coke."

"Help yourself," he said, waving his hand toward the Coke machine, "and while we're on the subject, don't tell your daddy you were down here if you get caught."

"Oh, I just never would," I said dropping coins into the machine slot. The machine hummed to itself for a moment and then an icy bottle of Coke bumped down its chute. "You can count on me, Darcy," I said, trying out his name, and with the strange taste of it on my tongue, I felt as if he and I were the only people awake on that summer night in Hooke's Crossing.

I sat down at the desk with him but before long the bell outside rang and he went to wait on a customer. You'll never tell him, I told myself. Then nervously I glanced outside. The driver was no one I knew. He stood talking to Darcy. Darcy laughed and pulled at his ear. I'd seen old men do that a lot. How could I tell him? Bending down quickly, I took the bottle of whiskey out of the desk and poured a big shot into my Coke. Then I sat back and crossed my legs.

When Darcy came back we talked. "Did you see Henry Fisher's new car?" "Who's going out for football this year?" "River's down. Bone dry at Fletcher's Creek." And all the while I was poised at the very edge of my courage to ask him what I'd come about. But the more we talked, the stranger the notion of asking him at all became.

The next few times he left to go outside, I laced his drink along with mine. His smile was more serene and secretive with every splash of whiskey. I was getting very drunk. It was late and when I looked out the window, I thought the station lights must be too harsh, too white to look at head-on from the still, dreamy darkness outside. The moths hitting against the bright windows seemed big as birds.

84

After a while, Darcy pulled the bottle out and held it up. "Goddamn, girl, you've been drinking my whiskey." His smile was gone.

"Just a little," I said, sitting up in the chair a bit straighter.

"A damn sight more than a little, I'd say. Your father'd put my ass in a sling if he found out. What are you trying to do to me?"

The drone of the air conditioner rose to a roar in my ears. Oh, he was angry and he would never tell me what I needed to know and I would be alone for the rest of my life with my terrible peculiarity. I laid my head on my arms and began to cry.

"Hey, now, Ellen, quit that. I mean it." His voice had softened a little.

I lifted my head and choked out, "I just wanted to ask you something. I couldn't do it without the drinks."

Those man's hands danced in front of me as he raised them and said, "Whoa, I don't think I want to hear anything you've got to get drunk to tell me."

"Darcy, I've got to ask you something real important. I've just got to know because . . . because I've got this friend and I promised her I'd ask you about it. She's awful upset."

"I sure hope your friend isn't pregnant." His smile was gone and I thought he looked very old under the lights. He rubbed his eyes.

"No, it's not that, honest. She couldn't be because she can't even do it."

Darcy sat back in his chair with the look of a man opening a bullpen. "Do it?" he said.

I squirmed in my chair. He wasn't going to be any help. He didn't even know. "You know . . . do it . . . with a boy."

"I see. Okay. What does your friend want to know?" What a stupid idea it had been to come to see him at all. It reminded me of going to see Dr. Charles and having to tell him things about your body you didn't want anyone ever to know.

"Well, why can't she?" I shouted in desperation.

"Well, I'm sure I don't know, Ellen," he shouted back.

Ah, the tears were torrential. I shook with the power of my sobs.

"Okay, okay," he said stroking my hair. "Come on. I'm sorry. We'll talk about it. Come on." The weight of his hand on my head seemed more than it could bear, as though my skull were no more than eggshell. I pushed his hand away and raised my head. Glaring at him accusingly, I said, "I don't know how to tell you now."

"Umm," he said, "let's see. Where are you having trouble? . . ."

"My friend," I reminded him.

"Your friend, right. Where is your friend having trouble . . . uh, doing it?"

I put my head back on the desk and mumbled into the darkness of my arms. "The boy's thing won't go in."

I could hear the quick intake of his breath but his voice was very calm, just like Dr. Charles talked to you, like nothing surprised him. He said, "Was this the first time your friend ever did it?"

"Yes." I raised my head again.

"Okay," he said, "this is what I think the problem is . . . the boy didn't break the . . ."

Yes, yes? He stared at the ceiling while I held my breath.

"Jesus, I don't know another word for it," he said at last.

"What? What word?"

"He didn't break the cherry. Do you know what that means?" He was beginning to look angry again.

"Why didn't he, Darcy?"

"Ellen, how the hell should I know?"

"Maybe there's something wrong with the girl," I suggested softly.

"Is that what all this is about?" he said laughing. "No, no, honey, the girl's okay. I think probably your friend's boyfriend just needs a little more experience.

Not that I'm recommending he get it with your friend, mind you."

"The boy said he'd done it lots of times."

"Well . . ." Darcy said shrugging, laughing.

I could see he didn't believe me, but it didn't matter. The girl was all right. I'd imagined a whole life alone keeping my strange secret and never having a husband or babies. The girl was all right.

"Hey," I said, "the girl's still a virgin, isn't she?"

Darcy considered. "Sure. Why not?" he said. Then we both laughed and sat back in our chairs with pleased grins. I thought we had done very well with such a serious subject and I congratulated myself on thinking of Darcy to ask. Under the desk I kicked off my shoes. My feet felt very naked in the chill of the air conditioning. I wondered if Darcy thought I was pretty, and then quick as the flash that passed between my thighs, I wondered what it would be like to kiss him. I looked at Darcy guiltily as though I'd said it aloud. He was still looking very pleased with himself. He leaned back in his chair.

I sipped my Coke and said, "Can I ask you something else?"

"Ask away," he said.

"What does 'beat off' mean?"

Darcy's chair lurched as he tried to right it. Regaining his balance, he peered across the desk at me. "Ellen, go home."

Years went by after that until Darcy and I began to talk again. But in those years between whenever I'd see him around town, he seemed a friend of mine. As if in knowing that one secret, he could divine others I'd never told him. When we met again at the Blue Moon Cafe, our conversation seemed as old and long as Bip and Daddy's.

In the yard in the breeze from Bright River, Daddy was saying "Tut, tut," as Bip pointed to one of Matisse's pictures in the book. Five nude women, faceless and graceful, danced on the page. Daddy drew back from the picture. "It's everywhere these days," he said shutting the book with a decisive thump. Mama seemed roused by the sound and rose.

With a grin, Bip signed and Mama, saying nothing, disappeared noiselessly into the house.

"You're glad?" Daddy said. "Don't be flip. You've been raised to know better than that. Some things are private."

Bip formed a question.

Daddy's face reddened. "Because decent people know enough not to show their bodies."

Bip signed.

Daddy yelped, "God, that's who says and only an idiot would have to ask."

Bip rose and stalked toward the front of the house. "I forbid you to ride that motorcycle," Daddy shouted. Bip didn't turn around. Soon we could hear the scream of the engine of the bike. Bolting up from his chair, Daddy started after Bip. And I, hearing a car in the driveway, followed Daddy. As we came around the side of the house, we caught sight of Bip on the bike. He was already moving toward the street. My date for the evening had driven into the driveway. I waved to him as Bip pulled around his car. When Bip gave Daddy and me a brief glance, Daddy called quickly, "Bip, come back here."

But Bip, cutting the bike hard into the street, chose not to see. As he approached the corner of our street, he thrust one arm in the air and raised his middle finger. My date, stepping from his car, snickered. Daddy's back stiffened and he yelled after Bip, "For Lord's sake, Benjamin, your mother or your sister might hear you!"

Jessie

Was it a vision, or a waking dream?
Fled is that music:—do I wake or sleep?

—KEATS

IT was Saturday and I was supposed to go out with Darcy. I had decided to go and then not to go a thousand times that day. But even at evening when the stars were poking tentative holes in the sky over the mountain, I couldn't make up my mind. Fresh from a bath that I told myself I would have taken anyway, I looked at myself in the mirror in the bathroom. I was a good-looking woman, I decided. But that thought didn't help. It was much too frail to bear the weight of confidence. What on earth will we talk about if I go? I wondered, this ex-high-school-English teacher coming up fast on an age to be called an old maid and this farmhand. Oh, I knew he wasn't really a farmhand. His family had suffered reverses—Darcy apparently being one of them. Everyone, of course, knew the story of his father's scandalous land deal and his subsequent suicide. It didn't matter. It was just that Darcy was so different from the other men I had dated, so different from Stephan. Stephan was head of the English department in the girls' school in Baltimore where I had taught. He was tall, ethereally thin and we read poetry to each other. I had loved it when the color rose in his face and his voice trembled with the joy of the words. I had fancied him a young Byron, passionate and willful. God, what would Darcy and I find to say to each other at the Blue Moon Cafe?

And all through the misgivings, I was dressing, applying my makeup, brushing my hair. I was moving with no volition, like a boat carried on the water toward its destination.

When I went downstairs, Dad was sitting under the reading lamp with his newspaper. He laid the paper in his lap as I entered the living room. I sat down, arranging my dress over my knees. Dad waited patiently for me to tell him where I was going. All that week I hadn't mentioned the date to him. I had kept thinking I wouldn't go at all.

"I'm going out with Darcy Blunt," I said.

"Oh?" He was very surprised. "I'd think about that if I were you. Darcy's a nice boy, but he ain't too . . . steady."

"He's not a boy, Dad, he's a man."

"That's why I'd think about it," he said.

I laughed. "It's just a date. I'm taking my own car, so if he gets too wild, I'll just come on home."

"That's a grand idea, Jess, your own car," he said as I rose. He stood too and walked me to the back door.

"I don't suppose I could ask you not to go," he said. I shook my head and kissed him on the cheek.

"It's not that I don't like the fellow, Jess."

"I know Dad. Don't worry, okay?"

"I suppose," he said as I closed the door behind me.

Outside, walking toward the car, I thought, I'm really going. I felt light-headed. My hands were cold and numb. It's only a date, I told myself sliding behind the wheel. The dogs all lifted their heads at the sound of the engine starting. Queenie's pups' eyes had opened the day before. The little dogs scrambled to the fence and danced on short fat legs.

The last time I had had a date, I'd felt like a young girl. At twenty-six, I didn't feel young anymore, and I didn't know if my dress was right. I'd never been to a bar before. But I did know I was going that night and it had nothing to do with what Darcy and I would talk about. It had to do with Darcy, shirtless, pitching shucks up on the truck as his back shimmered like satin in the

September sun. It had to do with his jaunty grace that made him seem as if he were free from what other people thought of him. And it had to do with his smile that said I was pretty long before he ever asked me out, his smile that promised whatever I would dare to ask. Oh, it wouldn't be much that I would ask. Just the thought of his being a keeper of the mysteries of the flesh had been enough to draw me over the quiet borders of my life. It was dark, this attraction, and modest, the earth breathing sweetly through the flowers of a night garden that sheltered secrets I only needed to know were there.

I pulled down the driveway, out of sight of the house and stopped the car. My courage had failed and I sat, my heart pounding, looking out over the fields. The night air was crisp. In the autumn, there's a sigh of movement that rises and falls, day and night. It's not only dried leaves stirring in the wind. There are sounds the whole busy earth makes in preparation for the winter. The ground shifts with a soft moan, hardening itself before snow and ice mark lacy death's-heads on its soil. And small creatures are hurrying everywhere in the fields and woods. They are pressed by the cool warning of the first frosts into burrowing, into flight, into death. I was saddened by the thought as if spring would never come again, as if the fiery richness of autumn meant nothing. But it wasn't the earth that had been struck into some spiteful everlasting winter. It was only me, haunted by the aborted fertility of my body, who brooded on death.

The moon had risen over the trees. It washed the fields in a light clear as tears and the ground seemed rubbed raw with only the stubble of the crop left. The sky licked the wounds of the earth. Suddenly I felt chastened. The fervent constancy of the moonlight chided me. I leaned my head back against the seat and closed my eyes. An unlikely peace stole over me and I thought of Darcy's face that day in the kitchen. "Why don't you give my company a try?" I nearly laughed out loud. When Stephan had first asked me out it was in a note he

93

had written to thank me for some extra work I had done for him. In the PS he had reworked a line from Thomas Hardy we had been discussing to invite me out to coffee. Maybe I was no match for Darcy. Yet his face was clear before me. Oh, no you don't, Darcy Blunt, you won't get the better of me. I let the brake off and there was a stirring in my chest that felt like singing. Here I come, Darcy, I thought. I hope you're ready!

I drove to town and then down by the water. I stopped the car and stepped out into the dirt parking lot. The Blue Moon Cafe was by Bright River. It overlooked the water and a short pier ran off the back. Under the moon, the river flowed dark and sullen, oily slick where the moonlight splashed the ripples. I straightened the skirt of my dress and buttoned one more button at the neck. I tried to remember how I had walked when I was meeting Stephan and had wanted him to love the look of me the minute he saw me. But I couldn't remember; I only felt awkward and too tall.

Inside, a jukebox was playing. It was early in the evening and the music was subdued. Cigarette smoke rose in ragged blue tiers toward the ceiling. People at the bar and tables turned when I opened the door. Their faces told me my dress was all wrong. All my confidence drained away. My hands began to tremble and I crossed my arms. I looked around, careful not to catch anyone's eye. Darcy wasn't there. I looked at my watch, a little show for the other people in the place. She must be meeting somebody, she's checking her watch. It was already past nine. I would have turned and left except I thought that would look foolish. Instead, I walked to a table as if there were nothing strange about my being there. There were faces there I had seen around Hooke's Crossing. Some of them watched me curiously as I seated myself at a small rickety table.

Goddamn you, Darcy, I thought as I ordered a drink and turned toward the jukebox. I sat there staring at the liquid red lights, seeing nothing. I even tapped my foot as if I were keeping time to the music. One drink and I would go. Oh, Dad was so right. . . . "Darcy . . . ain't too steady." I felt like I was glowing in my embarrassment. I was conspicuous, vulnerable, my aloneness advertisings things I didn't mean at all. If I ever saw Darcy Blunt again, I would . . .

There was a touch on my arm and Darcy stood there grinning. "Well, Miss Jessie. I'm sorry to be late, but to tell the truth, I didn't think you'd be here."

I wanted to slap his face and clenched my hands in my lap. "I told you I would be."

"Yeah, but it's hard to tell with girls like you. Sometimes they lose their nerve."

"Well, this one didn't."

"Jessie," he said still smiling slyly, "I'm sorry. Sometimes I get called away on business." He sat down at the table.

"I don't remember asking you to sit down." He squeezed my arm absently as if he hadn't heard me, then he called the waitress over and ordered drinks. I glared at him across the table.

"What you need is to smile more, Miss Jessie." He settled his arms on the table and smiled possessively at me.

"I don't need the advice of a man who can't even get to a date on time."

"We renegades are good for other things. We're just not known for being on time."

"Is that what you consider yourself . . . a renegade?"

"I know what you're thinking . . . the Blunts are all bankers but that's only half the story. It's my mother's people that are interesting, you see. They got a renegade or two hidden away in that family history. Real interesting." He winked at me like people wink at children they're teasing inviting them to share the joke.

"I'm going home," I said and picked up my drink, planning to toss it down defiantly in one last furious gulp. I raised the glass quickly to my lips and drank. The whiskey exploded in my mouth like brush fire and burned down the length of my throat. Darcy, smiling, watched

95

me as I felt the heat rise in my face. I willed my features into a smile and rose.

"Hey, come on," said Darcy, "sit down and I'll tell you a story. Let me redeem myself. Just one little story and a drink."

"No."

"What's the matter, Jessie, you afraid of me?" He reached out and traced a finger lightly on my arm. His touch left a trail cool as a sigh on my skin.

"No," I said again and just at that moment the drink I had had burgeoned in a yellow bloom of light inside my head. I sat back down.

"All right, then. You got your drink?" I nodded numbly and clung to the empty glass. "Now, bear with me here," he said. "This is a story about my great-great-great-grandfather. His name was Ambrose Darcy and he lived in this little town in Scotland. And that's where all the Darcys he ever knew had lived, so it never occurred to him that he might live anywhere else. Well, one Sunday Ambrose was sitting in church and he nods off. His neighbors weren't too happy about that because they figured he was probably sleeping off a drunk. Now, it was true that Ambrose had been known to tilt the bottle from time to time. So maybe he was sleeping off the effects of the night before or maybe he wasn't, but he slept through the whole service. And while he was peacefully dozing there, the rest of the congregation stood up to sing the last hymn, which just happened to be 'Amazing Grace.' Do you know it?" I shook my head.

He sat up straight in his chair and sang out in a strong warm voice that rose above the jukebox. " 'Twas grace that brought us safe thus far/ And grace will lead us home." Several people around us turned to look at him, then shook their heads and smiled. But Darcy didn't seem to notice them. He was leaning across the table, intent on his story.

"Well, just as they hit the last lines, my great-great-great-grandmother lets the old man have it in the knee

96

with her foot and he jumps up. He's on his feet when they finish, but he's still groggy, trying to place where he is and wanting to make a good show like he never missed a thing. So, he calls out loud enough for everybody to hear him, "And a grand old girl she is too, that Grace."

I laughed.

"Nobody'd have anything to do with him after that. Although there were some at the time who said the incident was only the last straw on old Ambrose. But Ambrose said to hell with the whole bunch of them and sailed for America." He finished and sat smiling at me.

"You're not as charming as you think you are," I said.

"But damn near."

"I'm still thinking of going home."

"I didn't ask you out to fight," he said. "Relax and we'll have some fun."

The funny thing was, we did have fun. We talked and laughed and I thought how odd it was that I didn't love him and yet I felt the same current of excitement I'd felt being with Stephan as if love were less than I had thought. In the smoky heat of the Blue Moon Cafe, love seemed an unnecessary frill that not too long before I would have had to place on the simple act of Darcy sliding his knees between mine under the tiny table. People were up dancing and the music surged and swelled around the small room in waves. The floor trembled under my feet and I imagined the Blue Moon Cafe had slid down its hill and was rushing along on the current of the river.

"Are you glad you came, Miss Jessie?" Darcy was saying.

"Yes," I yelled, "yes, yes."

"I sure do love to see you smile," he said.

"Can we dance?"

He lifted me laughing into his arms to dance. On the dance floor, the music seemed to be playing inside my head, striking a beat in my temples. An excitement, sharp as an electrical shock, rocketed down my spine as Darcy pressed his fingers into my back. His thighs rubbed against mine at every step. His breath was warm on my cheek. I pressed my face to his neck and inhaled the odor of him, his after-shave, the soap in his clean shirt. And underneath the civilizing smells the warm vital odor of his skin came to me like a wicked, thrilling secret. We swayed to the music. I think we must nearly have stopped dancing altogether. Darcy wrapped a strand of my hair around his finger and said into my ear, "Jessie, do you want to leave here?"

I felt jarred to attention. I pulled away from him. "You don't waste any time, do you? I ought to slap your face."

"You can do that if you want to," he said laughing, "but I had the real distinct impression you didn't expect me to come courting. I'm not exactly your kind of man."

My face burned to hear him talk like that to me. I nearly lied, told him he was wrong, but I felt so completely caught out, nailed dead to rights under his sardonic smile. "I can't stay all night," I said.

"So you don't worry Daddy?"

"That's right."

He pulled me close again and we danced in silence for a while. I leaned against him but I had retreated from him, saddened that Darcy's indelicacy could call up the same liquid weakness in my body that I had felt just glancing at Stephan through his open classroom door. I had to make myself hurry by, not stop to watch him lecture. He would pace the front of the room, his fingers jabbing the air to make a point, his hair tousled, his clothes rumpled as if he had more important things to think about. The girls in his classes leaned toward him attentively and some of them sent him love notes. Oh, I never heard about the notes from Stephan; the girls themselves told me. When I asked him about them, teasing him, he seemed surprised at my interest. "Oh, don't you suppose everyone gets them?" Then we both laughed trying to imagine dry, dour Art Starkes in chemistry getting a love note from a student.

I was even smiling to myself a little thinking of it when Darcy whispered in my ear, "Why don't we go to Jeff Maynes's place before it gets too late. Jeff's gone to Baltimore." He kissed my cheek.

"I'll take my own car," I said.

"Whatever you like."

And later when I was following him over rutted country roads toward Jeff's house, I was shaking so badly, I could hardly keep my foot on the accelerator. The night air swept through the car, cooling my skin, burning my eyes. Half-formed doubts rose and were carried away as I sped along behind him. The night seemed fated, inevitable. As the car hurtled along, I pictured myself on the deck of a ship . . . Captain Ahab's whaler no doubt. The wind rushed over me and the ship coursed through the night seas, a fire on the deck glowing like a great red heart in the darkness. I was breathless with excitement. I would meet myself as another kind of woman on that loveless ground with Darcy, a woman I thought would surprise Stephan, perhaps disgust him. I was surprised myself and I raced along the back roads of Hooke's Crossing wildly wondering if I would see it through. Would I dare transform myself into someone who might never have loved Stephan at all? My hair streamed back from my face and I imagined that it must look like wings.

We bounced up one last dirt lane and Darcy stopped at what was little more than a shack set in a wide field between two stands of woods. The moonlight passed calm blue fingers over the land and the trees. We stopped our cars and Darcy got out. His footsteps were loud in the stillness. A big white tomcat crept out of the shadows. "Come here, Sam," said Darcy. He leaned down toward the animal who hissed and drew away.

"Hey, compadre, it's me," he said, extending his hand again. The cat crooked its tail and ambled back toward the house.

"Moody bastard," Darcy said walking toward my car. "He knows me as well as he knows Jeff. He just wants to make me look bad." He really seemed insulted.

"Maybe he thinks you should have phoned before you came over."

"By damn, Jessie, I think you're right." He opened my car door and took my hand. "I'll apologize to him the first chance I get. Jeff's got about a dozen cats around here," he said as we walked toward the door. "Sometimes at night, everywhere you look you see big yellow eyes."

"I see. We're being watched you mean."

"Not by anybody'd who'd tell."

"I'm not worried about that," I said.

"Well, in case you ever do."

There was a surprising awkwardness to Darcy once we were inside the tiny house. "You'll have to excuse the place," he said turning on the lights. "Jeff's not much on housekeeping." I closed my eyes for a moment, dreading a sordidness, but Darcy needn't have apologized. Jeff's house had an odd male harmony to it that I liked. I tried to imagine Jeff there playing the banjo propped in one corner or washing the dishes that rested in a rack on the sink. A cat with an owlish face regarded us from the top of the refrigerator.

Darcy offered me a drink with a worried hospitality. I shook my head and we stood in the small living room saying nothing. Darcy stood close to me. He wasn't a big man and he didn't loom over me as Stephan had. We looked at each other and he shrugged helplessly as if he could think of nothing else to do and took me in his arms and kissed me. His mouth was sweet with whiskey and a heated longing quivered over my body. When he pulled away he said, "Well, all right, then." We walked into the bedroom. He smoothed the unmade cover of the bed. Three cats leaped to the floor and disappeared into the light of the door. When we sat down on the bed, Darcy was solemn, just as I wanted him to be. He ran his hand down my neck and I felt lost in his eyes as if I were staring into the poignant depths of a night sky. Only for a moment, just as we lay back on the bed, did Stephan's sharp-boned, nervous face appear in my mind. Panic rushed over me. But Darcy, unknowing, comforted me with gentle fingers as he undressed me and himself. I closed my eyes and I was falling free, my arms outstretched, aching to embrace the whole fine fever of Darcy's body. He sighed against my ear, sliding down the same bright tunnel of desire. And, then, I was like water beneath his weight, supporting and rocking him effortlessly.

Afterward, clearheaded and watchful, I lay beside him. We had talked for a while and now Darcy's eyes were closed and his breathing even. I rose gingerly and began to dress. Darcy's voice made me Jump. "You okay, Miss Jessie?"

"Yes, I'm fine, Darcy," I said and I was. I checked myself for the bitterness of shame but there was none. I touched his cheek briefly and turned away.

"You are fine," he said. I couldn't see his face but I could feel his smile through the darkness. As I leaned over to put on my shoes, my belt cut sharply into my waist. I was reminded of the unseen deformity there, but for the moment I was untouched by it. Being with Darcy seemed like a revenge against the disease, as if it were scalded by the reproach of his semen.

"I'm going to go now, Darcy." He stirred in the bed.

"Don't get up," I said. I liked the thought of leaving the little house by myself, walking out into the moonlight as if I knew all the night by heart and wasn't afraid.

"I'll call you, Jessie," Darcy said drowsily.

"No," I said and with two of Jeff's cats at my heels, I let myself out into the moon-washed yard.

Ellen

. . . I never saw him like anything so much until afterward when he said it was the most disgusting thing a girl could do. What is wrong with me? I just wanted to show him how much I loved him, but I always do the worst thing. I hate me. I hate to go to church. And God must hate it that I sit right up front like I should be there. I pray as hard as I can that Jerry will love me again and everything will be like it was before. But losing Jerry is probably God's punishment and I will just have to accept it. . . .

HOT, hot summer air. It was breathless, steamy with humidity. The heat was like a sound in the air as if we could hear the river flow all the way in the middle of town. That evening in our yard, Daddy had set sprinklers out at the bottom of the lawn. In the field beyond there was a deep hole, the foundation of the new building. The newly turned earth was red, a bloody gash in the heart of the meadow.

"I didn't even see the little fellow." My father's voice rose in the stagnant air. "He was there so quick and then it was a terrible mess of blood and fur and grass."

I was putting off going inside to dress for a date and I sat on the steps feeling heavy as the heat. Mama knelt in a flower bed by the porch. Gnats buzzed in a cloud around her face and she swatted at them with one hand while she weeded with the other. Daddy, sitting side by side with Bip, looked anxiously out toward the field.

"I feel like a murderer. It's the damned work going on back there." He glowered at the construction site. "A rabbit would know better than to be that close to the house unless it was disturbed." We all nodded silently.

Daddy had run over a rabbit while mowing the grass. When he had first told the story at dinner, there had been tears in his eyes. And we all, Bip, Mama and I, had turned attentive faces to him. We had consoled him and talked about it all through dinner.

"The blade cut the scut off neat as you please when it

hit," Daddy went on with a shudder. I wondered how long he would talk about it. Bip already was staring off across the yard.

"Poor, dumb creature," Daddy cried.

"Think of something else," Mama said abruptly. She rose and drew her gardening gloves off. Slapping the dirt from them sharply, she disappeared into the house. Daddy turned his attention to me, the last of his audience. "It was a terrible thing, Ellen." I wondered how much the small animal's death had really touched him. I knew he loved the drama of it, loved to move people with his words. He would, I was sure, tell the story to everyone who came into the store the next day. When I was younger, he would recite a passage from Shakespeare he had learned in eighth grade. " 'Blow, winds, and crack your cheeks! Rage! Blow!/ You cataracts and hurricanes, spout / Till you have drench'd our steeples, drown'd the cocks! . . .' " he would begin. Striding around, he waved his arms, and in a voice deeper than he had ordinarily, he would shout Shakespeare's words. He would cry from the depths of his chest: ' "You sulph'rous and thought-executing fires,/ Vaunt-couriers of oak-cleaving thunderbolts,/ Singe my white head! . . .' " and his hand would fly to his head and stand his hair on end. ". . . 'And thou, all-shaking thunder,/ Smite flat the thick rotundity o' th' world!' " I had trembled in a mixture of embarrassment and excitement to hear the way he rolled the strange words around on his tongue and spat them out in exotic shapes.

When he recited, Mama sat looking straight ahead with the careful expression she wore when people told her things she didn't want to hear. My father's father was alive then and living with us. His face glowing red, he would clear his throat over and over while Daddy recited. Daddy's voice would rise to cover the sound. " 'Crack nature's moulds, all germens spill at once/ That makes ungrateful man!' " Daddy would end panting. His face would be exultant for an instant as if he expected to hear applause. Did he soar then, I wondered, on Shakespeare's high-blown words? Was he lifted on the echo of his voice above his father's polite distrust of unnecessary words, above Mama's patient indulgence? I don't think it was the words themselves that he loved, not the way a reader may love words. I had never known my father to read anything but the newspaper and the encyclopedia with Bip. No, it was his own voice sounding the words that exhilarated him. And thinking of it, I hoped that he was free in whatever small vanity he imagined for himself. Free in that one moment before Grandpa would say with a final clearing of his throat, "Well, yes, Melvin, isn't that dandy?"

"Poor, dumb little creature," Daddy said again softly. Bip pointedly opened the encyclopedia and pushed it into Daddy's lap. When he had my father's attention, he thumbed eagerly through the pages and pointed to a heading.

"Metaphysics?" Daddy said with a laugh. "Oh, come on, son, I just had to give up on that one."

Bip shook his head and pointed to himself, grinning.

"Oh, you got through it, huh? Then explain this to me, if you please." Daddy's finger moved rapidly down the page as he read quickly under his breath. "Aha, Mr. Smart Guy, explain this to your old father: '. . . in Kant's view, the mind furnishes the archetypal' "—Daddy faltered over the word—" 'forms and categories (space, time, causality, substance and relation) to its sensations, and these categories are logically anterior to experience, although manifested only in experience.' Now what on earth is that mumbo jumbo?"

Bip looked perplexed and twice his hands rose and then fell to his lap. Finally he shrugged.

"Exactly what I thought, you didn't understand it either. I just had the good sense not to waste my time reading it once I could see they weren't saying anything."

Bip held his hands up. "Wait." He signed intently.

"Oh, they're talking about what's real and what's not. Well, they sure did a lot of fancy dancing on a simple subject. I've heard these crazy arguments before. Barney Sloane loves to talk about this stuff. There'll be a bunch of us in the store and he'll start. He's never going to let any of us forget he went to Harvard for that law degree when he could just as easily have gone to State. Anyway, it doesn't take a college education to tell you what I tell him." Daddy clamped his hand over the back of Bip's chair. "If I can feel it, it's real. If I can see it, it's real. If I can hear it, it's real. If . . . well, you get the idea."

Bip's eyes were lit in triumph. He signed in grand gestures.

"God?" said Daddy. "No, I've never seen Him or heard Him."

Bip signed and slapped his knees with finality.

Daddy smiled placidly at him. "Faith is how I know He's real, Bipper. Faith."

Bip's hands stabbed the air, insisting on his point, but Daddy was unmoved, sitting serenely in the dying light of the sun, shaking his head slowly.

Bip had lost for once because he thought he could banish God as if He were a shadow trick of words, and doubt was the only sleight of hand necessary to make Him disappear. If it were as simple as Bip imagined I would gladly have put aside this God who had damned my immortal soul to hell. I would have held Him in my head like an idea and changed my mind. That may be the way God begins . . . as an idea. My first memory of Him is a friendly father face in a Sunday school picture at the Morningside Methodist Church. But before I was grown He had become all the blue of the sky. He swam in the world like all the colors of my eyes. Impossible to distill my small life out of such enormity. And He inhabited every nerve of me and could electrify my whole body at the very thought of evil because by then the threads of my faith were too closely woven with the notion of sin ever to pluck them free. Yes, if it were as simple as Bip thought, I would have begun with a new idea and made a god who had no name, a god who loved me. As it was, I supposed that with the way I'd lived my life, I would always find myself cold with terror in those rare dizzy moments when I caught sight of eternity.

I shivered on the steps above Daddy and Bip. I remembered the comfort of innocence, remembered going to sleep as a child feeling invulnerable in God's love. But I had laid me down to sleep since then too many nights in a man's embrace, taking comfort where I found it in a small circle of animal heat.

Bip sighed in exasperation. He waved his hand in the air, dismissing what had gone before. When he began to sign, his body had the watchful tension of a cat.

"I'm glad you see my point, son," said Daddy. "What is it now? If everything you see or hear is real, yeah . . . what about people who what?"

Bip spelled out a word in sign. Daddy repeated the letters slowly: "H-A-L-. Hallucinate? For god's sake, Bipper, we're talking about normal people here."

Shaking his head in disgust, Daddy waited for Bip to reply. But Bip only crossed his arms over his chest and tapped his foot angrily.

Suppose Bip had told Daddy what he had told me. On drugs, Bip said, he had seen trees clear and crystalline as ice. He said his motorcycle turned to water beneath him and he had been carried as if on a single wave for miles and miles one night. He said he had watched from some distance to see himself shrink to the tiny seed of the moment of his conception. A moment too awful for me to think of for myself when my father would just have rolled away from my mother's body to sleep. No, I put it right out of my mind and imagined myself bursting into being somewhere in the open air like the sun rising out of a sea of foam. Bip was convinced that what he saw when he was tripping were not dreams or tricks of the drug. He believed they were as real and true as anything he knew when he was straight. Wondrous Bip.

In the yard, he tapped Daddy roughly. His hands made forceful gestures while Daddy watched him.

"What are you talking about?" said Daddy. "Let me repeat for you one more time. If I can see it, it's real. If

I can hear it, it's real. If I can touch it, it's real. If I can taste it, if I can smell it, that's good enough for me.''

Bip signed, his jaw in knots.

"I said what?" Daddy sputtered. "Because you can't hear, sounds don't exist. Ha! That's not what I said.''

Bip nodded adamantly and Daddy rose from his chair. "No, sir, that is not what I said. I'm going to move the lawn sprinklers.''

He started across the lawn and Bip, his hands jammed in his pockets, rose and walked toward me. He sat down on the step below me and stared at his feet. Daddy turned to us from the bottom of the yard and called, "We're talking about normal people.'' Bip continued looking at his shoes.

"Ellen," Daddy said over the shush-shush of the sprinklers, "tell him I said we were talking about normal people.''

I put my hand on Bip's shoulder and he turned to smile at me. Below us, Daddy resumed his chair and swatted at the gnats shimmering ephemeral as a ghost over Bip's empty chair.

"Come on, son," said Daddy. "Come on back. We're really dragging our feet on this volume.''

I pushed Bip gently and he went to sit again next to Daddy. As soon as Bip was seated, Daddy began to read aloud. " 'Midsummer Eve.' Huh, it says here it's June twenty-third. Now that doesn't seem like the middle of the summer to me.''

Bip pointed to the encyclopedia.

"Oh, yes, I see," said Daddy, "the summer solstice. Still, they might have called it New Summer Eve or something.''

Bip shrugged.

"It is important," Daddy said. "I've taught you to question things, haven't I? Not to take things on blind faith. That's all I'm doing here. Just because some old Greek said that June twenty-third is the middle of the summer doesn't mean I have to accept it. The Greek civilization collapsed like a house of cards, you know.''

110

Bip signed.

"Yes, yes, good thinking, Bipper. Another calendar or a warmer climate."

" 'Throughout Europe,' " Daddy read, " 'peasants often celebrate by lighting fires in the streets and marketplaces. Although the fires were often blessed by priests, the celebration was generally conducted by the laity.' Well, you can tell it's a Catholic holiday. They bless everything in sight." Daddy chuckled.

I blotted at the sweat on my neck with the collar of my shirt. I knew I should have begun dressing for my date but I didn't want to go into the hot house. But before long I heard a car in the driveway. When my father turned toward the sound, Bip followed his gaze. I got up quickly and stepped inside. I stopped behind the screen door and stood in the deep shadows of Mama's plants, watching my date come around the side of the house into the backyard. His name was Ted and he was a tractor salesman. Daddy had met him the day before at the Dairy Maid Luncheonette and had invited him home.

Through the screen I watched Ted walk toward Daddy. They shook hands. I could see the high, hard curves of Ted's arms below the short sleeves of his shirt. I imagined his thighs rubbing against the light summer pants he wore. Later, I thought, I would run my hands over his legs and feel the fine woolly hair there. I knew I would take him, number thirty-seven on The List, and hold him to me dreaming of love. Where were the priests to bless these unholy fires?

It was nearly dark on the porch as the sun faded. The odor of potting soil in its densified fertility rose in the close air. Mama's hanging plants made exuberant splashes against the twilit sky. I sighed, feeling unhurried in the heat. Daddy and the young man stood talking in the yard. My thoughts moved like sleepy fingers testing the muscled contours of Ted's body, then turned, unmindful as sleepwalkers, to a night with Darcy.

I had been at the Blue Moon with Tom Drager and he had gotten drunk as usual. Darcy offered to take us home rather than let Tom drive. I had danced with Darcy at the Blue Moon but we had never been out. After we left Tom off, Darcy wrestled the top down on his old convertible and we drove out the state highway, talking and laughing as if it had been our date from the beginning. Then he turned onto a rutted dirt road that brought us out just beyond the fence of the Highway Drive-in Theater. Although it was only a short way off the main road it seemed very isolated. Its big screen rose, pulsing light like a spaceship, out of the woods that surrounded it. It's darker than anywhere in the woods at night, as if the trees have caught the darkness and forced it to the ground. And there's a rushing sound there like something huge breathing in its sleep. I sat close to Darcy and we stared ahead at the movie as if we had paid to get in. On the screen two big heads mouthed distant words into the air. The trees behind the screen shifted in the flickering lights like thoughts the big heads were thinking.

"You want to go in and watch the movie?" Darcy asked.

"No, thanks."

"Good, because I don't have any money. We would have had to climb the fence."

"I used to do that when I was in high school," I said, "and sit in the chairs in front of the snack stand."

Darcy slapped his hand. "Oh, man, I wish you hadn't said that."

"What?"

" 'Snack stand.' Now I'll have to have some popcorn."

"Oh, I'd love some too."

"Well, that's it, then. Come on, you can boost me over the fence."

We got out of the car and Darcy took my hand. I was reminded of the night in the gas station when I was sixteen and his hands had been so frightening. I locked my fingers in his as we began to pick our way through the underbrush toward the fence. There was music playing

112

on the screen and Darcy and I were in a movie of our own.

"Over here," I whispered when we reached the fence. I remembered the very best place to go over. He took a running start and then leaped straight up catching the top of the fence. He thudded against the wood like a bug on a windshield.

"You're not very sneaky," I said.

"Well, I'm no damn Tarzan. Come on, give me a boost."

Shaking with laughter, I pushed at his feet and at last he pulled himself over the top. "Think of me when I'm gone, honey," he grinned as his face disappeared over the fence.

I huddled by the fence pretending to be brave. I felt like a kid again, like when I'd first started dating and didn't know how every date would end. Laughter bubbled in my throat. Before long, Darcy's head emerged over the top of the fence. He held a box of popcorn in his teeth. He jumped to the ground and popcorn exploded out of the box like confetti.

"Ha," he said, "bet you didn't think the old man could do it."

"I don't think you're an old man," I said and he put one hand behind my head and kissed me quickly on the lips.

Back in the car, Darcy produced a half bottle of wine from a tangle of clothes in the backseat. We settled back and stared up at the screen.

"That's better," said Darcy. "You should always have popcorn at the movies."

We sat in silence for a while, eating popcorn and passing the wine back and forth.

"How come you go out with Tom Drager?" he asked. "It doesn't look like much fun."

"Well, I'm not in love with him or anything like that. It's just something to do. I'd never go to the Blue Moon by myself." I crossed my legs.

"If you ever did, I'd dance every dance with you."

"Would you?"

"I'd even pick you up and take you out but I don't guess your daddy'd like that."

"No."

"How old are you now, Ellen?"

"Twenty-two."

"Huh, double twos. I know a girl in Baltimore who says every number means something but I don't know what twenty-two means."

"I guess you know a lot of girls."

"Is that what you hear?" he asked.

"Oh, I hear a lot of things. Do you ever hear anything about me?"

"Like what?"

"Like I know a lot of men. Do you know what I mean?"

"Why do you think I ought to know that?"

"I don't know. You always treat me like I'm another kind of girl. It makes me feel dishonest."

"What kind of girl are you?" he asked and over the fence a pale blue sky appeared against the night's faint stars.

"Well, I'm not a virgin."

"Hell's bells, Ellen, I'm not either," he laughed. "What kind of girl does that make me?"

"It's not the same, Darcy."

"It's not? Then you must have done something different to lose your virginity than I did. I'd sure be interested to hear about that."

His voice was tender and I meant to laugh. But instead tears leaped into my eyes and ran down my cheeks. There were flags flying on the screen's blue sky. Darcy put his arm around me and I slid my hand over the outer side of his thigh. My fingertips traced the lean jut of his hipbone just above his belt, then lingered in the concavity of his lightly haired belly. He moaned softly and I closed my eyes, wondering if I loved him.

Out in the yard, Ted and Daddy had started toward the house. I turned from the door and walked into the kitchen. Passing behind Mama who stood at the sink, I said, "I have to change my clothes."

"All right," she said. "Wear something nice. We don't know this boy. No blue jeans."

I could hear Daddy's voice as they approached outside. "I told Gret . . . that's Mrs. Gibbs, you know . . . that boy is probably just as pleased to meet a nice girl for a change."

While I was dressing, I could hear them all in the living room. I knew just how they would be sitting in the heated air that surrounded us all like tepid water. Mama would sit to the left of Daddy on the couch. She would be watching Ted for any lapse of propriety. Bip would sit somewhere central to the speakers. Ted would be facing Daddy uneasily and I knew Daddy would talk on and on until I went down.

" . . . one of the best darned tractors you can buy." Daddy's voice came to me from below. "From what I hear in the store . . . Did I tell you, Ted, I'm manager over at Myers' Hardware? And I hope you'll excuse me tooting my own horn when I tell you I'm the first manager they ever had there wasn't a Myers." I tried to imagine the polite interest in Ted's face in the small silence that followed.

"Anyway," Daddy went on, "from what I hear in the store, it turns more dirt than any of the others in the same amount of time. I got a theory about tractors, Ted. You're a smart boy, I know, but let me tell you where you and your company can improve your product. . . ."

And on and on, my father's voice. It filled the house and brooked no interruption. I brushed my hair down over my breasts. Men love long hair.

"Oh, Ellen's a pretty girl, all right," Daddy was saying downstairs.

"Melvin," Mama admonished him.

"Now I'm not boasting. I'm just a man who believes in telling the truth." Everyone laughed.

I took a last look in the mirror. Oh, Ellen is a pretty

girl . . . I was nearly humming. I grabbed my purse from the dresser and started downstairs.

"And she's not just pretty," Daddy said. "You won't find a sweeter girl anywhere."

When I came into the living room, Daddy and Ted turned to smile at me and Daddy's words settled over me like Cinderella's magic gown. He believed it and for a moment I did too. But then Ted stood up ready to leave. His pants rode easily at his waist and creased slightly above the bulge of the crotch. My breath caught in anticipation. I smiled up at him and took his arm as Daddy ushered us toward the door. Outside, the darkness was still thick with heat. Red roses spilled down the trellis at the side of the porch. Their perfume, wild and fruity, swam around us as we went down the steps.

"Good night, you two," Daddy called behind us, "have a good time."

Lilly

"You were on television? Really, Mama?"

"No, I didn't see it. Gran and I don't own a television set. Sometimes we stop and watch it if Coburn's has one going in the window. Remember Coburn's?"

"Oh, well, it's not much anyway."

"Hey, I did see pictures in the paper, though. All those people in California marching against the war."

"I can't believe you were there. The pictures I saw, somebody'd taken them from overhead."

"Yeah, like in a plane. But that way it just reminded me of the time the dime store had the contest to guess how many Ping-Pong balls. All those heads and everything."

"No, no, Mama, I know it's serious. I do. I'd march myself if they ever did it around here. I would."

"I love you, too, Mama."

SOME memories are like photographs, still and flat. A detail here, a detail there, just enough to count an event remembered. But there are others . . . the good Lord save us . . . that have caught a time up whole. No small reminders, these memories, where time itself is brought up short and stops forever in your mind.

It was an early winter day. The day before I had been to the river and seen a huge flock of Canada geese fly over, all their shadows passing like ghosts over the water. They seemed to fly along with the current, setting their course perhaps by Bright River. To see the geese meant it was winter for sure, and on the morning I'm thinking of there was ice on the birdbath in the backyard. In the late afternoon, I went uptown to shop for dinner. My coat felt cumbersome and even too warm as I walked from Winger's Bakery to the butcher. Several of the shops along Hooke Avenue had drawn their shades against a sun hanging low in the winter sky. I saw Henry French, the owner of the Heavenly Rest Funeral Home. We stopped a moment to talk. His wife had had her appendix out the week before. He told me she was weak but up and around a little. "Good for her," I said. As Henry walked off down the street, I found myself too warm in the late rays of the sun. I began to take off my coat. "Lilly," called a voice behind me.

When I turned, Cora Carey was coming toward me. She wore a fur coat with large fuzzy buttons that reminded me at the time of teddy bears with rhinestone navels. She walked rapidly, eagerly, talking in a confidential voice before she even stopped.

"Oh, Lilly," she said laying her hand on my wrist. I had one arm out of my coat while I balanced my packages with the other. "I've just heard, Lilly. It can't be true, of course."

"What can't be true?" I asked irritably. Cora always wanted you to dig information out of her, information she was dying to tell you.

"Well, never mind," she said, "you'll find out soon enough." A wind from the river traveled down the street and the sculptured curls on Cora's head held stiffly against it. It was amazing what they could do with hair nowadays, I thought; Cora's hair had always been straight as a stick. Really, she was so annoying. I made to turn from her but she held my wrist fast. Her eyes were glistening with the excitement of her news. "I will tell you this," she said breathlessly, "go right home and wait there."

The first pang of alarm passed over me. "Cora, tell me. Is Darcy all right?"

"Oh, it's not Darcy, Lilly, it's . . . But I'll not say another word."

"Cora Carey, so help me," I said sharply, "you had better tell me this minute."

"Well, they say . . . and mind you, I don't believe a word of it . . ."

"Cora!"

" . . . that Aaron is being arrested for a land deal he made in Anne Arundel County." I stood there stupidly for a moment, my coat hanging from one shoulder. Cora's eyes hungrily searched my face.

"That's ridiculous," I said at last.

Cora licked her lips. "That's just what I said, dear. They say he and Curtis Ward sold the same land over and over. I said it was ridiculous."

"Good-bye, Cora," I said, drawing my coat around me. I began hurrying home, laughing nervously to my-

120

self. Aaron arrested, impossible. His face was before me all the way home . . . the clear gray eyes, the stern chin. Just the night before he had been talking about Ed Chapman being caught with his hand in the till at the granary. "They should put him in jail where he belongs. Stealing is stealing whether you hit somebody over the head to do it or not." It was so like him, that straightforward judgment. And he was right, of course, but I couldn't help thinking of Ed's wife and children.

"I wonder what will happen to Evie and the children," I said.

"That's really no consideration, Lilly. The man is a thief," answered Aaron. Mercy in his mind was only incidental to the law. Aaron arrested. It could only be a mistake.

I felt naked as I walked down Broad Street, imagining for the first time in my life the eyes behind the shades and curtains watching me. How many of my neighbors had heard the terrible story? There would be plenty I knew who wouldn't be sorry to hear.

My hand was shaking when I opened the front door of our house. I tried to remember if Aaron had ever mentioned this particular deal. But no, Aaron rarely talked business at home. How did such a story get around town? I wondered. I thought of myself, as I had been, leaving the house to shop earlier. How strange to be so unsuspecting, as if bad news would announce itself through some vibration of the air if we were only alert enough. Yet stranger still is that once we are attuned to trouble, our fate *is* carried to us on the air.

There was stillness in the house that sent another wave of fear over my heart. "Aaron," I called, "Aaron." He was in the house. I would have staked my life on it. And the house was alive with an urgency, the walls seemed to lean in and whisper. . . .

"Aaron?" I said, walking softly down the hall.

I could see into the empty parlor. The dining room and kitchen were just as I had left them not two hours before.

"Aaron!"

I came back down the hall, running by then, my ankles wobbling in my high-heeled shoes. Up the stairs I ran.

"Aaron."

Our bedroom was empty, the coverlet on the bed slightly rumpled as if someone had sat down on the edge. In our house, no one was allowed to sit on a bed once it was made. Aaron wouldn't have it. Ordinarily, the bed coverings were smooth and undisturbed as placid water.

"Aaron."

Darcy's door stood open on an empty room. But in the back bedroom, the attic door stood slightly ajar. There is a worn dusty odor to an attic, an odor of things long put away and useless. The smell had traveled down the attic steps and hovered, out of place, in the small, cheerful bedroom. I had stopped running, was in fact immobile. I stared at the crack in the door and felt as if my terror would draw me, thin as a scream, through the narrow opening. When I began to walk toward the attic door, I was nearly on tiptoe. My breath was loud in the room. I crept up the steps one by one, wincing at every creak.

The attic was palely lit by two small windows at either end. I saw him right away, just as my eyes rose above the attic floor. He was hanging, limp and still, by a rope around his neck. The rope had been tied around a center rafter of the house. His chin rested on his chest as if he were deep in thought. An old chair lay on its side a few feet away. His shoes, dangling only inches above the floor, were shiny and black. Aaron shined his shoes every day. He was still in his business suit and his face in the soft light was the blue of a vein seen under the skin.

Aaron.

I didn't even go the rest of the way upstairs. Later, I thought that I had failed him, wouldn't even meet him face-to-face on his most terrible day. Instead, I turned

122

and ran, panting and gasping for air, down to the second floor and on to the first. There was no room for air to flow into my throat. It was as if I too had a rope wound in a grip around my neck. There was a pressure in my head, the picture of his body growing too big to hold inside my mind.

In the kitchen, I grabbed up a butcher knife from a drawer. I tested the blade carefully against my fingertips. A cook knows a good knife. Then holding it point down, just as I'd been taught, I ran back up to the attic.

I circled his body. Would death be less painful for us if the dead disappeared? Is it the body they leave behind that makes us think we can call them back?

"Aaron," I sobbed.

I pulled the chair he had kicked away up close to him. "Just you wait, dear," I said to him as I climbed onto the chair. His body leaned against mine. It was warm with a gentle weight to it. I sawed at the heavy rope, picturing somewhere in my mind that when I was done, he would step lightly down to the floor and walk away. The knife was dull against the rope. It was hard work and the muscles in my arms burned. Working the knife back and forth, back and forth through the tough fibers, I wondered where he had gotten the rope. Did he stop at Myers' Hardware store on the way home? Did he and Melvin Gibbs discuss what rope would be strongest? I could see him there buying it, exchanging a few words with Melvin as he pocketed his change. I turned the angle of the knife and got a deeper cut. It was merciful the way my mind shrank to hold only the task at hand. The knife, its blade blunted by then, gnawed through the last few threads and the rope parted with a whispered snap. When Aaron fell, when his body hit the floor, the whole house shook as if lightning had struck it dead center.

Aaron.

Ellen

. . . Daddy doesn't know anything. He thought it was really neat that I was going out with Craig because he knows Craig's father and because Craig plays football. It was neat all right. He took me out parking the very first thing on our date. Then he ripped my blouse and made me do it with him. He said if I'd done it with all those boys, I could do it with him too.

He was so disgusting. I could smell his sweat and his spit was all over my face. I lay as still as I could and pretended it wasn't even me under him. I just pictured myself sitting up in the front seat, all cool and smelling my own perfume and watching him and some poor, dumb girl doing it in the backseat. If I could just have concentrated hard enough, I'll bet I would have laughed. His ass is *enormous*. Ha-ha.

𝕔 THE sun was low in the sky. It was late August by then and darkness settled sooner. The sky, raked by jagged streaks of red, shimmered golden in the heat. The steel framework of the building was black and skeletal against its glow. The building rose five stories in the air and big fat crows perched tiny as sparrows on top.

Under the evening sky, Daddy sat, his back to the building. He sat stiffly like someone pretending not to notice some obvious disgrace. Yet he was talking about it even then, talking about it as he did so often, chewing over his resentment like a dog worrying a wound. Weeks before he had called the building site "a running sore." Liking the phrase he said it over and over. "What's to be done about that 'running sore'?" he said that night, calling up to me where I sat on the steps. Bip, pacing by Daddy at that moment, stepped behind his back and signed to me. "It's the fastest sore in town." I suppressed a laugh and Bip wandered off, scuffing a green trail through the cut grass that had dried gray as old hair over the lawn.

"Do you remember the petition, Ellen?" Daddy called from below. "Do you remember?"

"Yes."

Bip marched back and forth behind Daddy, reversing his direction every few steps with a smart turn.

"So who was it then that did something about it at the

very beginning? Who was the only one? Answer me that."

"I know, Daddy."

"Well, then, case closed. Not another word needs to be said." He settled his arms over his chest as if my answer had truly put the matter to rest. He puffed out a great sigh and nodded his head. Bip had jumped up and caught hold of a low tree limb. He hung there by his hands, his head cocked thoughtfully like someone listening very hard.

"It wasn't my fault!" Daddy shouted suddenly. "I did everything I could."

"I know, Daddy."

"Two people signed my petition. Two! Alvin Briley and old Mrs. Shanks. He was so drunk, he would have signed his own death warrant and I don't think she heard a word I said but she's too vain to admit it."

"She's awful deaf now," I said.

"Don't I know it. Nobody cares," he said bringing his fist down on his knee. Bip swung back and forth on the tree limb. Daddy turned and swatted him on the leg. "Come on down from there, you darned gorilla."

Bip dropped to the ground. When he sat down next to Daddy, Daddy opened the encyclopedia, then slammed it shut. "Nobody cares," he said to Bip. "Art Cramer said, 'What difference does it make? This is getting to be a real progressive little town.' Imagine that. He's nearly as close as we are. George Fogelmeyer said, 'Thank God it isn't a Minute-Mart, then all that trailer park gang would be up here,' as if that was the point."

"You tried, Daddy," I said.

"Yes, I tried and that's all you can say even on Judgment Day. Isn't that right, Bip?"

Bip regarded Daddy motionlessly for a long moment, then nodded his head like someone shaken awake.

"Well," Daddy sighed opening the encyclopedia again. "What'll it be tonight, son?"

Bip shrugged. "You pick," he signed.

Daddy laid the book open between them. "Here's an

128

interesting one . . . melody." Bip shook his head impatiently and tried to turn the page.

"I know," Daddy said. "We're past here but we didn't do this one."

Bip leaned toward the book and he and Daddy read down the page.

"Do you understand any of that?" Daddy asked when they both lifted their heads.

Bip nodded.

"I mean think of it," said Daddy smiling in wonder, "you don't even know what any of that means. You've never heard a tune."

Bip tapped his forehead and moved his fingers in a slow dance around his ears.

"I don't mean the vibrations you feel from a radio or a piano," Daddy said stubbornly, "I mean a melody, a tune."

Bip's hands moved more insistently at his ears.

Daddy pulled a handkerchief from his pocket and wiped his face. "I don't buy it, no, sir. It says right here, ' . . . melody is believed to have been derived from the patterns of spoken words. . . .' "

Bip shook his head emphatically.

"By God!" Daddy exploded, sweat streaming down his face. "If you're too deaf to talk, you're too deaf to hear music." He flipped the pages of the encyclopedia angrily.

Bip clenched his fists and lifted his head. He pulled his lips back from his teeth and he might have been laughing. He sat there taut, suspended as if he were caught by some sudden vision behind his closed eyes. I thought of him as I had seen him several weeks before. I had been riding home late one night out on Myers Road. The moon was full and the fields along the road swayed under somnambulent shadows. I had seen Bip riding on his motorcycle. He rode by the side of the road, keeping close to the fence there as if he were setting his course by it. The bike, bucking and plunging over the rough ground, had a milky opacity to its chrome in the moonlight. When my headlights found him, his face was transfixed, mad as if it were full of the moon and the violent motion of the bike. By the time I had turned my car around to catch up with him, he was gone. When I turned off the engine to listen for him, the night was still.

Later, I told him he must be careful. I threatened him, told him I would tell Mama and Daddy. But Bip only laughed and cupped his hands together. "I am safe," his hands said.

"Molecules," Daddy cried clapping Bip on the knee. Bip jerked his head around quickly. His eyes were wide as if he were surprised to see Daddy in the chair beside him.

"It's always good to know about science, Bipper."

Bip nodded.

"Listen, listen," Daddy said. Bip watched his face. "Let's see what you remember from what you read. If you divide a molecule of water what do you get?"

Bip stared away. He folded his hands in his lap. In the deep summer grass, his tennis shoes were very white. Mama had washed them that morning and they had hung, puckered and forlorn, on the line all day. While Daddy watched him, waiting for an answer, Bip rocked his feet heel to toe, heel to toe faster and faster until they seemed to be running by themselves in the grass. He signed offhandedly.

"Ha!" Daddy shouted, making me jump. "More water. That's what you'd think. But no. . . . 'splitting gives something that is not waterlike in character, but something else, perhaps hydrogen and oxygen. . . .' "

Bip put his finger to his temple and pulled an imaginary trigger.

"Yes, you forgot, didn't you?" said Daddy. "You wouldn't think it, would you? That's like me having a snake or a bear for a child." Daddy shook his head. Bip's shoes had walked a hundred miles since he had sat down.

Daddy laughed softly to himself and Bip and I, wrapped that summer night in our own secrets, would have been stranger to my father than snakes and bears. My brother jumped up jittery on drugs my father had never heard of. And I, restless and sad, idly imagining lying with a new man. It's only when a man and woman are brand-new to each other that their powers are perfectly poised. The mystery allows every dream. The primal complement, grip and thrust, is clear, and we can rock together in the clouds with the roar of great stone gods.

I would drive that night the fifty-five miles to the Red Rooster Bar and Grill. There, to strut along the bar and make them look, those boys, those men, hands around their glasses and heels hung over the rungs of the barstools. I could walk as though I wasn't afraid, as though I never cried or hurt or broke because no man wants to hear about my heart starred by scars. I could do that and at the same time look for love beyond every bend in the bar and every stain on the sheet.

Yes, yes, I thought, I would go to the Red Rooster and meet a new man, a man who would gather up the muddled edges of my life and suggest an order to a future that slipped and slid under the touch of the man I loved. Darcy. Unreliable, unapologetic, only working half the time and drinking the rest of it. A man no one would marry. How had I fallen in love with him when I needed a man so badly who could do me some good? Did Darcy know I loved him? Did he know I wished I didn't? Perhaps he loved me too.

There had been a night not long before when Darcy and I had walked down from the Blue Moon Cafe to the ferry. A waning moon dipped in and out of ragged clouds as we came down over the riverbank. Below us we could see the two lights on the front of the ferry bobbing in the darkness as the flat-bottomed boat shifted in its moorings. The two lights at the rear rode the water in splashes of gold. We could hear the gentle idle of the small motorboat attached to the ferry's side. It was this small boat that propelled the larger craft over the cables that ran from shore to shore.

As Darcy and I approached, one car sat on the ferry and Charlie Bates, the ferryman, perhaps waiting for more cars, stood leaning against the railing of the boat. It was late and there wouldn't be many more. The ones that came would be mostly strangers passing through Hooke's Crossing into the next state.

"Could we ride for a while, Charlie?" asked Darcy, and we stepped aboard over the clanging metal ramp. The car waiting to cross had tags from the state across the river. Its window was rolled down and the driver tapped his fingers impatiently on the side of the car.

"Depends if you got fifty cents," said Charlie.

"I got better than that," said Darcy and pulled a pint bottle of whiskey from his jacket pocket.

"Welcome aboard, then," smiled Charlie through the gaps of missing teeth. When we were children Mama always said not to speak to Charlie when the family rode the ferry. "He's not a nice man," she had said mysteriously and I had thought maybe he was the devil. And indeed, the light that played over his face showed his gray hair wild and grizzled, his one eye gleaming and the other eye blind with the milky iridescence of a pearl. Darcy passed him the bottle and the old man drank and wiped his mouth. "I could shove off anytime," he said.

"You just say the word," said Darcy.

Charlie fastened heavy chains along the open widths at the front and the rear of the boat. Then he worked some levers and the ferry began its slow quiet chug across the river.

When he returned to Darcy and me, he squinted at me through the darkness. "Yes, sir," he said pointing at me, "I know who you are, Miss Gibbs. I see your daddy regular at his store up there."

"Now, Charlie," said Darcy handing him the bottle again, "we don't want Mr. Gibbs to hear about us being out here. He's got this fear of water that makes him unreasonable about Ellen being out on a boat. You understand."

The ferryman cocked one eyebrow at Darcy. "Nobody never hears nothing from old Charlie. Not that I couldn't tell plenty if I wanted to." I shivered as the old man hunched into the slight wind from the water.

"I'll bet you could tell a tale or two," said Darcy.

"That's just right, I could." Charlie nodded vigorously. "One night," he whispered, the words hissing through his broken teeth like wind under a door, "a man paid me a hundred dollars to take the ferry over after closing."

"A hundred dollars!" Darcy whistled.

"A hundred dollars, that's right, and both of you know him. That's right."

"Somebody everybody knows, huh?" said Darcy.

"That's right and I seen what was waiting for him on the other side or better to say 'who.' And that's all I'm saying about her." The old man turned suddenly then and went to sit on a metal stool at the back of the boat. He crossed his arms and set his one good eye on the shore across the water. Darcy and I went to stand at the front of the ferry. The two lights there undulating over the current seemed sunk in the water, fire reflected from the bottom of the black river. Darcy held my hand.

"That would be old man Myers, I guess," said Darcy.

"Who?"

"Myers of the hundred-dollar-bill."

"Oh, Darcy, you don't think that old man will tell Daddy, do you?" I said.

"No, Charlie never told about it. It was Mr. Myers himself who told that story one time when he was lit. He told it to Webb Dickerson . . . you know that barber that used to work for Bill Muller." I shook my head.

"Yeah," he said, "it was after some big business lunch they gave Myers over at the Moose. On his way home, he decided to get his hair cut. And Webb said the whole time he was up in the chair, old Myers just kept saying, 'Yes, sir, Webbie, that was some woman. That was some woman.'" Darcy laughed.

"There aren't any secrets in Hooke's Crossing," I sighed.

"Not many," Darcy agreed.

"Sometimes I just hate this town. It's like your history is all written for you from start to finish and you can't ever be anything but what everybody else decides you are. When I was away at college I promised myself I'd never come back here."

"Yeah, when I went in the service, I said the same thing."

The ferry glides over the water and I can barely see Darcy's face. "Why did you come back, then?" I asked.

He laughed abruptly. "After I'd been gone awhile, it just seemed to me that any place was as good as another as long as it wasn't Laos. Why did you come back?"

"In college, I fell in love with a boy who said he believed in free love and then after a while he said he was too embarrassed to go with a girl with a reputation like mine." Darcy laughed again. I slapped him on the arm.

"I should have known you'd like that one," I said. "At least here I know what the rules are."

"Don't be too hard on your friend at school, honey. Hardly anybody ever breaks loose. People always think they got a bead on freedom but mostly they get it wrong somehow."

"You don't seem like that. It looks to me like you just do whatever you want to."

His eyes took on a sudden gleam as the moon passed from behind a cloud. He regarded me with a half smile. "Is that how it looks to you?"

"Don't tell me any different, Darcy. That's how I like to think about you," I tell him smiling back.

"I'm not like that, you know, living with no rules. It's just I have to figure out the rules for myself now."

"Isn't that good enough? Isn't that what you want?"

Darcy looked away. His face was serious, as if he hadn't thought of it before. "Ask me that on different days, Ellen," he said at last, "and you'll probably get different answers."

"Okay, I'm asking today."

"Today . . . today, I'm with you and that's breaking rules a lot of other people might have. So today I'm glad

I make my own." He drew me to him. "Tell me you're glad too," he said.

"You don't need me to tell you that."

"Tell me," he said, squeezing me and kissing my neck until I was choked with laughter.

"I'm glad!"

"Swear it."

"I swear."

He released me then and I stood beside him in the circle of his arm. Clouds scudded over the moon again and the river turned black, and depthless, weighted as if it were deadly still. Only the lights of the ferry betrayed its motion.

"What about the other days, Darcy?" I asked him, resting my head against his shoulder.

"What do you mean?"

"You said to ask you if you were glad on other days." He pulled away from me and turned to face the water upriver.

"Other days? It's like . . . what is it like? I know," he said with a sudden grin. He swung his legs over the side of the boat and set his feet along the narrow ledge of metal just above the water line on the outside of the ferry. Holding to the railing with both hands he pulled himself erect. "On bad days, honey, it's like this." He let go with one hand and hung out over the water at a precarious angle.

"Darcy!" I cried.

"It's like this, like you're looking out over the edge," he called to me, the breeze lifting his hair gently and laying it back into place again as he swung over the water, "and all you know about the darkness is what you can prove to yourself."

"Darcy, please come back on here. I'm afraid." I turned and the man in the car looked over at Darcy and then, yawning, looked away. Charlie turned on his stool and shouted, "Darcy, get back on board here. It's rascals like you that are always requiring the bother of fishing you out. Get aboard!"

With a grin, Darcy vaulted back over the railing. "Charlie, you old philosopher," he called, "you're one hundred percent right. It's always the rascals that need fishing out."

"What?" said Charlie and twisted his body sharply to train his good eye on us. The sounds of the woods swelled like a single voice as we approached the shore.

"Nothing," called Darcy.

"Good," said Charlie, "I'm sick of messing with you." The ferry hit the opposite shore with a bump. The ferryman turned the little boat on the side in a wide arc to reverse its direction. The ferry shimmied underfoot like some outsized dancer. Charlie fastened the big boat to the ramp and Darcy unfastened the chain at the front. The car drove over the ramp and up the steep incline of the shore.

All three of us stood in silence watching it go. Its lights glowed red in the darkness, then disappeared. Darcy took the bottle from his pocket, uncapped it and raised it to his lips. "Charlie?" he said when he was through and held the bottle out to the old man. Charlie wiped the bottle with his sleeve and drank. After he had handed it back to Darcy, Darcy held it out to me. But I couldn't bear to drink after the old man and I shook my head.

Charlie shuffled back to his stool and sat staring toward the glow of light from Hooke's Crossing that showed over the ridge on the far shore. Darcy and I stood looking downriver. The breeze had stiffened and Darcy gave me his jacket to wear. The moonlight spattered over the wind-stirred water in sudden flecks of silver. I held Darcy's hand and traced his fingers to their base, pressed the ridges of flesh in his palm.

"Did you ever have your palm read?" I asked.

"No, I don't believe in that stuff."

"Well, I'm a palm reader. Let me read yours." I smiled up at him.

"Okay," he said and held his hand out to me. In the dim light of the ferry's lamps, I studied it, frowning.

"It says here you like me," I said glancing up at him.

"Well, honey," he laughed, "you're amazing. You've made a believer out of me," and he kissed me.

We parted as a car horn blared in the night. When we turned we could see headlights at the ramp on the Hooke's Crossing shore. "Darcy, boy," called Charlie, "we're agoing back."

Charlie worked at his levers and Darcy pulled the chain back up. The ferry moved away from the shore as Darcy began to sing,

> "If I were young and dreams were new,
> I'd love a girl who looked like you. . . ."

He held me, stroking my hair, and it seemed to me his voice fell through the air and lay upon the water with the same bountiful serenity as the satin ripples in the ferry's wake.

"I am king," laughed Daddy loudly from the yard and I felt as if I'd waked from sleep.

"See?" Daddy said. "It says here under 'monarchy' a king is a ruler of something for his lifetime and I guess I'm supreme ruler of this family until such time as the good Lord sees fit to call me. What do you say to that, Bip?"

Bip made a mock bow and Daddy laughed.

"But look here," Daddy said, "I'll grant a constitutional monarchy with you and Ellen and Mama as Parliament."

Bip's eyes were on Daddy's face with a curious concentration, as if he were looking through my father's skull at something behind him. He began laughing before Daddy finished speaking, but Daddy didn't seem to notice. He patted Bip on the back. "You and Ellen and Mama as Parliament," he laughed.

Bip looked away. His feet had resumed their long walk and the last rays of the sun sent tall shadows sprawling like giants fallen down across the yard. Bip smiled softly into the evening air as Daddy turned the pages of the encyclopedia. I wondered if Bip was thinking of his girlfriend. She wasn't his first. He'd had several from school. But the one that summer was the young wife of a farmhand out on the Wesley place. She would see Bip when her husband went to town to drink. When Bip described her to me, his gestures were gentle. His hands slid slowly through the air to tell me about her cool, smooth skin.

Whatever he was thinking of, he was remote. And in the yard, Daddy seemed all alone in a kingdom where nothing existed but things that began with the letter *m*. Oh, not unmentionable *m*'s of course, like misery, menstruation, or madness. He was sealed off from Bip and me by some trick of light, some strange arc to the summer air. And I could barely see him, riding as I was on that wild curve away through hours at the Red Rooster Bar, riding in my mind to those moments afterward lying beside a man, not feeling finished, just resting. The surge that brought us together lying in abeyance in a dark pool, power waiting like water dammed or eyes closed. I've been sleepy then, lying quietly while the man in guarded silence may be thinking of anything but sex . . . stock commodities, torque conversions, or just the next six-pack of beer. And I have loved the stillness of their bodies then, have loved the delicate weight of their manness, soft as the petal of a rose. Whipped cream soft, so soft it could be a breath blown against my fingertips. Perhaps I've loved these moments most of all.

Ah, but I can't deny that there have been other times when I've been with a hard-on man and seen it spring up hard as a hammer, straight as an arrow and high as the Washington Monument. Hallelujah! Then, then I could have stood right up in bed and saluted.

"Mongoose," Daddy said, "hmmm, interesting, huh? They really do attack snakes like they say in the stories. It says here, '. . . even the largest and most poisonous snakes are attacked by these little animals which avoid the poison fangs of the reptile with great agility.' "

Bip bent his arm at the elbow. His fingers and thumb were pressed together at the tips. He moved his arm sinuously; it could have been boneless. Then his hand darted with a startling quickness at Daddy's face. Daddy laughed and Bip struck again, opening his fingers as wide as they could stretch near Daddy's throat. Was Bip the mongoose or the snake? I couldn't tell. "Okay, Bipper, that's enough," Daddy said irritably and waved Bip's hand away.

But Bip feinted again and again just out of reach of Daddy's slap. "Stop it!" Daddy shouted. "You're acting like an idiot."

Laughing, Bip looked away, refusing to see what Daddy said. His hand made several more passes at Daddy's face. At last Daddy's hand shot out and caught Bip by the wrist. Bip struggled against Daddy's grip until his young face was red with anger. Daddy's face was the red of exertion.

My brother continued to strain against my father but his arm was caught fast. A smile of triumph broke over Daddy's face before he released his hold. Bip folded his arms around himself and turned away.

My father rose from his chair with nearly a swagger and called to me, "No date tonight, honey?" I shook my head.

"Well, then let's you and me take a walk down to the drugstore. I like to show off my beautiful daughter."

I walked down the steps of the porch. When I took Daddy's arm, I felt him square his shoulders.

"And I can certainly use the pleasant company," said Daddy staring down at Bip who still sat in the yard. But even if Bip had turned to look at us at all, it would have been too dark by then to see my father's face.

Jessie

Beside the autumn poets sing
A few prosaic days
A little this side of the snow
And that side of the haze.

—EMILY DICKINSON

AUTUMN was quick and hot, racing over the earth like brush fire and scorching the fields to a dry brown. The last of the hay was baled, and all of Queenie's pups had been sold except for the breech pup, Ginger. Dad had kept her to breed in the spring. The farm is at rest in the late fall and the long evenings pass aimlessly like rambling stories you've often heard. After dinner Dad would fall asleep, his newspaper, half-read, across his lap. It was new to him, this sleeping so early in the evening. And I worried about him sometimes because he seemed so tired. He might sleep all evening, his long limbs spilling crookedly out of his chair. The reading glasses he had pushed up on his head reflecting the light unblinkingly like watchful gray eyes. Dr. Charles had told us that Dad's heart was a bit weak and that we should think of hiring someone to help around the place come spring. Dad had said maybe Darcy could come a day or two a week.

Darcy hadn't called since our date. I hadn't seen him in town. I was surprised by the loss I felt. I had told him not to call, had told him quite specifically. I told myself that in the last days of autumn while I tugged up the withered tendrils of my spent garden. I told myself that while I rearranged the jars, bright and opulent as gems, on the canning shelves. It wasn't that I wanted him: It was only that I needed to know he wanted me. It was so important then. Women divide their lives by love lines,

143

measuring time by the men we know. Our thoughts of love always seem of a whole piece as if each man were connected to all the others by a dense tangle of clues that will lead to some indisputable conclusion about ourselves. And it seemed to me that Darcy's not calling affirmed Stephan's not loving me, because even my sweetest memories of Stephan always seemed set in some time of deadly innocence. The Sunday mornings that I had loved when the sunlight spilled over the windowsills of my apartment and warmed us like cats as we lay on the floor reading the paper, all of it . . . the smell of coffee brewing, the quiet rustle of the paper, Stephan's lips, his hands, the bright blond hair on his toes! . . . every bit of it seemed some awful seduction to pain, some dark introduction to my own unlovability. Stephan had discovered it and Darcy was even quicker to see it.

It had crossed my mind to go to the Blue Moon some night as if Darcy only needed reminding that he wanted me. But the strongest memories I had of Stephan were the bitter ones of the end. I hadn't been able to believe he didn't love me anymore. Even knowing there was another girl, I couldn't let him go. I cried and cajoled for his time. I shamed him into not abandoning me altogether. The last time I called him was a week after his wedding.

"Please, Jessie," he had whispered into the phone, "please don't do this. You're too good for this." I knew in that moment he didn't believe that anymore and I hung up and called Dad.

"Dad, I'm coming home."

"Well, ain't that grand, Jess. When can I look for you?"

"I'm going to stay for a while. I'd like to move back just for a few months," I said.

"I don't recall a holiday at school right now, Jess. Are you sick?"

"I'm quitting my job."

"Oh?" There was a long pause.

"Stephan and I broke up," I said at last.

"It's not like you to take things so hard, Jess."

"Dad, I just want to come home." I began to cry.

"I can come with the truck whenever you say."

The months had gone by with my thinking that each new season on the farm would find me healed. But even after two years had passed, the humiliation I'd felt with Stephan seemed as sharp as if he had only just left me. Oh, if life were fair, love would leave you when you didn't need it anymore. It would, like an arc of electricity, stop when one pole was removed. If life were fair, love wouldn't stay behind to burn up whatever heart you need to love yourself again. I couldn't go to the Blue Moon; I had nothing to spend on disappointment.

Instead, I stayed home and wondered why Darcy didn't call, pondered it as if knowing why would tell the story of the rest of my life. I wondered what he thought of me. Maybe it would have surprised him to know he was only my second lover. Maybe he talked about me to his friends at the Blue Moon. Or worst of all, maybe he never thought of me at all.

At twenty-six, I wasn't a girl anymore. All the women I'd gone to school with were married and I had wasted three years on a man who had decided he didn't want me after all. Does every woman assume she'll marry? Is Elinore Purdy surprised at her late age that no man ever came along to marry her? Who is it she dyes her hair bright red for? Who is it she hoists up her breasts into cavernous cleavage for? No one in Hooke's Crossing, it would seem.

It's said in town that old Miss Hicks who taught senior English at county high had a fiancé who was killed in World War I. And they say she never got over her broken heart. How would it be if I went back to teaching in the county? Would they say . . . even before I knew that no man would ever claim me . . . would they say, "Poor Miss Talbot. She went off to the city and got her heart broken. She was never the same."? Suppose no one else ever loved me? Would I always be sad, then? I imagined that I would feel like half a set, one eye, one hand. Not useless surely but impaired.

And all the time that fall as I passed these things through my mind, the thickening walls of my uterus swelled. But even when my belly became distended, rounding to a purposeful globularity, the idea of what was happening to my body came and went dimly like something glimpsed from the side of the eye. It seemed lodged stubbornly out of sight in my mind, a small detail difficult to remember. Oh, I knew it was there. I even made plans to call the doctor, but somehow the day never seemed right.

By December, I couldn't button my pants, and winter, creeping silently over the mountain, surprised us with the prim white of new snow. It was late afternoon and the sky had cleared. The sun had set and its last light, held a moment longer in the brilliance of the snow, lit the kitchen. I was cooking dinner and had reached up to a high shelf for a bowl. My hands were high above my head, my shirt hitched up above my waist. When I set the bowl down and turned, Dad was standing in the doorway, staring at me incredulously.

"Why, Jess, I believe you're expecting," he said in wonder.

I was caught, mute, the blood rushing into my face.

"Ain't you?" he asked insistently.

I stared at him. My mind seemed to whirl at some dead center where thoughts came and darted away half-finished. There was a scalding memory of the time my father had opened the bathroom door and found me naked. After he had quickly closed the door, I had hugged my arms to my breasts and though not large, they had seemed an ostentatious armload. In that moment, I would have lifted them away from me, given them up, smoothed myself over with the bland rubbery skin of a doll and been grateful for the sly pink blank between my legs where my sex should have been. I would have done anything to have spared my father and me the embarrassment that was so acute and silent that it left us uneasy with each other for weeks.

And there I was, more naked before him than I had ever been, the secrets of my body, evil secrets now, before his reluctant eyes. My father's face was patient, concerned, but with the same hopeful lift to his eyebrows he always had when I had a problem. "You could always look after yourself, Jess, since you were a little bitty thing," he would often say to me and his eyes would light with love and pride.

I began to feel calmer. I took a deep breath to speak. I could already hear myself saying, "Now, Dad, everything's going to be all right." But Dad spoke first.

"I believe any baby's a wonder, Jessie," he said, "and I'm not ashamed of you."

Then as if it only needed to hear the word, the flat gray plane in my mind that had held the fact of my barrenness almost as an afterthought exploded in an overwhelming shame. I tugged my shirt down over my belly. There was a malign deceit to that roundness there, a roundness of vitality, of life proceeding in some slow, merciful continuity. That was the roundness that attracted my father's assumptions. Yet it was illness masquerading as health, this deformity swathed in the shape of hope. It was an indecency my father could never imagine . . . a woman's body too self-absorbed with filling its own womb with useless tissue to bear a baby.

"Answer me, Jess," Dad said, "you're going to have a baby, ain't you?"

"Yes," I said and it was done.

He bit his lip, studying my face. "I wonder," he started, cleared his throat, "I wonder what we ought to do."

"I don't know, Dad."

"Was it Darcy Blunt?"

"Dad!" I couldn't look at him.

"He should know, Jess."

"No!"

My head spun, trying to untangle the lie. Words crowded into my mouth and died there.

Dad looked away. "A baby," he said. "I'm going to be a grandpa," and a smile he couldn't quite conceal crossed his lips for a moment.

Turning toward me he said, "We should make plans, Jess."

"Not now, Dad. Please." Tears stung my eyes.

"You think you might get married?"

"No."

"Jess, look here, don't cry. If you should think of keeping this baby, I wouldn't mind," he said. "It ain't the best way to have a baby, but it might not be too bad."

"I wouldn't keep it," I choked out.

In the days that followed the terrible cruelty of what I'd done closed over my heart to lock the lie like iron. My father didn't mention it further except for shy suggestions that seemed to burst from him against his will. "The back bedroom might be good for a baby. It's on the sunny side." "Could put a swing in that maple out back. Good strong limbs."

"Dad," I said sharply each time, "forget about this baby."

Another snowstorm hit and the snow lay so heavily, chastening, immobilizing, a vast power squeezing the earth into an icy ball. Our lane had snowed over and Dad and I kept busy in the house. One overcast afternoon we decided to paint the kitchen table and chairs a bright yellow. Dad painted the tabletop in slow, deliberate strokes, laying the paint on in silky swaths. The shiny yellow paint had a misplaced cheerfulness to it in the gloom of the kitchen. Dad and I agreed there would be more snow by evening. There was a knock at the door. I glanced questioningly at Dad. He shrugged, avoiding my eyes.

When I opened the door, Darcy stood there. His face was red from the cold. There was snow caked nearly to his hips where he had waded through the drifts. Even before the door was completely open, he was saying, "Damn, Jessie, you could have told me."

"How . . ." I began. When I turned, Dad stood by the table. The paint from the brush in his hand dripped glossy little puddles on his one shoe. I shoved the door back against Darcy but he caught it with the flat of his hand before I could close it.

"I sure didn't walk all the way up that driveway out there to get the door slammed in my face," he said. "I'm coming in to get warm at least."

He pushed the door open and came in rubbing his hands together.

"Get out!" I screamed, hugging my arms around the protrusion of my belly. "Get out!"

Darcy tried a grin that failed. I could hear Dad behind me. "Now, Jess."

I whirled on him. "You! How could you? How could you do this?"

"I thought he ought to know."

"Thought he ought to know? Well, you know what? It isn't his. It belongs to someone else. It might belong to four or five other men. How do you like that?"

"I know better than that, Jess. It was Darcy's right to know," Dad said. He was calm. It was one of those rare times when my father had made up his mind.

"Jessie," Darcy said, "I agree with Cecil. Now here's what we're going to do. . . ."

"You get out of here. This has nothing to do with you," I said.

Darcy turned to Dad. "Cecil, I think one thing we're talking about here is money. I want to do what's right." Dad looked relieved, believing, I suppose, that the conversation had taken a sensible turn.

"Well, hell," I said, "let's not worry about money. We'll just sell it off like we do the pups."

Darcy and Dad regarded me warily and without once looking at each other, they edged away from me and closer together. I hated the way they watched me, bewildered. For them, my anger sprang from a source too foreign to trace. They seemed somehow unfairly protected from my anguish by the closed, invulnerable planes of their bodies. I felt light-headed and hot. There was a sound in my ears that beat with the urgent shudder of a bird caught fast. I screamed at them. "You can't have my baby. This is my baby."

It was only after I had run from them and locked myself in my bedroom that I could say to myself, There is no baby. There is no baby. Of course there was no baby. I fell asleep across my bed.

In the morning, the snow we had looked for was fallen. I went down to the kitchen when I heard the scrape of the snow shovel on the back walk. I wanted some time alone before I faced Dad. I felt numb, as blank as the new snow. I had promised myself to tell Dad the truth. I knew that when I spoke, the words would sound very far away and I knew that Dad would never quite know what to make of me again.

The shovel rasped against the pavement outside as I entered the kitchen. Dad stood at the stove pouring himself a cup of coffee.

"Who's out back?" I demanded, knowing.

"Darcy," he said matter-of-factly. "Couldn't very well send him home in that snow last night."

"What do you want, Dad? What is all this about? Do you want Darcy to marry me, make an honest woman of me?"

"That's up to you and Darcy. It was just snowing too hard to send him out is all."

Oh, God, I thought, how could it have gone this far? "Dad, listen . . ." I said and the back door banged open, sweeping a sugaring of snow over the kitchen floor.

"Morning, Miss Jessie," Darcy smiled and shook the snow out of his cap. I turned away. Putting on his coat, Dad said, "Going to feed the dogs. Thanks for shoveling, Darcy."

"No problem, Cecil," Darcy answered, but Dad, his coat only half on, was out the door.

As I moved to leave the room, Darcy caught my arm. "Jessie, just hear me out. That's all I ask."

"I don't want anything from you."

"Listen to me," he said, tugging on my arm. "Just listen to me."

I sat down reluctantly at the newly painted table. Darcy sat down across from me.

"You going to listen to me?"

"What is it you want?"

"That's right. Let's get right down to business. Jessie," he said, "I want to be a father to this baby if you would keep it."

"Darcy . . ."

"I know what you're thinking. I'm not much good. I know that. I just state it as fact, not for sympathy."

"Sympathy hadn't crossed my mind."

"Good. Because that's not my point."

"What exactly is your point?"

"Well, in the first place I don't believe you'd want to be married to me. I tried it once and I'll tell you honestly I wasn't much of a husband. Not that I don't think you'd make a fine wife for somebody. It's not that."

"How dare you?" I said, the blood rising in my face. "Whatever made you think I'd want to marry you?"

"I don't think that." Darcy quickly put his hands up in front of him. "No, wait. That's not what I think. I just thought . . . under the circumstances . . . under the circumstances, Jessie . . . marriage might be on your mind."

"I'd sooner marry a tomcat," I shouted.

"Easy now," said Darcy; "we're in agreement on that at least, no marriage. See how well things are going?" He grinned across the table.

"Things aren't going well. This is an absurd conversation. What on earth do you want with a baby?" God, what was I saying? Why was this conversation proceeding as if it had a destination or even a point of departure for that matter?

"Just let me try to explain it to you. That's why I'm

151

here, to explain it all to you. I've been thinking about it a lot since Cecil told me and for a while I didn't come up with much. But then Sunday night I was walking home from the Blue Moon and I stopped and was just looking up at the stars. I was right there where Tubber's Flat Road runs onto Broad. You know how you can see all the way down to the river there. Well, anyway, this feeling came over me while I was standing there like the sky knew me, like my name was written up there someplace if I only knew enough to see it. And like every different turn my life might ever have taken was written up there too, clear to see as the stars if I only knew how. And it took my breath away, Jessie, because there it was, the whole sweet package of all the choices I'd ever have just waiting for me to find them. You see what I mean?"

I frowned. "Not really. Are you trying to say our lives are fated?"

"No, no, Jessie," he said. "It's not fate if there are choices, and that's what I'm talking about see . . . choices. Look, that baby's name is already written up there too and he must already have his own set of possibilities. Not many yet, maybe no more than he could count on whatever fingers he's got now. And, Jessie, I stared up at the sky, stared till my eyes ached just like I'd be able to see what all might happen to that baby if I just looked hard enough. Then finally, I just sat right down on the ground and it hit me, see, it hit me. One possibility that baby could have for sure, by jumping Jesus, was me in his life." Leaning across the table, he let out a bark of laughter. There was a thin beading of sweat over the bridge of his nose. "See?" he crowed. I drew back.

"Darcy," I said carefully, "this baby is not yours. I swear to you."

He leaned back in his chair and sat staring at the floor. His fingers worked nervously on his knees. Then he raised his head and pointed a finger at me. "What we have here, Jessie, is a misunderstanding. Otherwise, you'd see it doesn't make much difference if the baby's mine or not. Wanting to be a father to this baby doesn't have to do with claiming my own. It has to do with me making the choice to be important in somebody's life."

"Darcy, that's crazy," I exploded. "You don't just go around taking up babies for your own just because you're lonely or your life needs a boost. Stray cats, stray babies, that's insane."

"It's not just for me, Jessie. The baby would have a father who loved him and that's real important."

"You're not the father!"

Darcy sighed deeply. "Listen," he said patiently. "Loving a child isn't blood answering blood like a lot of people think. It's not sudden like that, where you take to the kid the minute you see it, just knowing it's yours. That's not the way it happens. For Tim and me, it's like, it's like . . ."

Darcy propped his chin in his hand and we both gazed out the window. Three chickadees hopped across the snow, barely disturbing the surface. Dad was pushing snow out through the gate of Queenie's kennel. Queenie and her breech pup marched along behind him. Darcy sighed again and opened his mouth to speak.

"Darcy . . ." I said. I wanted him to stop. I was privy to the secrets of his heart under such false pretenses, I felt as guilty as if I had been eavesdropping. But Darcy leaned into me, pressing on.

"No, listen," he said. "Gradually is the way it's come up on Tim and me. Like we were sewing something with a needle and thread and it comes together just a little at a time until nothing can shake it apart. Knowing your own might be the first prick of the needle but time is all the rest."

"Darcy, you always surprise me."

"That's what all the women say," he said. I turned from him, smiling absently. He touched my arm. His fingers were very warm and I shivered.

"I just wanted you to know," he said, "that I know about loving a child. How did I do?" His voice was soft and he stroked my arm.

"Do you always trade on your charm?" I asked him.

"If that's all I have to trade."

"Oh, look," I said waving my hand impatiently, "it doesn't matter. I'm not keeping this baby. That's best for everybody."

"You're right. Best for everybody," he said taking his hand from my arm. And then tears sprang into his eyes.

"Darcy, I'm so sorry. I never wanted you involved in this."

"Hey now, don't be sorry," he said wiping his hand across his eyes. "It was too much to ask. It was just I wanted that baby so bad. Lately, I've been having this feeling like I forgot something I need to know, like I set something important loose in the world and lost it. And it seemed like this baby had something to do with getting it back. It's crazy."

Darcy and I were silent and outside we could hear the snow blowing off the roof and hissing against the trees.

"Darcy," I said, "thanks for coming. Really, I appreciate it."

"You know, Jessie," he said, "it was so strong in my mind how it was going to be with you and me and this baby, it was like I'd already seen him. Crazy, huh?"

"Yes," I said, and for a moment I could see a little girl standing in our backyard on a summer day. Her hair was fine and yellow as corn silk. A breeze lifted the hem of her blue dress above her straight strong legs. She was smiling, this child, and if she'd been mine I'd have put her hair in braids.

"Crazy," said Darcy shaking his head.

"Yes," I said and he rose from the table. He put his coat on.

"Well, look, could I come around, keep in touch?" A mischievous smile crossed his face. "You might change your mind."

I stood too and pushed the chair carefully under the table. "I won't change my mind, Darcy. And I really don't see the sense in your coming here."

"Miss Jessie, don't be so hard," he said seriously.

"You could be kind enough to let me ease my conscience."

My face flamed and I turned from him. "Oh, come if you like, then."

"I will," he said behind me. "That's a promise."

When I heard the back door close, I sat down again at the table, my back to the window.

I was amazed. The two of them, then, Dad and Darcy, seeking comfort from this perverse womb that could nurture nothing beautiful. I sat tracing the slick brush lines of yellow paint with my finger. Then the back door opened with a rush of cold air and Dad called, "Any chance for breakfast this morning?"

Lilly

"What is this you're talking about, Mama? A dream?"

"Uh-huh, you're in the water and you come to a window and look in?"

"My window? Really? And you see me. I bet I look back out at you."

"Yes, yes, I do see it. You in the water outside my window. You look like the picture Gran has of you and your hair is waving in the water like it's wind. I can just see it!"

"Oh, I don't guess so, Mama. You mean dreams travel from one person to another like sending a letter? No, Mama, I don't guess that's so. But maybe. No. I don't know."

DARCY left home in the springtime. The river breathes easier in the spring like a great sigh for winter's passing. It fills up with melting snow and ice and churns along in full voice. I remember how that year I drew in so greedily the expectant muddy scent of the thawing river as if I couldn't quite believe that the earth had come full circle once again. And indeed only months after Aaron's death the earth seemed very fragile to me, its stately endurance tenuous under the impact of my own tragedy.

The night before Darcy left for the army, we sat on the front porch. It was the first night it was warm enough to sit outside after sundown. Crocus pushed like strong green knuckles up into the flower beds along the front. And the newly leafed trees were lacy under the street-lights. Darcy sat perched on the porch railing. He was hunched over and looked very small and boyish to me from where I sat on the porch swing.

There is a stillness in some spring nights before the crickets begin their summer song. Ivy says that Otis proposed to her on just such a night and that she felt as if the darkness were holding its breath to hear what she would say. She was surprised too when she answered yes. My son and I were silent the night before he went away. The only sound was the porch swing creaking irritably on its chains.

Darcy, don't go, I said to myself. The words echoed

in some hollow place that lent no strength to say them aloud. His profile, silhouetted by the streetlight, was sullen.

"It's too bad you won't finish school," I said.

"Don't worry, Mama, I'll finish in the army. I told you."

"Well," I sighed, "I guess I just hate to see you miss the football games and dances, those things."

"I've been to plenty of dances. Besides I'm almost eighteen."

I had to smile at the world weariness in his voice. My seventeen-year-old son off to join the army. He was a child, his beard like a smudge above his lip. He was a child, yet I could remember that when I was seventeen I'd felt grown up, probably more grown up than I felt that night on the porch with Darcy. But I resisted thinking of him as a man. I had never once allowed myself to say to him after Aaron's death, Now you're the man of the house. I thought often in those months of Dorothea Beck and her son, Tom. I would see them in town, always together. Tom, grave, courteous, touching his mother's elbow as they crossed the street. He would be carrying her packages and at such a young age, he was barely distinguishable from the father who had died years before. It was as if his mother's need for him had constricted his heart and accelerated his aging. I hated that woman in her pheasant-feathered hats and her bland acceptance of her son's devotion. I hated her because I felt the same need, dark and cavernous, dangerous, open up in me. And in the end, it was wanting him never to leave me that let me let him go.

"All I want is to put Hooke's Crossing behind me," he said and set his chin grimly.

"Yes, go," I whispered.

"Not because of you, Mama. I wish you'd go too."

"Where in heaven's name would I go?"

"Any place is better than this town," he said. "I could send you money. You wouldn't have to worry."

"I've lived all my life in Hooke's Crossing. I expect

160

I'll die here too." And my own death did seem very near at the sound of those words as if Aaron's death had cut my own time short.

"Well, I plan to send you money anyway."

"I won't need it. With the job at the stationery store, I can take care of myself."

"God, I hate him," Darcy said, his voice breaking.

"Darcy, I can't stand to hear you talk about your father that way."

"You must hate him too," he said.

"No."

Whenever I thought of Aaron in those days, there was a nerveless calm in my mind. It was a merciful waiting, a brief blessing like the numbness after a tooth is pulled. I felt nothing at all.

"I won't forgive him ever."

"Hate hurts the hater worst of all," I said and even to my own ears it sounded like a bit of school-yard wisdom that wouldn't bear much looking at . . . "sticks and stones may break my bones . . ."

"He left us, Mama," Darcy cried. "After all the talk he did about responsibility, he left us in the worst mess of his life."

"He couldn't bear the shame, Darcy. Your father was a proud man."

"How can you say he couldn't bear it. He didn't even try!"

I could see the tears, silver in the light of the streetlamp, begin to slide over his cheeks. I leaned over and took his hand, an almost man's hand, rough though not yet hairy, my child's hand enclosing mine.

"You have to take the good things about Daddy and keep them because that's all you have now that can help you at all. I know sometimes you two didn't get along but . . ."

"I never hated him like this, though." He swallowed several sobs. "Not like now. He was a goddamned liar and a big goddamned phony and a coward. I hate him."

I drew back from his rage and with nothing to say, set the swing to rocking once again.

It was probably the force of Darcy's bitterness that carried him over the chasm of his father's death to a new life. Or maybe it was only his youth that took him as a boy to war. But he was gone quickly and I was alone to untangle the knot of my loss.

Ivy has said she always feels one event away from being overwhelmed. As if she will reach the limits of her endurance in the very next moment. She is afraid there will be one last thing . . . too much pain, too much time, too much weariness perhaps . . . that will topple her over into madness. She worries terribly and constantly, peering into the darkness of the future, trying to decide just what it might be that could bring her down. "I couldn't have stood it, Lilly," she would say when we talked of Aaron's death. "You're so brave."

But was it really bravery simply to go from one thing that needed doing to the next? Where was the courage in plodding gratefully through the busy welter of details that come with a death? Check the deed to the house, Lilly. Call Rudd Burnes about Aaron's insurance, I'd tell myself with no thought of what would happen to me the next month, the next week, or even the next day. I was a swimmer treading water. Powerless and dazed, I was only waiting to be washed ashore. Is that what Ivy has admired, that hanging on? Then it seems to me that it's only the believing in being washed ashore that can count as strength and in that case, bravery is nothing more than hope.

Now where that hope comes from I couldn't say. It didn't even feel like hope at the time. Lord knows there was no promise of joy. No, it was dull and dogged like the beating of my heart and the only proof of it is that I'm here now and not swinging from a rafter like Aaron. And whatever it was that sustained me was drawn out of some necessity much deeper than circumstances because the usual comforts of habit and appearance were gone. As it all unraveled, we found out that Aaron had been in land speculation for years. I had never known, but that was so like Aaron to assume that I would have no interest in such things. The first deals he had made had apparently been aboveboard. He had even made a bit of money. But later, when the state highway was rerouted, he had lost everything we owned except our house.

And later I remembered nights when I would wake to find him standing at the window. "What is it, Aaron?" I would ask and he might reply, "Nothing, dear. Something I ate perhaps." How desperate he must have been to have been driven into something dishonest and how little good his surrender had done him in the end. There was nothing left and the transformation of Darcy's and my life was complete and immediate with Aaron's death.

The day after he died, I went with Aaron's brother, Ben, and my mother-in-law, Hannah Blunt, to see Father Brennan at Saint Matthew's. Aaron's father had refused even to have anything to do with the funeral of this son who had died out of grace.

When we arrived at Saint Matthew's Father Brennan sat behind an old scarred desk. A confusion of papers was strewn across the top. The priest was old, a small man with the thin-boned look of a frail child. Hannah pulled a chair right up to the desk while Ben and I formed a rear guard behind her. She wore a black hat with a large felt rose and a fox-headed fur piece that stared balefully over her shoulder at Ben and me.

"John," she said leaning forward and addressing the priest, "I cannot imagine why you've refused to perform the funeral Mass for Aaron. You've added enormously to the grief I already have to bear."

"I'm very sorry, Hannah," said Father Brennan. "You must know I feel great sorrow for you and your family."

"Ah, then you'll do it," she said, clasping her gloved hands with a little pat of satisfaction.

"No," said the priest.

"We have so much to discuss," she said as though she hadn't heard him.

"We have nothing to discuss, Hannah."

"John," she said, "Dr. Charles has listed the cause of death . . . on legal documents, mind you, John . . . as a heart attack." The rose on her hat trembled earnestly.

Father Brennan eyed her impassively and when he spoke his voice grated softly like a pencil scratching across paper. "Everyone in town knows how Aaron died. You may have gotten Bob Charles to support this charade of yours but I'll not do it. I'm too close to judgment now, Hannah. Bob only has to answer to the state medical board. Aaron will have no Mass in this church. He cannot be buried on consecrated ground; he took his own life!"

The old priest closed his eyes as if he were exhausted by the force of his words. Hannah rose and Ben and I trailed after her out the door. "If his father had come," she hissed as we left the church, "the old fool wouldn't have dared refuse." There was no doubt that Jonah Blunt was a powerful man. He had begun a law practice in his hometown and by the time his sons were grown, he had sat as municipal judge for many years. He had twice been mayor of Hooke's Crossing and had presided over the Moose, the Knights of Columbus and the Rotary. Yet, for all that, I don't think even he could have moved Father Brennan.

But Hannah held his refusal to intercede with the priest against her husband until his death, which wasn't long after Aaron's own. All of Hooke's Crossing laid the death to a broken heart over his son. Ben moved to Baltimore and every few years a Christmas card will arrive from him. The cards always bear a photograph of Ben, his wife and two children posed around a dog who looks newly washed and brushed. There is only the stamped message and their names inside.

For Hannah, it would seem, her family had disappeared with Aaron's death and Ben's leaving. She had been a pleasant enough mother-in-law through the years and certainly a dutiful grandmother to Darcy. But the day of Aaron's funeral, she told me, "My son was raised to be law-abiding and God-fearing. What happened to him after he married you, I don't know. But I do know that you're the one to pay for this terrible stain on Aaron's soul." And neither Darcy nor I have heard from her from that day to this. She retired into her house then, and her maid, Mattie, still goes about for her. She's an invalid now, I'm told. There's no question that Aaron came by his pride naturally.

Actually, Hannah could have put more faith in her neighbors. There were powers of memory and custom that would have kept the people on Broad Street from turning their backs on her. It is possible to survive scandal in a small town. In my mind I always picture all the people Aaron and I had known running like a pack of scalded dogs at his death. But actually it must have been more gradual than that because it wasn't the slip of the noose around Aaron's neck that sent me from proper to common in the eyes of Hooke's Crossing. It wasn't even the taint of thievery from the land deal. No, it was being poor that cut the ties between me and my old friends. Being poor came upon me suddenly like disease and raised the same fear of contamination. It was the stink of poverty that made my family's shame unforgivable. Then the scandal became a magnet that drew every past indiscretion to it . . . Ivy's Mr. Stanton, Darcy's trouble in school. It was the loss of our money that made it seem as if we had been found out at last and forced to give up a respectability that was never rightfully ours. For all the fine talk about Christian charity and the evils of wealth, there's always the idea behind it that anyone who is poor has done something to deserve it.

It's not that there were no kindnesses. Rudd Burnes, Aaron's partner at the bank, came to see me a few days after the funeral. In the front room, he sat stiffly, his hat on his knees. As we talked, his eyes kept wandering uneasily toward the ceiling as though a vision of Aaron hanging in the attic might appear there. I knew how he was haunted by the awfulness of it. For many nights after Aaron died, I would awake suddenly in the middle of the night certain I had felt the house shift again under the impact of his fallen body.

"Lilly," said Rudd, "I hated to bother you with this. I know your lawyer will take care of the liquidation for you. He will be able to secure the house for you, I hope."

"Yes," I said, "thank God."

"Do you have what you and Darcy need right now?"

"For the moment. I'll be taking a job in two weeks."

"Oh? What will you be doing?" He looked at me hopefully.

"Will Enderly has taken me on at the stationery store."

He winced. I suppose he couldn't help it. "Oh, God, Lilly, your father would roll over in his grave."

It would have been then that I could have comforted him like the old friends we were. We had been in Cotillion the same year and danced solemnly, counting off the steps when Rudd's slicked-down head had been no higher than my shoulder. We had made our First Communion together. I had even kissed Rudd a time or two when we had played spin the bottle at birthday parties. It would have been the most natural thing in the world for me to have confided my confusion and fear to such a dear old friend.

Yet, by his very remark . . . "your father would roll over in his grave" . . . I could see the gulf that had opened between us. Rudd imagined me still sustaining myself in the embrace of old friends. Perhaps he thought of me soothed by the cool hand of the Church. What he couldn't have understood, what I barely understood myself, was how those lifelong friends even if they had cared to keep up the old ties could so quickly come to belong to another time that seemed so far behind me then. I left the Church the day Aaron died, for the God of Saint Matthew's seemed a great grim Mouth clamped shut upon a word of mercy, silent on the subject of my grief.

I looked at Rudd, his onyx cuff links winking like small bright eyes at his wrists, the blueness to his jaw

166

from a recent shave, the seeming indiscretion of the powdered red line where his collar had chafed his neck. How could I explain to him a life that had overflowed like a flooding river and obscured every familiar shore? What would he have made of a woman who managed that life like someone rushing around a flood plain gathering in armloads of water and trying to pat them back into place? Oh, my composure was that precarious, that lightly held that it could bear no sound of doubt.

"Rudd," I said with a level gaze, "I'm not taking up streetwalking. For heaven's sake, I'm not afraid of good honest work."

I'd heard a woman say that in the bank one day while I was waiting for Aaron. She was a big woman in a faded housedress and her hands were rough with dirty broken nails. And it was her hands that seemed proof to me that she meant what she said. In my front room that day with Rudd, I hoped that I sounded just like her because the only shape I had to give my life at that moment was what I could pretend to know.

Rudd, his face flaming, drew papers from his briefcase. I studied my own hands lying in my lap. The veins showed a delicate blue through the pale skin and my nails were pink and glossy as seashells. Ah, I was afraid. At the time of Aaron's death, there were women in town who worked. They were mostly girls passing time until they married. And then there were the older women who worked, women my age . . . Wanda Choate keeping books out at the lumberyard, Kitty Boone serving drinks at the Blue Moon. Life had gone wrong for them somehow. They, like me, all seemed unlucky survivors of some misfortune to their men. Goodness knows, Hooke's Crossing made only a grudging place for them as if we all believed that the Indians may have had the right idea in burning up the widows with their men. Where did those women I had seen around town draw their strength? I wondered. How did they live in that unprotected state of manlessness that seemed in itself to invite new disaster?

"I'm very sorry, Lilly," Rudd said formally, his eyes wandering again to the ceiling.

"Of course."

"Well," he continued briskly, "I hope I've brought something that will help a bit. I've talked to the board at the bank and we all agreed that despite the . . . uh . . . circumstances, Aaron gave us a lot of fine years at the bank and we can, with a clear conscience, give you half of his pension. I don't know if you could live on it but . . ."

I drew a deep breath. I could nearly feel Aaron's presence in the room charging the air with outrage.

"I don't need your charity or anyone else's," I said and rose.

Rudd stood too. "Lilly, please reconsider. So far as I'm concerned that money is rightfully yours."

"I don't say things I don't mean," I said and showed him to the door.

I can't say I never regretted it. Ivy says there's something wrong with somebody who'd rather eat bean soup for a week at a time than look the fool a little. She's probably right. But I never could make myself go back on it even though I sure had a lot to learn about living without money.

There's a look to being poor. It can be subtle . . . maybe it's only the way someone has of picking up his feet and putting them down again. Or maybe it's no more than an expression on someone's face. Before Aaron's death I would have supposed . . . if I had thought of it at all . . . that breeding was what kept that look from you no matter what the circumstances. I would have imagined that even in a desperate situation, I could have pinpointed those small signs of loss well enough to fool my neighbors. I might have pictured myself walking along Hooke Avenue, a well-considered set to my head and no one the wiser to how difficult my life had become. But I needn't have worried about the finer points of looking poor. Before the first year was out, a small black hole that I couldn't afford to have fixed appeared on a tooth not too far back in my mouth. And when I went to take my winter coat out of the attic, two moths rose wanly from its now shabby folds like the final puffs of smoke after a fire. How strange to find that only money fixes being poor.

Oh, I shouldn't complain. I could just get by and really I could have tried harder to keep up appearances. Aaron might have said I had no pride. Ivy says I have too much. And the people on Broad Street must very soon have been saying, "Lilly Blunt, pathetic. Oh, my dear, even a bit seedy." They must have talked about how quickly I went down. Maybe I was even dotty in their eyes. I wondered myself, in fact, because after Darcy left I would find myself muttering under my breath when I was alone. I'd seen my mother do that when she was old and senile. And in the big old empty house, I sang songs aloud, songs I'd forgotten I knew. "Daisy, Daisy, give me your answer true. . . ."

There were things I could have done to put a better face on it, small things that wouldn't have cost me a cent . . . wear a hat uptown as I'd always done before, show up for the Ladies Guild at church. But early on, I knew I couldn't do it. I didn't want ever to be caught playing the lady of Broad Street to the back of Lydia Atwood's coat as she dashed around an aisle in the grocery to avoid me. Or ever again to be taken unaware at my front door by Harriet Archer with a bag of her old clothes. "Don't feel bad about taking these," she chirped. "You know my maid, Mary, has just gained too much weight to get into my clothes anymore. It would be such a favor you'd be doing me, Lilly. You know how I hate to waste."

"Then why don't you put Mary on a diet?" I snapped and slammed the door. No, I'd been turned out by my old friends, and to take on the trappings of my old tribe would have been like begging to be taken back. I was thorny about it, I'll admit, and I suppose I am to this day.

I couldn't even bring myself to be gracious to the few

people who tried to maintain contact after Aaron's death. I remember one terrible dinner with Jane and Rudd Burnes. Dinner was over and Rudd had gone off to his study or somewhere. Jane and I sat in the front room with our coffee. We had spent many evenings like that when Aaron was alive, but this evening was strained and Jane went on and on about some wallpaper she had bought for the front hall.

"It's navy blue, Lilly, in the background and it has a small white print, oh, shaped like little teardrops or maybe they're little acorns no bigger than this." And when she held up the tip of her little finger, her hand trembled and a great wave of loneliness passed over me.

"Oh, you don't care a thing about this, do you?" she said as tears rose in her eyes.

"Not really," I said and the evening soon ended. What would it have cost me to lie? Jane was a good-hearted soul but certainly not strong enough to bear my bitterness which was deep and lingers only slightly dulled by time even now.

Sometimes someone I used to know will come into the stationery store. And in that little awkward silence that falls after I've rung up their purchase, they may say, "Do call me, Lilly." I could let it go for what it is . . . a small politeness to be ignored. That is what I always tell myself later, but before I even think about it, I hear myself saying. "Why that would be lovely. When is a good time?"

I can't leave well enough alone, it seems. I wonder what makes me always want to stick a finger under the scab to see what's there. Ivy never could stand it.

Dear Ivy. I don't remember being lonely then except for Darcy. Ivy and I were always together, alone together as we'd been as children on the riverbank. Naughty children rolling our eyes at the thought of what our mother would say at the sight of us. And as I remember it, time passed then much as it had when we were children. Flowing like a summer river, unfurling slowly from where we stood and drawing the eye always to the horizon.

Often when it rains at night in Hooke's Crossing there will be a mist that trails gauzy tatters over the black river and sometimes even makes its way into town. The night Darcy came home from the army, it was spring-time. The trees were deep green and fat with rain and the mist churned along in the gutters of Broad Street. Under the streetlights, the road was shiny and black as patent leather shoes. A pear tree had strewn its blos-soms, round and bright as dimes, over the wet surface.

All day I'd waited for Darcy. I'd checked anxiously at the front windows since I'd gotten up. Ivy had come early in the day to wait with me. She had a bad cold and she'd sniffled and dabbed at her eyes all through the long day. At nine that night I told her to go home.

"Darcy must not be coming today," I said. "You go home now and rest."

"Oh, no, honey, I'll wait."

"No," I said firmly, "you go home."

"All right," Ivy sighed, her eyes swollen and red from her cold, "but only if you call me the minute he comes. Promise now."

I promised her and she left. It was nearly ten. I sat in the dark in the front room staring out the window. The raindrops pocked the street in tiny pools of light. A car stopped in front of the house. It was a taxicab . . . a strange sight in Hooke's Crossing. Darcy! I jumped to my feet. Under the streetlight, my son stepped from the cab. He dragged a duffel bag behind him. I had started to turn from the window when someone else climbed out of the cab behind him. It was a girl. I squinted through the glass trying to make her out but I couldn't see her well. They started up the walk as the cab pulled away. The girl was carrying a big suitcase. She and Darcy disappeared from view for a moment and then the front door swung open.

"Mama!" a strange deep voice called. "Mama!"

I walked to him then, his name caught in my throat. I

had told myself before he came, We'll be strangers to each other. It's been three years and he's been to war like a man. Like a man. He's not a child, I cautioned myself. But when I saw his face, when I felt his presence under my fingers, he was my child, composed of my memories, memories that had abided for so long that the child was marked in the face of the man as plainly and tightly as the bones beneath the skin. And he was mine by the claim of those memories. Ah.

"Hi, Mama," he said stepping back and laughing. He had to pull my arms from around his neck. He stood holding my hand. "Mama, Mama," he said, "this is Evelyn." Smiling, he turned toward the girl.

I'd forgotten about her, standing shyly behind him. She was a pale girl, her skin milky with spots of bright pink in her cheeks. Her hair was black and choppily cut around her face. She had on a shirtwaist dress. All the other young girls I'd seen in town were wearing short skirts but Evelyn's fell to the middle of her calf.

"Hello, Mrs. Blunt," she said and looked me so directly in the eye, I knew it took all her will to do it.

"Hello, Evelyn," I said, "won't you come in?" A formality settled over us. "Do come in."

No one had been to see me in a long time except Ivy. I wished with all my heart that Ivy had stayed. Darcy and Evelyn were smiling and taking seats on the couch. I turned a light on and sat down across from them.

Darcy, his arm around the girl, talked nervously. There was an edgy vigor to him that struck the sad quiet air of the house and set it to singing. I hardly heard what he was saying as if it were more than I could do to take in the sight and sound of him at once. He and the girl had a short conversation about the bus ride from New York. I sat watching him hungrily, the familiar curve to his lips, the constant restless motion of his body. He was leaning forward wiping his sleeve briskly back and forth over one shoe. Then he was sitting back smoothing the girl's short dark hair. And he was talking, talking.

"Boy, don't you know it's good to be home," he was

saying. "Yesterday this time I was in New York City and a week ago I was on the Mekong headed home." The foreign word and the easy way he said it suddenly made him seem far away as if I were dreaming and he had never come home at all. I sat forward and took his hand.

"Boy, don't you know it's good to be home," he said again. The girl giggled behind her hand. "I stayed in New York a couple of days, Mama. You know how it is, celebrating. I met Evelyn there."

"Is that so?" I said. "So you're from New York City, then, Evelyn."

"Yes, I am," she said.

"Well, I'm sure you find it very stimulating to live there."

I'm not sure how I had pictured Darcy's homecoming, but I certainly hadn't counted on making small talk with a stranger. "So much to do there, I hear."

"Yes, so much," she agreed. Beaming, Darcy turned his head from one to the other of us.

"Boy, I never could keep a secret," he said, laughing and hugging Evelyn close to him. "How should I put this? Let's see. Mrs. Blunt, meet Mrs. Blunt."

"Darcy, you don't mean . . ." I said.

"That's right, Mama, we're married." When he turned toward me, I could smell whiskey on his breath.

"Well, I never . . ." I said, and tears were quick and uncontrollable. Was this what it meant, then, giving your boy over to a man? This sharp, unexpected severance. This seemed so much more final than his merely going away. It was like putting something precious in your pocket for safekeeping only to find later that it had slipped through a hole that you knew you would never have noticed. "Without even telling me," I sobbed.

"Now, Mama," said Darcy, kneeling by my chair, "we thought about calling you. Honest. It was just love at first sight for us. Everything went so fast and I said, 'Shoot, let's just get on home and tell Mama face-to-face.' Didn't I say that, Evelyn?"

"Oh, yes, several times, in fact." The girl nodded emphatically.

"But, Darcy, married!" I cried.

"I'm twenty-one, Mama," he said standing. "You're looking at a man who ran the Reds back where they belong."

I wiped my eyes, embarrassed by the tears there. "Well, it's over and done now, I suppose."

"That's the spirit, Mama," he said.

"My son is very impetuous, Evelyn," I said.

"Don't I know it," she said smiling up at Darcy. Then we all laughed harder than the remark called for.

"I knew you two would hit it off. Didn't I say to you on the way down, Evelyn, you were going to love my mother?"

"Yes, you did. You did," said the girl, smiling and staring down into her lap.

Ellen

. . . Ray said more and more people are beginning to realize how oppressive and dehumanizing the old systems are. He said the world will be new and beautiful soon with everybody free to love their bodies and their spirits. I can feel the power of it building like a wave. College has been the best time of my life!

I'll always love Ray for all the things he made me think about. I'll always love him even though he was such a funny man in bed. It was as if he had to think about everything he was doing. And he was so worried about how I was feeling that sometimes when my eyes were closed, I was sure he was watching me. Then I would just lose the mood thinking about opening my eyes to see if he really was looking. . . .

A late summer evening. Mama and I sat on the back steps, a basket of corn at our feet. We were shucking the ears and had begun a small golden pyramid on a towel between us. Bip had missed dinner again and Daddy was alone in the yard. Moving his chair into the sunlight, he seemed to retreat before the long shadow of the nearly completed building. The heavy equipment machines that sputtered and roared through the day leveling the parking lot sat idle. Muscular and pugnacious, they squatted under a bloodred sky. And slick from an afternoon rain, they seemed to sweat in the sullen August heat.

One night a week before, Darcy and I had parked where the parking lot would be. We pulled in behind the building, out of sight of my house. The moon veiled by the haze from the earth met the sky with the wispy white outline of a spider's egg. And the big machines hunched like prehistoric beasts in the slender shelter of the building.

The shadows of the construction site were jumbled and sinister like a graveyard at night. After we turned off the motor of the car, we sat for a while talking idly. The top of the car was down and we drank the last of some beer we had bought.

I yawned. "I guess I better go home. I have to go in early to work tomorrow," I said.

"I guess," said Darcy and began backing the car out.

"Wait a minute," he said suddenly. "We can't go home yet. We're going for a ride." He stopped the car and got out.

"Come on," he said and I climbed out on my side. He took my hand and we started over the uneven ground. The newly graded dirt was strewn with buckets and old boards. Darcy stepped nimbly around them, leading me behind him.

"How can you see those things?" I said.

"Old trick I picked up in Laos, seeing in the dark."

He stopped at a dump truck and opened the driver's door. The heavy door swung open with a metallic snarl. Hoisting himself up, Darcy looked inside. He felt along the dashboard and then dropped back down to the ground.

"Did you ever drive one of these?" I asked.

"Nothing to it," he said, raising the hood. It rose with a screech of hinges.

"You never told me you drove one of these."

He leaned over the fender and put his hand to the engine. "Nothing to it," he said.

His head disappeared into the shadow of the hood. He hummed under his breath. A sharp buzz of electricity crackled blue for a moment, then stopped. For several more minutes, Darcy worked under the hood. "Hell," he said dropping to the ground, "I can't jump it."

"I don't care," I said. "Come away from there, you'll get hurt."

Darcy slammed the big hood down and leaned against the truck. He folded his arms. "Hell," he said again, "I thought we were going for a ride." I laughed to see him so disappointed.

"I'll be honest with you," he said earnestly, "I never did drive one of those things, but I just bet there's nothing to it. We could have gone for a ride. Maybe gone over to see Jeff. You know he'd a got a big kick out of that, you and me pulling up in a dump truck."

"Darcy," I said stepping back from him, "you're just not going about this the right way."

I kicked off my shoes and climbed onto the front of

the truck. I pulled my skirt up to my hips and straddled the hood. The metal was gritty under my thighs and moonlight shimmered in pearly puddles over my knees. I raised my arm over my head. "Giddup!" I shouted laughing.

Darcy stood on the ground looking up at me. "Honey," he said, "you look like something that would come riding through the dreams of the luckiest man I know." He started toward me.

Smiling down at him, I unbuttoned my blouse and bared my breasts to him. I held my arms out to him and the moonlight splashed milky rivers down my arms and over my fingers. He stopped as though struck still and gazed up at me. His eyes in the blue ache of the moon were pools that might have touched the heart of the earth. He whistled under his breath. "Jesus," he whispered, "let the light shine on me."

Then he reached up and gathered me to him. He carried me toward the car, his hand cradling my head, his fingers tangled in my hair. And where his lips were pressed to my temple, I would have sworn I felt his pulse and not my own. "I love you, Ellen," he said. "I love you."

In the yard, I stared down at the building, thinking of that night with Darcy. I wondered what I would do now that I knew he loved me. "Are you finished, then?" said Mama sharply at my side, and I realized I had been sitting, my hands lying idle in my lap, while Mama shucked the corn between us. Daddy sat in the yard studying the encyclopedia.

"Oh, I'm sorry," I said and picked an ear from the basket.

"Gret," Daddy said looking up, "did you know we only see fifty-nine percent of the moon from here?"

"Is that so?" said Mama. We were working rapidly then, Mama and I. The leaves pulled off in thick, papery handfulls and the spermy odor of raw corn rose in the air.

"Just a little over half. Think about it," said Daddy.

"Well," said Mama, "yes."

Daddy looked expectantly toward the porch. Mama laid an ear of corn bare in two quick strokes while Daddy turned and, with a sigh, closed the encyclopedia. He glanced up toward the driveway and then sat fingering the pages of the book as if he expected Bip any moment.

I wondered if Bip was spending his time with his girlfriend. Her husband must have been gone a lot. Bip didn't tell me where he went. He was distracted and vague when I talked to him. He was careless with his drugs and sometimes in those days I cleaned up after him. But I hardly thought of my brother at all then. I imagined that he was in love like I was, turned in on himself and dreaming through his days on memories of the night.

Daddy, bumping his knees on Bip's empty chair as he turned again toward Mama and me said, "You know, Ellen, I always thought when you got married, we could have the wedding here in the backyard. Of course, that was before they built this . . . this monstrosity. Money-hungry mayor and council sold us right down the river. Every time I think of it . . ."

"Well just don't, then," said Mama.

"Don't what?" asked Daddy.

"Think of it."

"They might as well have laid every last one of those bricks over my heart," Daddy said loudly.

"Melvin," Mama said sternly. "You're right, Gret," said Daddy, "there's no point in talking about it. A man knows when he's been licked. He knows when he's been run to ground. That's not to say I didn't give it a good fight. Nobody could say that."

"No, nobody could say that," said Mama.

"Everybody in town talks about how hard you fought," I said. Mama gave me a sidelong glance of irritation.

"Do they really?" said Daddy grinning. "I'm just darned glad somebody noticed. It wasn't much, you know. A few letters. Still nobody could say Melvin

180

Gibbs didn't have his say. They really talk about it downtown, huh?''

"Oh, yes," I said, not regretting the lie at all.

"In my book, it's a man's duty . . ." Daddy talked on and drowsy in the evening heat, I pulled halfheartedly at the leaves of the corn.

"You going to stop altogether now?" asked Mama over Daddy's voice. " . . . if no one takes the time to voice an opinion, why then it's just like the fellow says we get the kind of government . . ."

"No, Mama," I said and began working faster again. But in some unhurried place in my mind, Daddy's voice faded . . . "we deserve, and God knows what. . . ." and I lay next to Darcy after making love the night he'd said he loved me. It was quiet then in the long backseat of his car, quiet like the still, small space between two breaths. And I lay looking at the stars above us, tremulous in the misty sky. I thought about other times I'd lain awake after making love. My eyes would feel stung open as if they were electrified along the lid and I would be guessing what that man might be thinking of me. I would be concentrating, trying to divine his thoughts out of the silence. But with Darcy I slid easily into sleep. In his satisfaction, he would open to me and embrace me like long calm fingers unfurling from a fist. And I would sleep gliding on the miracle of his easy touch.

"Ellen," Daddy called from the yard. I turned to him. His smile was impish and he crossed his legs with elaborate nonchalance. I knew he would tease me.

"Yes, Daddy?"

"What's the story on this David Everett? He seems like a real nice fellow."

"He's nice enough," I said.

"A little birdy told me he wishes things were a little more serious between the two of you."

"Oh, Daddy."

It was true. David did love me and he was a good man, solid and sure. When I had first met him at work, he was head of the accounting department. He had told me then that he expected to be a vice-president within three years. He had had several promotions since then and his name just in the past few months had indeed been mentioned as a likely vice-president. And when he told me he would love me forever, I believed him. David was a tidy person and things stayed put in his life. He wanted to marry me. It's not that I hadn't considered it. David would make a good husband and I would have loved him if I could. But there was something frightening in the certainty of his love. I had never once told him anything that touched me any deeper than the morning's weather report and yet he loved me. What was it he was in love with? Did he make me up in his head or was what he saw all he required? Either way, when I kissed him, a little sigh of impatience in me always seemed just a moment away.

"Don't wait too long, honey," Daddy admonished. "You'll end up an old maid." He laughed heartily.

"Daddy's right," said Mama, stacking the last ear of corn on the pile between us.

"Oh, Mama, I . . ."

But as I began, we heard the sound of Bip's motorcycle nearing the house. We all looked toward the driveway. The engine stopped and Bip appeared around the side of the house. His clothes were wet and he was smiling foolishly. In the grave intensity of the red sky, his eyes were luminous and glassy in his pale face.

He passed Daddy without a glance. As he came up the steps and his face became level with Mama's, she signed, "Were you caught in the rain?"

Bip nodded.

Mama's hands gave sharp orders. "Change your clothes. You'll catch cold."

Bip threw his hands up in exasperation.

"Do what your mother says!" Daddy thundered from the yard. His face looked nearly as pale as Bip's. Bip didn't turn toward him at all. He only brushed between Mama and me, stepping high over the pile of corn and slamming the door behind him.

"You know," said Mama, "that rain didn't do him any good. He looked feverish already. Did you notice, Ellen?"

I shook my head. Daddy slapped the top of the encyclopedia in his lap. "What's gotten into him?" he demanded. "I can't imagine. I shouldn't have let him have that motorcycle."

"*I* never wanted it," said Mama. "I didn't want him to have the crazy thing."

"Oh, it's not that." Daddy waved his hand in dismissal. "He went back to school this year and came home a different person. I don't know. He could be a stranger for all I know. What's wrong with him?" My father's voice rose. He threw the encyclopedia to the ground. When Bip came out, they would fight, I knew. A heaviness settled over my heart. The raw red light of the sky made it seem as if the air were already charged with their anger. And I thought to smooth the evening, soothe my father, and I said, "I think Bip's in love."

At that my father's face brightened. "No kidding? The Bipper has a girl?"

"Yes," I said.

"A girlfriend. Well, how about that? It just goes to show you can't keep a good man down. Deaf and still he's got a girl. It's the old Gibbs charm, wouldn't you say, Gret?"

Mama gave a small smile but Daddy didn't look her way.

"Who is it?" Mama asked.

"I don't know," I said. "Don't tell him I told you, please, Daddy."

"Mum's the word," Daddy grinned. "So that's where he goes. I can't think of any deaf girls nearby though. He knew some at school, I know. She's not from those apartments, is she, Ellen?"

"I don't know." I was already sorry I'd told him.

Daddy perched on the edge of his chair, enjoying the news. "You better watch out, sweetheart. Your brother will be married before you. Wouldn't that be something?"

When I didn't answer he said, "The bloom can go off even the prettiest rose."

It was true. Women can get a certain look to themselves when they've been passed over and disappointed by men too many times. It's a look of the spirit trimmed like a light turned low and women get it when nothing in love is new anymore, nothing . . . not even the hope they don't dare show in their faces for fear of seeming ridiculous. I'd overheard a woman in a bar one night talking to a friend. "God, men," she said to the other woman, "I don't remember them all. They just come and they go and you know what I mean." They both laughed, harsh, ugly laughs. This woman in the bar was tough-looking, old, rolled over, walked over old and *she couldn't remember them all*. Ah, now, it's all right, I said to myself, smoothing out the little ripple of fright that passed through me at her words. The trick was in the remembering and I had my List. I'll remember them all. I won't forget a single man who ever crossed my body. Not the ones I loved and not the ones I only knew for hours who passed through my life as though they were marching over a bridge that connected them from one love to another. Not a single one.

Bip appeared at the door in dry clothes. He smiled down at Mama and came out onto the porch. Mama rolled up the towel around the corn we had shucked and lifted it into her arms. "I'll get you something to eat," she said to Bip and rose. As she passed Bip at the top of the steps he touched her arm and raised his hand toward his mouth.

"You already ate?" said Mama. She leaned back against the porch railing and hugging the corn close to her, scrutinized Bip as if she didn't quite believe him. Bip kissed her on the cheek and walked down the steps. Taking his seat next to Daddy, he picked the encyclopedia up from the ground. He turned to the back of the book. Looking at Daddy, he patted his hand down on a page. Mama still holding the corn continued to stand at the top of the steps. She looked down at Daddy and Bip.

" 'The moon,' good topic, Bipper," Daddy said eagerly. "Your mother and I were just discussing that before you came."

Daddy skimmed the page, reading under his breath. " ' . . . size . . . one fourth that of earth . . .' 'The mass of earth is eighty times greater . . .' "

Bip, grinning, pretended to take notes with rapid strokes of his hand.

"Ha! Here we go," said Daddy, "listen to this. . . . 'Not an entirely dead body, it nevertheless has virtually no weather and no sound.' How about that? If we all went to the moon, Bip would have to show us around. That'd be a real switch."

Bip's eyes narrowed and he signed tersely, "Maybe I wouldn't."

"Now, son," said Daddy, "I didn't mean anything by it. We're just talking about the moon, that's all. You're awful thorny lately."

Bip pecked the air with one finger.

"I'm not picking on you, Bip. I didn't say one word about you missing dinner again, now did I?" Daddy's voice had lost its good nature.

"It doesn't matter," called Mama from behind me. Bip, turned away from her, shrugged sardonically.

"It is a big deal, Benjamin, because it's common courtesy to let your mother know whether you're eating dinner here or not."

"It doesn't matter," Mama repeated.

"It does matter!" Daddy shouted.

Bip rose and started for the driveway. The sky had the heated glow of fire and the light cast my father and my brother into sharp relief. Daddy grabbed Bip's arm.

"You're not going out!" Daddy roared. Bip threw his arm off but Daddy made another lunge for him and caught hold of his collar. As Bip tried to turn, Daddy jerked him up short and my brother faced him, glaring furiously.

"Going to see your girlfriend?" said Daddy, fairly crowing. Bip, too caught off guard to conceal it, gave up a moment to a look of surprise. Then he nodded defiantly.

"What kind of girl is she that you can see her anytime?" asked Daddy, his face full of malice. "You're gone all hours of the day and night. What kind of family does she come from that her parents allow it?"

Bip signed slowly, his fingers stiff with rage.

"Oh, she's a woman, is she? Some old deaf woman." Daddy laughed breathlessly.

"Ssshh, ssshhh," said Mama. She set the corn down on the porch. The towel opened slowly and as the bright ears tumbled to the ground below, Mama stepped quickly down the steps into the yard.

Bip's eyes were golden in the light of the sky. He signed expansively. My father let go of his collar and stood with his hands on his hips.

"Oh, ho, she's not deaf? Then what does she want with you?"

Mama was nearly running when she reached my father. She laid a restraining hand on his arm, but he seemed not even to know she was there.

Bip took a step toward Daddy. Glowering, he formed a circle of his one thumb and forefinger and ran the middle finger of his other hand through the circle.

The blow was quick and sharp to Bip's face. Daddy's breathing was audible. Sweat streamed down his face and in the red glow of the evening burgeoned like a bloodstain on the front of his shirt.

"You damned animal!" he gasped. "You freak!"

Bip strode off across the yard. At the corner of the house, he turned. His face was contorted. The veins in his neck writhed like snakes caught under the skin. He opened his mouth and his lips formed carefully around the agonized sob of his voice. It was a cracked, toneless croak and the words were utterly clear. "I hate you!"

186

Jessie

Let us lose sight of ourselves, and break the mirrors.
For the fierce curve of our lives is moving again to the depths
out of sight, in the deep dark living heart.

—D. H. LAWRENCE

WINTER had come. Iron-cold and gray, it brooded over the strange events of our house like a troubled witness. The harshness of the weather kept me indoors. It wasn't that I couldn't get out. It was only that I didn't care to. Dad went to town for whatever we needed and I waited at home. I was glad to give up going to town. I hated the river in winter. The water, slowed by the cold, takes on the wounded opacity of a blind eye. Fallen leaves, petrified by threads of ice, choke the gulleys close to the shore. And the leaves themselves seem no less trash than the blown-away papers and carelessly thrown cans and bottles that collect among them. It will all lie there just below the banks all winter until the river gathers strength in spring and sweeps it all away.

It is simpler where we live, without the moody river. Our small mountain seems constant, a contemplative bump in the earth. Too small to have weather of its own, it acquiesces under the storms from the north and effaces itself for days behind the veil of hazy air passing from the river and the town.

Dad and I began to settle in for winter as we always had known it, long and solitary. With a tacit acceptance, we planned many things to do around the house before spring. We knew that without work, time in winter can stop and catch you sad too far from spring. But those months were not like any of the winters Dad and I had spent. Darcy began to come to visit us, not every day, but often enough that Dad would sometimes stand at the window watching for him. His visits were always unexpected and he never promised from time to time to come again. But when he came there was fun in the house, something Dad and I had missed for a long time. We had comfort and quiet companionship, even an occasional joke or two. But there wasn't the stir of a holiday that Darcy always seemed to bring with him.

He brought us odd presents. For me there was a pair of funny-looking slippers that someone had told him were good for the feet. They weren't bought anywhere in Hooke's Crossing. I know that. And I wouldn't have been caught dead with them on my feet. He bought a finely carved pipe for Dad who had never smoked in his life. "I ran into this, Cecil," Darcy told Dad, "and I thought of you. Look at the face here cut as neat as you please." And Dad and Darcy sat looking at the pipe and discussing it as if it were the very thing Dad had been wanting.

Dad got the pipe out one night when Darcy had come. He filled it slowly, ceremoniously. He performed the ritual neatly and I was amazed to realize he must have been practicing. Darcy watched Dad's thoughtful gestures silently. When Dad put a match to the pipe a white puff of sweet smoke rose from the tobacco. Dad's eyes watered above the bowl. "That's it, Cecil. You got it," Darcy said. "Keep drawing. Don't let her go out."

Dad puffed diligently at the pipe until the bowl glowed red. Then leaning back and wiping the tears from his eyes, he beamed at Darcy.

"Well, there you go, Cecil," said Darcy clapping his hands. "You look just like a professor."

"Distinguished, you mean," said Dad posing with the pipe. "I look like I'd be a better grandfather than some old farmer."

"There's not much discussion there," said Darcy. "You are an old farmer. And I can't think of anybody'd make a better grandfather."

Dad's thin, ruddy face reddened with pleasure. He and Darcy laughed together and I was silent, smiling at their delight. I would never have believed how easy it was to slip into their dream. Like walking into the ocean and finding with a thrill of exultation as the water closed over your head that you could breathe.

One morning I woke to find the back bedroom painted a fresh light green. Dad smiled all through breakfast but neither of us said a word. When Dad went outside, I went up to the room. It was nearly bare with an old patterned carpet that in its newer days had bloomed with impossibly robust red roses. It was faded then, its flowers dusty and brown. I could remember a time when it had been in the living room of a house we lived in when my mother was alive. Walking into the newly painted bedroom, I could feel the ridges of the floorboards through the flattened nap of the carpet. I paused by the cedar chest that stood in one corner. Idly I lifted the lid. The odor of cedar leapt out into the room with the sudden vigor of a music box melody. It competed for a moment in the air with the fresh paint. I let the lid down and ran my fingers over the top where varnish, whitened and cracked with age, webbed the red wood. Through a window, a southern light, diluted by the winter sky, fell thinly over the clean green walls. I stood in the room with my hands folded over the swell of my belly and wondered if this was how madness began, with a single lie. Did it matter that I rarely allowed any discussion of the baby? Did it matter that I'd told them both that I was giving this baby up for adoption? Hadn't I warned them away from any long dreams of a child? Hadn't I drawn the limits of the madness? But if I could stand in the middle of that room and feel such contentment with the present, such hope for the future, did it matter at all that I told myself the truth in the middle of the night? I couldn't have said. That morning in that room the color of a freshly broken stem, the idea of a baby growing inside of me seemed far more possible than the cells of my body multiplying to no purpose.

And yet there's no way to forgive my deception. I go over and over it in my head trying to unravel the threads that made it up. I remember that in the beginning there seemed to be a plan for it all. And I remember how I intended calling the doctor from day to day. The hysterectomy could pass for a miscarriage and I would be free of the whole preposterous situation. There was no question of telling Dad or Darcy the truth by then. To have them catch me so needful, to make them witnesses to that intimate hurt so enormous that it only dared show itself in dreams and ludicrous lies, oh, it was unthinkable.

The shame is a straightforward sort of explanation and it could serve as the final word on all that came later. But it doesn't touch the truth of those tight white winter days that slid so easily one into another when Darcy was with us and I played at being pregnant. Perhaps it is impossible to say how Darcy's presence seemed to fix the boundaries of our lives on some far plane that accommodated the child of our minds. Perhaps if I could describe exactly the sound of the wind as it howled down over the mountain and prodded at our little house until it seemed lifted up like Dorothy's house in Kansas and hurled into a benign and trackless draft. . . . But no, that wouldn't quite do. I would have to tell, too, how inside the warmth that steamed up the windows until we couldn't see and the smell of hot food mingled with the secret of the baby to comfort and enclose us, just Darcy, Dad and me. If I could tell it well, say precisely how it was, would it explain the guiltlessness of my happiness in being there with those two men whose joy over the baby was pure of worry or plan? Would it be clear then how I came to see the grotesque mistake as a justice, a small recompense for my loss? I imagine myself telling someone else what happened. But of course the explaining is never done because even at the time there was a part of me always that watched in wonder as one day passed into the next without my doing anything to end the lie. There *was* that part of me, but it lived outside the winter somewhere as if it were something I expected to appear over the mountain like springtime and wake me from that winter dream.

But the winter was longer than I might ever have thought and even now there are mementos of the dream. There was an afternoon when Darcy, Dad and I sat at the kitchen table. We had been sitting for a while, talking quietly. Darcy was telling us about the time Elsa Potts had shot her husband, Bob, in the seat of the pants with bird shot. It was in the early days of their marriage and Bob had stayed late at the Moose Lodge. When he did come home, he found that Elsa had locked him out. As he came through a kitchen window, she opened fire on him. She said at the time she thought it was a burglar. But Bob . . . or so the story goes in Hooke's Crossing . . . was never sure exactly who Elsa thought she had caught coming through the window. And he hadn't been seen out after dark without Elsa in the thirty years since.

While Darcy talked, Dad tugged at one ear. He shuffled his feet beneath the table and shifted in his chair.

"Good golly, Cecil," laughed Darcy, "did somebody light a fire under that chair or did you just hear the story before?"

"No, no," said Dad, "that's a good story no matter how many times it's told. It's just I ain't much for sitting."

"That's something I have noticed about you," said Darcy, "you don't sit still for long."

"Well now, there was a time I'd sit in church with Jessie's mother for an hour or two at a stretch. Don't remember being bothered by that."

"Is that right?"

"Yes, hours at a stretch." Dad rose and leaned stiff-armed on the back of the chair. "I wonder what made it tolerable," he mused.

"Probably because you felt like you were doing something you had to do, attending to business, so to speak. You just like to keep busy, that's all," said Darcy. "You're a man of action."

Dad regarded Darcy seriously for a moment and then said, "Well, that's right, ain't it, Jess, I do like to be stirring around."

"You sure do," I agreed. "But you could slow down a little in the winter. You could rest."

"It ain't restful to me to be idle," Dad said stubbornly. "Winter sure can hang heavy on your hands."

"Hey, that reminds me, talking about a man with nothing to do," said Darcy. He stood and began rummaging through his pants pockets. "Look what I came across the other day." He drew a piece of shiny paper from his wallet, a page torn from a magazine and folded into a square. He spread it out on the table. There were diagrams up and down the page, obviously plans for something.

"What's it for?" I asked.

"A rocking horse," said Darcy, shooting me a questioning glance.

"Oh, no, Darcy," I said.

"Now wait a minute, Jess," said Dad.

"Look, Jessie." Darcy flipped the page over and there was a photograph of a little wooden horse mounted on rockers. It had been built and left in the natural wood for the picture. The featureless head for all its elegance had a chilly hauteur. But on each side was a sturdy wing that invited the grip of a tiny hand.

"I know how you feel about plans for the baby, Jessie," Darcy went on hurriedly, "but how about this . . . we could build this little thing just for the fun of it, see, just to give Cecil something to do. And then if you don't want it, we'll just take it over to the Methodist Bazaar. It'll be as simple as that."

"If it were painted," I said almost to myself, "it could have a funny face."

"Jessie, are you saying . . .?" Darcy began, but Dad had scooped the plans up from the table before Darcy could finish.

"Got some pine boards out in the barn. All we need's a straight one," he said putting on his coat.

When Dad came back with wood and tools, we covered the floor of the dining room with newspapers and spread out everything we would need to build the little horse. Dad studied the plans for a moment. Then he put the saw to the first board and the odor of freshly cut wood brought a stir of beginnings to the winter-logged house. He cut two narrow strips from the wood and, putting them into the bathtub, left them there to soak until they would be pliable enough to bend into rockers.

And for the rest of the afternoon, the three of us worked. We hammered and sawed and sanded until the sanding dust lay yellow as pollen over everything. The newspapers had rumpled and smudged under our busy feet and rustled like dry leaves when we walked. The knees of our pants were black from kneeling. And when it was nearly evening, the little horse took to its legs. We had set it in the center of the room. "He cuts a fine figure," said Dad proudly and Darcy and I nodded. We had painted its body and head yellow. Its wings were the bright red of the flower boxes Dad had painted the spring before. The last rays of the failing sun streamed through the opalescent depths of the frost on the windows. In the rosy light, an arc of shadow lay along the legs of the little horse and lent them an animated tension that made the toy seem drawn up straight and tall by a power of its own.

After an afternoon of noisy collaboration over our project, we were silent. Dad had taken the rockers out of the tub. They couldn't be added until later. They would have to hang in the basement to dry. He sat working them into gentle bows over his knees. Darcy, his hands in his pockets, his head thrust forward attentively, watched as I knelt before the horse, a small paintbrush in my hand. With a meticulous and tender stroke, I swirled blue paint into great wide eyes on its narrow wooden face.

"Aha!" cried Darcy as I sat back on my heels with a smile, "there's the crowning touch."

Soon after, we sat down to dinner as we had so often

together. But there was a difference that night as if we entertained a new guest. The little horse occupied the room as a charming fourth presence, constantly drawing our eye and conversation. "We'll call him Jake," said Darcy, "we'll call him Lem." "No, no, no," I laughed, "a name no one else has." Dad grinned happily, twice clapping Darcy on the back.

We were nearly finished eating when Dad laid his fork down hastily and rose. "Good Lord," he said, "I forgot to feed the dogs."

"Those dogs looked fat and sassy when I came in, Cecil," said Darcy. "They're not going to starve in an hour or two."

"Yes, Dad, finish your dinner," I said. "A few more minutes won't hurt."

"Well, maybe not," said Dad from the kitchen where he was shoving his feet into a pair of boots. Darcy winked at me when my father went out the back door.

" 'Well, maybe not,' " said Darcy, shaking his head. "That Cecil's a bird of the old school."

We both smiled and ate the rest of our dinner nearly in silence. When we had finished we sat surveying our work of the afternoon.

"Well, I'd say we were pretty decent carpenters," said Darcy.

"I'd say we were," I said rising and circling the horse. As I moved, its round wise eyes winked in and out of sight in the lamplight.

"Look what a handsome fellow he is, Jessie. Look at the sweep on his wing there." Darcy drew a bead on the horse with his thumb. "I believe he could fly if he wanted to."

I stood, my hands on my hips, regarding the toy. "No," I said, "he needs his rockers. Poor thing, he's grounded now."

"No. No, that's an animal built to fly. The rockers would just give him a running start like the wheels on an airplane."

"Spoken like a true dreamer, Darcy, but everybody

knows a plane can't get into the sky without wheels and a rocking horse can't rock without rockers.''

"Now, there it is, there's the kind of logic I'd expect from somebody like you. All he needs is a little encouragement, just a word from you to tell him he can fly. But oh, no, he won't hear it from you, Miss Jessie. You're a stickler for the law of gravity, I can see it. And you'd count our friend here out just because he's off his rocker.''

When I could only answer with a laugh, Darcy, with a satisfied grin, rose and lifted the little horse into the air.

Later, in the living room, Dad sat reading the newspaper. I sat with a book of poems open in my lap. The page was turned to D. H. Lawrence's "Snake." And although I looked down into the book, the words seemed to move under my gaze and take themselves off like Lawrence's snake. And all that was left of the poem in my mind was a vague picture of a man going for water in a hot, hot country.

Darcy, propped on one elbow, lay stretched on the floor. He held a can of beer in his hand. He never came to our house without a six-pack or two tucked under his arm. And since Dad and I rarely accepted his offers for a beer, he drank most of it himself. Darcy never seemed drunk no matter how much he drank. He never staggered or slurred his words. And if he fell asleep suddenly, talking and animated one minute and sound asleep the next, I could only assume it was the beer that made him do it. I'd never seen him when he wasn't drinking. I wondered sometimes why Darcy drank at all. I only drank for courage and he didn't seem to need any.

I smoothed the pages of the book in my lap and looked at Darcy. Dad had nodded off. His quiet snore was the only sound in the room. Darcy lifted the can of beer to his lips. When he tilted his head, his jaw was sharply drawn, his cheekbones taut against the skin. The shadows under his eyes seemed lightly drawn as if they would vanish easily in his smile. He's a handsome man, I thought. And I wondered at his being with us at all, his lean-edged energy at rest in our house. He had come into our life and become somehow an arranger of it. It was as if he became the storyteller of our life and through his words he set us all into configurations varied as the stars. His affection defined us in ways we'd never thought of. And in the evening of the day we'd built the rocking horse, I wondered if I loved him after all. Was it the beginning of love, that great tenderness that swelled in my chest at the thought of how the silence in the room lay so peacefully, so gracefully? Darcy's comfort in it seemed to give it the generous symmetry of light falling through a window. Wouldn't love be next after such pleasure in someone's company? Dad shifted in his chair and laid his head against the back. His face was hidden and his chin pointed at the ceiling. I rose and laid an afghan over his knees.

As I sat down, Darcy started up out of the silence. "Jessie, you ever think about raising this baby yourself?"

"I wouldn't think of it," I said wanting to end any discussion. That day had been a day when the dream that we all played at seemed self-contained. The happiness we'd all shared building the horse seemed to have cut itself free from the lie it was built on by the sheer force of our joy. A dream is fragile, whimsical, as a balloon on a string. Yet when a balloon is let loose into the sky, when it disconnects from whoever holds it it takes on a durability, a dignity of purpose that can make us believe it could float unharmed around the world.

"Did you ever think of maybe leaving Hooke's Crossing and having this baby?" Darcy pressed on.

"Darcy, I don't want to talk about this."

"No, listen, Jessie," he insisted, "did you ever think of that?"

"What's the matter," I teased, "are you afraid somebody will find out you got a girl in trouble?"

"It's not that, it's . . ."

"Can't have people knowing you got me in a family way," I said.

"Come on, Jessie, I'm serious."

"Don't want people to know you knocked me up," I said prodding him in the ribs with my foot.

"Jessie!" he whispered and glanced at Dad who slept on undisturbed. He turned again to face me and laughed quietly.

"I don't know what to make of you, Jessie. At one time I would have thought you would be too proud to have people talk behind your back like they would if they knew. But I believe your pride runs another way. You could carry that baby for everybody to see and they could all be damned."

I smiled at him, feeling a fierce strength at the thought of everyone knowing. Suddenly I wanted them to know; I wanted to parade my big belly for all of Hooke's Crossing. Then they would think for all the rest of my childless life that this womb had once nurtured another life.

"What about you, Darcy? How would you feel? Would you ever admit a part in this?"

"Of course I would," he said indignantly. "There's nothing people could say about me that hasn't already been said."

"Oh? This isn't the first time this has happened?" I asked.

"No, that's not what I mean," he said wiping his hand across his mouth. "Jessie, don't you ever get serious?"

"Well now, Darcy," I said enjoying his discomfort, "you told me once I was too serious. Now you say I'm not serious enough. I don't know what you want."

"I want to talk about the baby," he said.

"Well, I don't," I said sharply, and in his chair, Dad jerked awake with a startled sound. He shook his head. "Well, good night," he said and rose and left the room as if he'd never been asleep at all. Darcy and I laughed, looking after him.

"Dear Dad," I said.

"It must be awful hard to deny him this baby," Darcy said doggedly and I was washed in a great wave of guilt.

My secret felt like a splinter working its way to the surface as if I would, against all my instincts, tell Darcy. As if it would mitigate my blame if I could explain to someone how I had come to tell such a terrible lie to my father who never lied, probably never thought of lying.

And in the next breath Darcy said, "Look, Jessie, I'm sorry. I know you're doing what's best. Anybody looking at the two of us would know your judgment's better than mine. I don't have any right to question that."

His gaze was very direct and I studied his expression. It was a look men have when they tell you they respect a woman. It's for women they trust to say what they want, women who never throw them onto that emotional minefield where men are powerless to please because they don't know what's required. To Darcy, I was independent, dependable, tough-minded. In fact, he liked me for those very things. And I liked the way he looked at me because of it. If I had told him the story of the phantom baby, the look would have changed. Being Darcy, I supposed he would have pitied me. Poor, poor Jessie, wanting a baby so bad. Or maybe he would only see it as wanting a man so bad.

Either way, his eyes would have taken on the same look Stephan's had at the end when I begged him to love me. It was a mixture of pity and contempt and there was fear there too. A fear that he might somehow be made responsible for shoring up my weakness of heart or mind, however he saw it. And with Stephan's face before me, the moment to tell Darcy passed and something strong and utterly private closed around the lie again, wrapped it up close and secret like a baby in a womb.

I lifted my chin and smoothed my hair. "Yes, I think it's best," I said.

"Yeah." Darcy lay down flat on his back on the floor and closed his eyes. He still held a can of beer in one hand. His fingers were long and well-formed. I had a sudden vivid memory of his hands sliding slowly and lingeringly over my breasts the night at Jeff's house.

Cautious hands, touching me as though he were sounding my desire through his fingertips. Ah.

Darcy looked nearly asleep on the floor and when he spoke, it was a sleepy mumble. "Jessie, I'm going to spend the night if you don't mind. If I could just have a blanket or something."

"I'll do better than that, Darcy," I said softly, "you can sleep in my bed."

"No, no," he said his eyes still closed. "I'm not going to put you out of your bed. Just a blanket here on the floor will be fine."

"Oh, I had no intention of giving up my bed. What I had planned was to share it." And I laughed to see his eyes fly open.

"Jessie!" he cried sitting up to face me.

"I mean it," I said.

He rubbed his hand through his hair and sighed. "Jeez, Jessie, look," he said, "I can't."

"Why not?" I felt my face flaming and hated his seeing it.

"For one thing, you're pregnant," he said.

"It doesn't make any difference yet," I said needing to press the issue, needing to know the very end of it.

"It's not just that," he said.

An impertinent smile clung mercifully to my lips. "Oh," I said, "what else could possibly keep you from this unheard-of opportunity? Well, practically unheard-of."

"I've got a girl, Jessie," he said steadily, "and I promised her."

"Well, how nice for you," I said. The smile stayed in place making him fidget. "Do I know her?"

He hesitated a moment, studying my face. Then he said, "It's Ellen Gibbs." A slight girl, Ellen Gibbs, blond and pretty. I had seen her around Hooke's Crossing and not long before I had seen her picture on the engagement page of the paper.

"Ellen Gibbs!" I exploded. "She was engaged to be married the last I heard."

201

"She still is. I know, I know it's a funny situation but I promised her, Jessie, and she promised me."

"Does that include her fiancé?"

"Look, I told you it's a funny situation. We made our promises out of what we had."

"I see," I said crossing my arms over my belly, "and your sexual fidelity was the big sacrifice."

There was a flash of anger in Darcy's eyes and he said, "That's right. I offered my money and my Cadillac but she wasn't satisfied."

"Have you talked this over with her fiancé? He probably doesn't have any idea why it's so difficult to score with his little lady love."

"Jessie," said Darcy, "nobody talks like that about Ellen to me. I wouldn't have told you what I did except I thought you and I were friends."

"Friends?" I said and I could hear the hurt and anger quivering in my voice. "Is that what we are, friends? Does Ellen know about your friend's baby?" I wanted to stop. I clamped my mouth down tight, ground my teeth behind trembling lips.

"I never told her because I didn't think you'd want me to. Is that what you want, Jessie? You want me to tell her? I wouldn't deny my own child, I told you that."

"No, no," I said breathlessly, "this is just how I want it, just the way it is. Just like this."

"You call the shots," he said warily. I sat back in the chair and gazed down into my lap. When I opened the book there and fluttered the pages, they grazed the protuberance of my belly with tiny paper sighs. "Why don't you marry her, Darcy?" I said, and my tone was conversational, casual again.

"She's like you, Jessie, too smart to have me." He gave me a small smile.

"Well, I wasn't smart enough to know when to leave well enough alone it would seem," I said and rose. Darcy leapt to his feet, kicking his beer can over. The beer erupted white and foamy onto the floor. He didn't seem to notice.

"Jessie, listen," he said putting his hand to my face and tracing my jaw with his thumb.

"Don't let it worry you," I said and I knew my eyes, my voice, my skin were cool. But as I turned away, Darcy drew me into his arms. I didn't return his embrace, I only allowed him to hold me, my cheek against his chest.

"It's not because I wouldn't want to," he said and I could hear his breath quicken. He wants me, he wants me, I thought.

And I was calm as I pulled away from him and said, "I'll get you a blanket. You can sleep on the couch."

Lilly

"Mama, Mama, listen, you don't have to worry about the bomb."

"Yeah, I know. You told me you saw one go off in New Mexico. And look, you're still here, aren't you? See, it's okay."

"No, you don't have to worry about me either. I know how to take care of myself."

"Well, they taught us about civil defense in school."

"Civil defense. Where you get under your desk and cover your head if it's an atomic bomb and you go sit out in the hall if it's a hydrogen bomb. The walls are stronger there, you see?"

"Civil defense, Mama, civil defense."

"What? No, no, not devil defense, civil defense."

"Oh, never mind. It doesn't matter."

TIM. Tim. When he was just a little fellow, he would say his name over and over to himself until the word was only a hum. And the sound of it seemed to coil him down into himself, away from us and out of sight. His eyes would be lively then, his baby bald head sunk musingly on his chest as though even then he was picking at some matter beyond the wisdom of the rest of us. It's no different now the way his conversations wind round and round and disappear into unanswerable questions. I hardly know what to do with him.

One night this past summer, the three of us, Darcy, Tim and I, had walked down to the river with Jingles after dinner. The road to the river runs downward for a way just as you leave town. Then it turns uphill, so that the river takes you by surprise, coming upon it as you do from the top of that last steep rise. The road ends at the boat ramp where the ferry docks. It's a small ferry, holding no more than six cars at a time and it chugs at its dreamy pace back and forth all day on this river that divides two states. The riverbank on the opposite shore is woodland shaking loose its underbrush, like unbound and tangled hair, down to the water's edge. But the land on our side has been tamed into thickly grassed banks. There are picnic tables there to rent and a small store that draws its business from the ferry trade. We bought a soda pop for Tim at the store and walked down onto the grass to spread our blanket. Darcy set up the lawn chair he had carried down for me. Then he sat down on the blanket, taking a beer from the cooler he had brought. Tim stretched out beside him.

Jingles ran off up the river toward the lights of the Blue Moon Cafe. He ran and stopped, ran and stopped, never going where he couldn't see us. I had brought the newspaper to read but for the moment I was only using it to fan myself. The breeze from the water was slight but it was more than we had back in town. I sighed gratefully and the river rolled by below with the stately grace of a bridal train.

"Hey, Daddy," said Tim propped on one elbow, "how long would it take you to go from here to Alaska?"

"Is this part of your homework or something?"

"No. How long?"

Darcy lifted the beer to his lips. The sinking sun turned the can to gold. "Depends on how you want to go, plane, train, car," he said.

"I don't know. A plane, I guess."

"A day maybe. Shoot, I don't know. Why? You thinking about going there?"

"No, but Mama was. I'd be too afraid to fly there."

"Well, then, by golly, we'll go by car. We'll start tonight," Darcy said and ruffled Tim's hair.

"Aw, Daddy," said Tim.

"Come on, let's do it. Mama," he said over his shoulder, "Tim and I are heading west. What do you think?"

"Darcy, for heaven's sake," I said and shook out a page of the paper but the glare from the late sun was too strong for reading.

"No, I mean it. We'll do it, won't we, son?"

Tim sat up. He rested his elbows on his knees. "Maybe we would," he said.

"Then, let's do it." Darcy was half drunk and I could see how he ended up in Baltimore sometimes not knowing how he got there.

"I would if I wasn't . . ." Tim paused and rocked side to side. His blond hair, cut short for the summer, looked to be no more than baby fuzz in the concentrated light.

"Wasn't what?" asked Darcy.

"Wasn't . . ."

"Afraid?"

"Yeah."

Both Tim and Darcy were silent. Jingles came loping back just then. Out of breath and panting, he trotted onto the blanket next to Tim.

"Get off there," I said. "Tim, get him off. His feet are all wet."

"Go on," said Tim and gave him a shove. With a wary eye on me, the dog lay down in the grass. Darcy reached into the cooler for another beer. He took an opener from his pocket and punctured the top of the can. "Maybe," he said to Tim, "if we always wait to do something until we're not afraid, maybe we'll never do anything. Everybody's afraid sometimes, Timmy."

"Not you," said Tim.

"How do you figure that?"

"You were in the war and everything."

"Timmy, let me tell you something . . . over there it was being afraid that kept you alive. And I guess that's true most anytime."

"I'm afraid all the time, Daddy."

"Well, that's the trick, you've put your finger right on it. You've got to figure out first what's worth being afraid of, see? What are you afraid of?"

"Everything."

"Name one thing."

"I'm afraid I'll be crazy like Mama," mumbled Tim.

"Ummm," Darcy said considering. "Well, let's take a look at this. For one thing what's crazy to one person may not be crazy to somebody else."

"You don't think Mama's crazy?" asked Tim in astonishment.

"Wait a minute, wait a minute, I didn't say that. I will say this though. . . . I know a lot of people who are considered sane who cause a whole lot more trouble in the world than your poor mama. And don't forget, *she* knows what she's doing."

"You really think she does?" asked Tim.

"It stands to reason, doesn't it?" said Darcy.

"I don't know."

"Sure. Look at old Jingles out there." The dog was leaping into the air, snapping at the first fireflies. "Now, I might say, 'That dog is crazy jumping around after those bugs like a frog.' But he's probably got reasons of his own that make perfect sense for trying to put those little lights out."

Tim laughed and we all watched the dog for a while in silence.

"See what I mean, Tim? He's dead serious. There's a dog with a mission if I ever saw one," said Darcy and Tim laughed again. I had to smile myself at the sight of that silly dog. The fireflies pierced the lengthening dark with their tiny lights and I knew we would have to head back to the house before too long. It's never long between the first fireflies and the mosquitoes that drive you away from the water at night.

Tim's and Darcy's laughter was sweet there by the river. It was only Darcy who could really make Tim laugh, but I didn't think he was always good for the boy. Tim needed definite answers, not Darcy's kindly speculations. Tim's wondering was too deep and dark. You don't admit the possibility of ghosts to someone who's as haunted as that child is. On the way home that night when Darcy started off down the road to the Blue Moon, I said to Tim, "There was never a crazy person in my family, honey, or in your grandfather's family that I know about. And I can tell you right now that your grandfather's stock is too strong to allow any craziness to pass into you."

And indeed, I couldn't imagine that Darcy's poor, rabbity wife had left any mark at all on Tim, inside or out. She was a flighty girl, a bit stoop-shouldered as if she were trying to fold in on herself like a snail. She wasn't bad-looking. While it's true she was nearsighted and flat-chested, she did have good hair and as the boys in my day used to say, a well-turned ankle. But she never seemed to take any of this into account like most girls do in considering their advantages. She surely didn't think much of herself. She was fearful, as if a blow might strike, an insult drop the very next moment. And I suppose by way of protection, she apologized. She apologized for everything, Lord, she apologized for nothing. There was an apology in the set of her head, in the tremor in her voice. When Darcy was a boy and he was reprimanded for something, sometimes he would say, "Well, excuse me for living." Evelyn often made me think of that bit of smart-aleck nonsense because I believe that that was the apology at the root of all the others.

Evelyn worked so hard at not offending that sometimes she seemed barely to be there at all. There was something flimsy about her, wispy as high, windblown clouds. I have thought that Evelyn may even have welcomed her later madness. Certainly, it is more substantial than her sanity as I remember it. My memories of her for the most part have survived as snippets in which Darcy breathes a bit of heft into the small shadow she cast among us. I can see her on the first Christmas she and Darcy were with me.

There had been Christmas Eves with Ivy and Otis while Darcy was in the service. Ivy would never have let me spend a holiday alone. But they were small, quiet Christmases best gotten through with as little talk of the past as possible. There certainly had been no celebration in my house in those years. At first, it had been unseemly and later it didn't seem worth the effort.

But on that Christmas Eve with Darcy and his young wife, there was a bustle of joy in the house. We had a tree in the corner of the front room. It was strung with lights fat and gaudy as summer stars. A fire in the fireplace warmed the piney bite in the air. Darcy sat in a chair facing me. Evelyn sat at his feet, looking more like a faithful dog than I liked to consider.

"Can you smell the cookies, Darcy?" she asked, smiling up at him. All day, she had been excited, nearly gay.

"You bet," Darcy said. "It's been a long time since I saw a Christmas like this one. And don't think I didn't dream about them the whole time I was overseas. Yeah, this is about as fine a Christmas as I can remember." He poured himself a drink from the bottle of whiskey he had been given from the electric plant where he was working. The red foil box the whiskey had come in lay on a table nearby. "Happy Holidays" ran in continuous gold script round and round the box.

"When shall we open presents?" Evelyn asked. "Lilly, when did Darcy open his packages when he was a little boy, Christmas Eve or in the morning?"

"When did your family open theirs, Evelyn?" I asked.

"My family's Jewish, Lilly. We did things a little differently," she said.

"Jewish?" said Darcy sitting forward with interest. "You never said before. Just this morning we were talking about how we used to go to Midnight Mass."

"Well, yes," said Evelyn nervously. "I never said anything before because I was afraid you wouldn't like it." Darcy and I protested stoutly.

"I didn't know Jewish people wore crosses, dear," I said.

Evelyn fingered the gold cross at her throat. "Well, the thing is," she said, "my mother was Catholic and my father was Jewish. So we just celebrated everything."

A small silence fell as Evelyn looked from me to Darcy with an anxious bright smile.

I sighed to realize that this was another of Evelyn's lies. Her lies were constant and irritating and they seemed sometimes to just pop out of her mouth as though someone else had told them and left Evelyn behind to defend, in a sort of innocent desperation, some obvious untruth.

We never did get to know much about her because of the lies. When Darcy had met her in a bus station in New York, he said she was sitting on that big cardboard suitcase of hers and watching the clock as if she had a bus to catch. She told Darcy she was going out to see her father in California, but later when I asked her about her parents, she said they were dead. I believe there was an uncle in Idaho she used to call from time to time but we never saw him either.

And by that first Christmas Eve we all spent together, I found myself too weary with her pretenses even to wonder at the truth. I was only relieved when Evelyn seemed to have settled her latest fabrication to her satisfaction and we didn't have to discuss it anymore.

"So when shall we open presents?" she said cheerily.

"We always opened ours Christmas morning. Darcy liked to wait for the last possible moment," I said.

"I love suspense," said Darcy happily.

"Oh, I know you do," said Evelyn. "That's why you love those Alfred Hitchcock movies."

"I do not," said Darcy. "I liked the one we saw but I didn't like the second one at all."

"Oh, yes, you did," Evelyn persisted. "I remember distinctly."

"Evelyn, I did not. I ought to know."

"It doesn't matter," I said, "it's nothing to argue about."

Evelyn's eyes filled with tears. "You're right, Lilly. I'm sorry, Darcy," she said burying her face against his knee. "I'm sorry. You didn't even have to buy me a present."

"Not buy you a Christmas present?" Darcy teased her, leaning close to her ear. "Of course I bought you a Christmas present. Come on now, smile. It's Christmas and I don't want tears. Right, Mama?"

"Right. No tears," I said as warmly as I could manage. I'd seen Evelyn's tears too often to feel much sympathy.

"Okay, okay, you two," said Evelyn, laughing and dabbing at her eyes. "I'm just sorry, that's all."

What were the portions of love and fear that bound that desperately pliant girl to my son? There was a large measure of gratitude, that's for sure. And I have found gratitude to be a mean companion to love. Bitterness will work its way in underneath like a splinter in the skin and irritate the love to anger. No one likes to be beholden. There was no way out of it, I suppose, the grudge that Evelyn came to bear for Darcy and me. And it was fed, I'm certain, by the rage she must have borne for whoever beat her down in the first place. I believe that even now it's anger, still red and wicked as fire thorn, that stings her to craziness, sends her raging to the top of a lonely hill to confront the end of the world by a God too blinded by some grand fit of pique to pity the worst among us. And, looking back, it seems to me it was anger that brought about the astonishing changes in Evelyn, although at the time we laid them to her pregnancy with Tim.

I've heard of women whose hair went straight or got curly when they carried a child. I've heard of women who broke out in strange rashes or were cured of an allergy to strawberries. But Evelyn became simply and completely beautiful. I don't mean beautiful in the way an ugly girl can make a beautiful bride. I mean she was beautiful to anyone's eyes. The color bloomed in her cheeks and her hair, dark and lustrous, fell in a thick scattering of curls over her shoulders. Her eyes shone and most noticeably, her breasts grew large and round as cantaloupes. Those amazing breasts seemed to float there below her shoulders and I can only imagine that it was their presence that slowly lifted the set of her chin and changed the direction of her gaze.

When we went downtown everyone looked at her, people who months before had hardly been aware of her. Evelyn had been the one in a group that everyone forgot to say hello to. But when she was pregnant with Tim, she turned the heads of all the men in Hooke's Crossing, from that foolish Eli Berry at the drugstore, who leers at all the women, to handsome William Quinn. It was as if she were lit from under the skin. I used to picture the baby curled and shining like a glowworm inside of her. A happy, laughing baby I would have said.

Tim was born quickly. I was downstairs when I heard Evelyn scream, "Lilly, come help me!" When I reached the top of the steps, Evelyn lay on the hall floor where she had fallen, Tim lay wailing against her thigh, the cord a bloody snake between them. Evelyn's eyes accused me from a face washed white and waxen by terror. A shaft of light from a nearby window bisected the infant's face and dust motes like tiny golden fish swam above his head. For a moment, I stood there close to tears, touched by what came to me as a primordial daring in the way the china-thin bones of the baby's chest seemed thrust nearly to breaking by the force of his cries. He seemed to have taken great risk to suck in the air of this world. I shook my head. It was nonsense, of course. Baby's bones are greenwood tough and supple. Evelyn pressed her fingers into my ankle as I stood smiling down at the baby. "You could have told me how bad it hurts, Lilly," she said. "You could have warned me."

"It'll be all right, Evelyn," I said absently, wrapping Tim up in my apron.

Had Evelyn been in labor long? Had she been too shy to say? Or had Tim come too quickly for any of us to have done anything? Evelyn would never tell me. But she was unforgiving of the pain and Tim was mine from the beginning. Evelyn was slow in recovering; she seemed to feel it was hardly worth the effort, and stayed in bed for months. She had kept her extraordinary beauty and sometimes she sat up in bed gazing into a hand mirror. She would turn her head fretfully this way and that. Certainly she took no pleasure in what she saw. She seemed embarrassed by her sudden beauty and suspicious of whatever providence had brought it to her.

I wonder what thoughts she turned over in her mind as she lay day after day in that darkened bedroom. When she cried the tears slid from the corners of her eyes and slipped down to wet her temples. The fine hair there sprang up in damp little curls when she made no move to dry her tears. I remember Darcy sitting with her sometimes and I remember the silence that swelled out of their bedroom and down the hall to the nursery where I was with Tim. It seems to me that Darcy was with her a great deal but Evelyn has said that wasn't so. He drank with his friends every night, I remember her saying that.

To tell the truth, I couldn't say just how it was. In those days, Darcy held a steady job and I had quit work to stay home and care for Evelyn and the baby. And that time in my mind is filled with Tim. Oh, what a fine baby was my Tim, plump as Darcy had been frail. The solid healthy weight to him under my hands, against my shoulder, seemed like a blessing meant especially for me. He was God's restitution, a balance to the horror of Aaron's death. What I felt for that baby was like an aching greed. There could never have been enough to do for him to satisfy me. There couldn't have been too many mealtimes, too many baths. Sweetest of all were those hours in the night when out of the darkness and stillness of the house, one lamp would carve a place just big enough for Tim and me. I'd hold him long after he had fallen asleep, his heartbeat flickering light as a moth's wing against my breast. I'd hold him, half asleep myself, lulled by the faint purr of his breath while his mother slept fitfully and painfully in the next room.

In the months while Evelyn recuperated, she didn't interfere with my care of the baby. Even when she was out of bed at last, she seemed content just to pick him up from time to time and put him down again if he needed anything. She said she was still so tired. Oh, I didn't press her to help. I'll admit it. But it was never in my mind to deny Tim to his mother. If she had only asked it, I would have, no matter how reluctantly, turned his care over to her. As it was, it never came to that. A week or two after Evelyn was up and about, I came home to find her packing.

Tim and I had been for a walk. As I carried him upstairs for his nap, I caught sight of her through her bedroom door. She was folding her clothes into the old cardboard suitcase she had brought when she came with Darcy.

Entering the room with Tim in my arms, I said, "Why, Evelyn, where are you going?"

She had her back to me and without answering she continued to lay her clothes in the suitcase. "Are you going home?" I asked her.

She straightened then and faced me. "I have no home, Lilly," she said.

"That's silly, dear," I said, "your home is here now." Evelyn turned back to her packing.

"No, this is Darcy's home," she said, carefully folding an ice-blue satin nightgown she had bought for herself not long before. "Did you know he would always come back here no matter where he went? Did you know that when he went away?"

"I wasn't sure, to be truthful. It was like a death to me at the time."

"And you grieved for him, didn't you?" asked Evelyn, her voice wistful and faraway.

"Yes, I suppose I did."

"Will you grieve for me when I go away?"

"Evelyn, this is nonsense. You're not going anywhere."

"Will you, Lilly?" she said loudly. Tim started at the sound.

"Will I what?"

"Grieve for me." The pale blue gown slipped from her fingers to lie in a pearly heap in the suitcase.

"Evelyn, you must call Darcy or I will." Tim's eyes moved between his mother's face and mine.

"Oh, there won't be time for that, will there, Lilly?" Evelyn reached out and lightly stroked Tim's cheek with the back of her hand. Fear quickened in my heart and I took a firmer grip on the baby's back.

"Your family is here now, Evelyn," I said desperately. "I . . . I won't hear of your leaving."

"Don't worry," she said, closing the suitcase with two sharp clicks, "I'm not taking the baby."

At that moment I let her go, even wished her gone quickly.

"Why, Evelyn?" I asked almost idly, as Tim, restless, wound his fingers in my hair.

"Because other men will love me now. I don't have to settle for a man who collects flawed people like they were stray dogs."

She turned to face me then and she did look lovely standing there, defiant and . . . I wouldn't have believed it . . . proud. She picked up her suitcase and headed out the door with me close on her heels.

"What shall I tell Darcy?" I asked.

"Tell him I'm sorry. No. Tell him thanks but no thanks." She laughed softly to herself and clambered awkwardly down the steps with the big suitcase. From the top of the stairs, I watched her walk out of the door without a backward glance. The palm of my hand cradled the wondrous roundness of Tim's head.

And Darcy? Did he cry, did he rage? Later it seemed to me he drank a little more, was home a little less. But just at the moment of telling, he smiled a smile one might see on a parent whose backward child had made them unexpectedly proud. "Well, I'll be," he said, "I'll be."

Twelve years went by before we heard from Evelyn again. The way her mind is I would have thought she would have forgotten all about us by then. I wish she had. But out of nowhere she began calling Tim, and the way the questions have poured from him when he hears her voice, the way he draws that cockeyed comfort from her ramblings, I knew from her first call he had been preparing to hear from her for a long time. There's a longing in him for her that is deep, written in his blood perhaps. And his will in this matter is too strong for me to fight.

"Mama, Mama," he says anxiously into the phone, "do you remember when I was a baby?" Then she tells him stories I think he halfway believes of finding him beside a magic pond or his being torn from her by giant birds. And he says that this is better than not knowing her at all. "It was like going along like maybe you were

218

blind in one eye, only seeing half of things, you know. And knowing her lights up that blind side some way, you know? You know, Gran?'' he said wanting me to understand. And I pretended that I did. But my heart aches to think of his mother's mere mad presence soothing some vital spot in him that I, with all my years of care for him, can't reach.

It's not that I believe he doesn't love me. Tim and I live comfortably together, after all, with a great meeting of the minds in unexpected places. He's an odd duck, my Tim, and I suppose that I am too.

One evening not long ago I asked Tim to set the table for dinner. Darcy wasn't to be home. He and Jeff had gone to Washington to meet an old friend from the army. Tim got it into his head that the two of us should eat in the dining room.

"Tim, honey," I said, "you'd have to take all that laundry off the table first. It's just so much simpler to eat here in the kitchen."

"Come on, Gran," Tim pleaded, "just tonight. We'll have candles and everything."

"I don't know if we have any decent candles."

"Yes, we do," he said beaming. "I found them."

"Oh, for heaven's sake, what a bother it will be, Tim."

"No, look. I polished the napkin rings and everything."

The napkin rings were silver and had lain, black with tarnish, in a drawer since before Aaron had died. Tim had returned them to their refined gleam. I had a sudden vivid memory of my mother. Dressed for dinner, she surveyed the long cherry wood table we had at home when Ivy and I were girls. The evening light gilded the curve of her cheek and she folded her white hands before her. I could hear the sibilant friction of her light dress against her slip as my father seated her. When she slipped her napkin from its ring, she turned to Ivy saying, "Sit up straight, please, dear." I felt a great rush of love for her just then in thinking of that moment. I felt again the ordered serenity her attention to detail and her stiff-backed vigilance of our manners had brought to the dinner table. Unlike me, my mother had never questioned the importance of the unnecessary.

"All right, Tim," I said, "let's do it up right, then."

An hour later, I was presiding over the long polished dining-room table. Four candles lit the room. The dim, wavering light made the old wallpaper look nearly elegant again. The tablecloth, creamy with age, had belonged to my grandmother. It crisscrossed the dark wood of the table in a web of delicate knots. The silver cast its quiet gleam on the rosy undersides of Mother's good china. I had dressed for dinner in the best dress I had left. And although it was long out of date, it had the same almost-forgotten formality to it as the lavender toilet water I had dabbed behind my ears. I drew myself up and squared my shoulders against the back of my chair. I fancied that I looked like my mother.

"You look very nice tonight, Tim," I said, complimenting him on the tie and white shirt he had put on for the occasion.

"Thank you, Gran. You look lovely," he said with a grave courtliness. He lifted his wineglass with one finger carelessly crooked. I smiled. Tim was at ease that evening as though we often dined like that. I supposed that even before we had gone looking through those long unopened drawers, Tim had imagined himself sitting among the finery we eventually mustered. Was he a prince in his daydreams, a gentleman of means? Was he debonaire, heroic?

"Thank you," I said. "You remind me of your grandfather tonight, sitting at your end there looking so grand. We always ate in the dining room when he was alive. Afterward, it just seemed so big in here, your daddy and I began eating in the kitchen. This certainly brings back memories."

Tim sat forward. "Gran, do you think maybe memories could be passed along from father to son like the color of your eyes or something," he asked, peering owllike down the length of the table. He looked very much the boy again.

"Good heavens, Tim, how should I know? I don't suppose that's so."

"All I know is," he said placing his glass emphatically on the table, "I could swear I've done this before, eaten here like this with you." He sat back and folded his arms. And there was Aaron's implacability set unmistakably around his mouth. I would have wished that some of Aaron's stubbornness and arrogance would flow into this child who seemed, like overripe fruit, to bruise too easily. I would have given up some of his gentleness for a bit of his grandfather's starch.

"We all have those feelings sometimes, Tim, like something has happened to us before. It happens all the time. And there's a perfectly logical explanation for it just like there is when people think they see flying saucers."

"Maybe memories are like flying saucers and they just go winging around under their own power, you know," he said dreamily, tipping the wineglass to his lips.

"There're no such things as flying saucers. That's been proven," I said.

"Mama thinks there are."

"That should be proof right there that there aren't any," I said curtly.

"Maybe. But it'd be nice, you know, to think about somebody else being out in space and being better than us."

"Oh, Tim, that wine's made you silly. You talk like your father does when he's had a few beers." I said it with a laugh but a little chill breathed through me. I don't want Tim to pick up that subtle twist of mind, that way Darcy has of giving importance to whatever notion might pop into his head. It's Darcy's wondering that keeps him from getting about the business of life. And it's the weight of so much possibility, it seems to me, that bends him toward the bottle.

"I like Daddy when he's drunk," said Tim.

"Why?"

"Oh, I don't mean when he's gone around the bend like he says, but when he first starts out and he likes to talk."

"Well, for my own part, I'd just as soon see him sober," I said. The candlelight rippled over the walls like sun on the water.

"Remember the time Aunt Ivy got drunk?" asked Tim.

"Yes." I laughed. It was a New Year's Eve and Ivy had brought a bottle of champagne. I can do without it myself and only drank one glass. But Ivy had finished the bottle. As she drank it, Tim and Ivy and I all sat in the front room waiting to ring in the new year. It was late and Ivy had just said that Tim looked like Mr. Stanton. I must say that's the first I ever heard of *that*.

"Don't you think so, Lilly?" asked Ivy. "Doesn't he look just like Mr. Stanton?" She sat thoughtfully regarding Tim who looked questioningly from my face to hers.

"Ivy," I said sharply, "I never saw Mr. Stanton."

"Oh, you never did, that's right," she said crestfallen.

"Who's Mr. Stanton?" asked Tim.

Ivy turned to him in amazement. "Nobody ever mentioned Mr. Stanton to you?" Her eyes were wide and bright.

"No, ma'am," said Tim. "Who was he?"

"No one ever told you," said Ivy incredulously. The color was high in her cheeks.

"And no one's going to tell a twelve-year-old, are they, Ivy?" I said.

"Oh, Gran," said Tim, "please. I know a lot more stuff than you think I do."

"We're not going to talk about that either," I said.

Tim sighed disappointedly and Ivy drew herself up as if she had suddenly roused herself from the champagne.

"No, we most certainly won't talk about that," she said primly.

The church bells in town began to peal in the distance. It always seemed momentous to hear the bells toll at night as if they were still rung as they had been in the old days for all the births and deaths in town.

"Happy New Year," shouted Tim and jumped up. He kissed me on the cheek. And when he leaned over Ivy to kiss her, he whispered something in her ear.

"Curiosity killed the cat," she said taking Tim by the hand. "Your grandma's right, you're too young to hear about Mr. Stanton."

"I'm not," protested Tim, bad-tempered then by the late hour.

"Here's a promise, honey," Ivy said holding Tim's hand against her cheek. "I will tell you about Mr. Stanton. I'll tell you when you fall in love."

"Well, that'll be never," said Tim pulling away and flopping grumpily back into his chair.

"Do you think Aunt Ivy will ever tell me about Mr. Stanton?" Tim asked from his end of the long table as we sat at dinner those few years later.

"Well, I don't know," I said smiling at him, "are you in love?"

He looked quickly down at his plate and I knew that even though the dimness of the candlelight hid it, he was blushing fiercely. He gave me a warning glance and sat back in his chair with his arms folded across his chest.

"I didn't mean to pry," I told him. He said nothing.

I said, "I thought Aunt Ivy might have told you about Mr. Stanton that same night when you walked her home." Tim unfolded his arms at the change in subject and sat forward to pick up his wine.

"No, she never did," he said. "You could tell me."

"It's not mine to tell."

"No, I guess not," he said. "I wish she had told me that night."

"I remember watching you two go up the street that night. Ivy kept weaving back and forth across the sidewalk. She must have walked a million miles before you got to her house." I laughed thinking of Ivy moving off up the street with young Tim at her elbow. She went at a careful pace but even her greatest concentration on her

223

dignity couldn't hold her on course. Tim, keeping to her side, traced her unsteady steps. "You beside her there reminded me of Lester Haney trying to drive his Cadillac home after a night at the Blue Moon."

"Gran!" Tim remonstrated.

"For heaven's sake, Tim. I didn't mean anything by it. You know I love Aunt Ivy."

When his expression didn't change, I added huffily, "It's all right to laugh, you know."

"Not like that though," Tim said and his grandfather appeared in his face again as he set his lips in a grim line of disapproval.

Later, after we had finished the dishes, I could hear Tim upstairs moving about his bedroom while his radio played. Tim loves rock and roll music. Da da dum, da da dum, the music thudded overhead. When Tim and I went to Baltimore one day, that rock and roll music was everywhere, in the stores, in the restaurants, spilling into the streets from windows everywhere. There wasn't peace enough to think. But Tim was beguiled by the music, walked in time to it, humming to himself.

It's strange to me the way Tim is drawn to this rude loud music. His father loved it too I remember, but it seemed to fit Darcy with its wild angry rhythms. The part of Tim that answers to it is hidden from me. Da da dum, da da dum, it goes on and on and Tim's big feet above mark out a tread so light, he could be dancing.

Jessie

We are created from and with the world
To suffer with and from it day by day:
Whether we meet in a majestic world
Of solid measurement or a dream world
Of swans and gold, we are required to love
All homeless objects that require a world. . . .
—W. H. AUDEN

IT was a Sunday evening. I do remember that. It had been a pale hard winter day when the air was crystalline and painful to breathe. Dad had mended fences all day. He had seemed to be working only for the sake of working and had walked much farther than he needed to.

At dinner he was quiet, barely eating. I should have known from that that something was wrong. We always knew if an animal was really down when it stopped eating. But I scolded him . . . imagine! . . . for passing up the pot roast and carrots.

It was only later when we sat in the living room and his face was lit by the strong glare of his reading light that I really took notice of him. Even across the room, I could see a strange look to his skin. It had a flat gray cast to it, ashy almost, as if the grayness could be brushed away at a touch.

"Dad," I said, "how do you feel?"

"Not good, Jess. I'm awful tired."

"What's wrong? You said at dinner your stomach hurt."

"Well no, it's not a pain exactly. More a sick feeling and like a numbness down the side of my neck."

Fear prickled in my scalp. "We're going to the hospital," I said getting up quickly. I don't know what made me know so surely then how sick he was when an hour before I had hardly paid attention.

"Hospital?" Dad laughed weakly. "All I need's a good night's sleep, Jessie. Don't concern yourself."

"We're going now," I said and went to get his coat.

He didn't resist me anymore after that and I bundled him into his hat and coat. The truck was icy. Out in the air, Dad's breath rattled in his chest. Although he said nothing, I felt a terrifying imperative that ran between us like electrical current. Unwarmed, the truck lurched and bucked down the driveway. It proceeded reluctantly and was hard to steer. The steering wheel pressed into the swollen bulk of my belly. Dad seemed to be precariously bracing himself against the jolts of the ride.

Once we hit the state road, the drive was smoother. I felt Dad relax a bit beside me. His breathing labored loudly in the small cab of the truck. His face was ghostly in the light of the oncoming cars. His eyes were closed.

"Dad?" I said, jamming my foot down on the accelerator. "Dad?"

"I'm all right," he said but it was little more than a whisper.

Dad was drawing his breath with the sound of heavy chains dragging. Steering with one hand, I took his hand and kneaded it under my own. His hand was rough and bony, the knuckles swollen and gnarled. I pressed Dad's hand, pressed my will into his wide old bones as the scenery outside rushed by with the fluid flash of water. I drove not thinking where I was going, trusting Dad's hesitant breathing to direct me. I drove through the frozen blur of the countryside holding on to my father for dear life.

And just as we could see the lights of the county hospital, Dad said in a voice that seemed to whistle up from some great depth in his chest, "Jessie, you are my sunshine."

"Don't talk," I screamed, finally crying, the tears coursing down my face as I pulled into the emergency entrance of the hospital.

"My father, my father . . ." I gasped stumbling from the truck as two men in white ran from the doors. But before I could tell them, they had begun to lift him from the cab of the truck.

He lived through the night and when they settled him in the intensive care ward the next morning, I felt as if I were looking at him underwater. The bottle green light in the ward tinted his skin gray and turned the white sheets a pale phosphorescent green. His body seemed disjoined, broken in the bed. His long arms did not lie peacefully at his sides. They seemed strewn there, bent at odd angles as if someone had laid him down in a terrible hurry. As I watched him lying there, I realized that in all the images I have of my father in my mind, he is moving, working. His long lean body has no particular grace yet everything he does looks easy.

In the days that followed in the hospital, he slept most of the time, his eyes swimming under his lids like shy fish. He was dreaming, I supposed, dreams as deep as the sea-green light in the room. I stayed with him all through the days but at night they sent me home . . . to sleep, they said. Yet I didn't do much of that. I read far into the nights and was up early. In the mornings before it was time to go to the hospital, I took long walks along the dirt roads around the house. I strode along leading with the huge weight of my belly, cutting the sharp winter air, I imagined, like the prow of a big ship. I walked the roads in their icy stillness, my breath bursting into the cold in white blooms of steam. I needed to walk in the mornings before I could leave for the hospital. I felt driven from the house by an unfocused edginess that would grow until I could see my father. All the moments of the day tumbled helter-skelter toward seeing him and it was only the sight of his face that brought them into order. With him I was gathered into the center of some purpose the enormity of which I could hardly make out.

"Jess, I've been a lucky man," he said one day, his face dim in the quiet light of the ward.

"Have you?"

"Yes, I've had pretty much everything I ever wanted."

"I think you haven't wanted much," I told him.

"Is that the trick to it, then?" he chuckled weakly. "You think that's bad?"

"No, no, I envy you."

"Does that mean you ain't happy?" he said and his eyes, large and intent as a child's, searched my face.

"I hope I'm too young to make a judgment like that for my whole life." I turned from him. "Have some water, Dad," I said heartily.

Waving his arm in a weary arc of dismissal, he said, "You got a lot on you now."

"I don't think about it."

"That can't be true, Jess." In the gloom, his face appeared so dear to me my heart ached.

"Dad," I said gently, "I have made plans if that's what you mean. Nothing's changed."

He nodded and turned his head on the pillow. When he turned again to face me, his eyes were filled with tears.

"Jess, I know you're determined and I ain't saying I blame you. Ain't saying that at all. But if there's nothing to change your mind on this will you promise me one thing?"

"What is it, Dad?"

"Will you put the rocking horse by. Maybe put it in the attic for another time?"

"Yes, I'll do that, I promise," I said and held tightly to his hand.

When I stepped out of the intensive care ward that day I was surprised by the light through the windows of the waiting room. What had been a clear bright winter morning had turned into an afternoon heavy with the gray of snow clouds. It was only five days since Dad had had his heart attack and I sighed to think of going home to the quiet empty house. As I turned from the door of the waiting room, I heard, "Jessie!" And there in the somber silence of the hospital, sitting amid the determinedly colorful plastic furniture was Darcy. He closed the magazine in his lap and rose.

230

"Well, Miss Jessie," he said when he reached me, "your telephone out of order?"

"Darcy, I . . ."

"You could have called me. Did you think I wouldn't be interested?"

"You could have called the house," I said.

"I did. You never answered." He folded his arms and regarded me through narrowed eyes.

"I'm there in the early mornings and late evenings," I said. But I didn't offer it as excuse or information. I felt a sharp surge of anger with him, and I realized I had been looking for him every day as though he had to pass a test of affection by finding Dad and me in our trouble. And unreasonable as it was, five days was too late and he had failed. He hadn't loved us enough.

"I called a couple of mornings," he said.

"Not the evenings, I'm sure."

"What's that supposed to mean?"

"Too busy with Ellen Gibbs, I'd say."

"Whoa, Jessie, come on. Looks like I'm the only friend you got right now. Take me for what I'm worth." He rocked back on his heels and looked at me seriously.

"I'm sorry," I said, tired and not sorry at all.

"You must know how much I care for Cecil."

"Yes."

"And you too," he said touching my chin softly with his knuckles.

"I know." And I did.

"Friends?" he said offering his hand.

"Friends."

"Okay," he said, "tell me about Cecil."

"He may be dying, Darcy. I'd like to put a good face on it for you but that's the truth of it."

Darcy winced, saying nothing.

"I've been living with it for days. This may be the end for him."

"Okay, okay," said Darcy, "I heard you the first time. You're giving up on him a little early, though, aren't you?"

"If you're going to be here, you might as well know it, Darcy." My voice had taken on the same tone I used to use on recalcitrant students. "It won't be long until he's dead."

"God, Jessie," he said reaching for my hand, "don't say it again. Nothing can prepare you for it."

"I believe I am prepared," I said trying to pull my hand out of his.

He thrust his face down close to mine. "No matter how many times you say it," he said holding my hand fast, "it doesn't make it easier."

"Thanks for the consolation," I said angrily.

"I'm here for the duration, Jessie, and I can't lie about what I know. You and I don't lie to each other."

"No, we don't," I said and found tears rolling over my cheeks. Darcy pulled me to him, and washed in the subterranean murkiness of the winter-lit waiting room, I sobbed against him.

And Darcy did come every day. He sat in the waiting room, leafing through the same old magazines, slipping out for a drink occasionally. Sometimes he stayed until the heavy blue winter evenings drew frost in tiny cracks on the hospital windows and I left to go home at night. Did he know how much I needed him in those days? Could he imagine the time I spent with my father even though we never talked about it?

There were days when I was so frightened by my father's weakness. The conversations between us then were like that of two strangers snowbound in a bus station . . . friendly, tentative, impersonal. Easy conversation, one might have said. But it wouldn't have been true. Those words that I spoke had been pacified into their comforting blandness by their long passage through the fear in my heart, over the thin jitter of my nerves.

"What was for dinner last night, Dad?"

"Oh, meat loaf and green beans."

"Was the meat loaf good? It can be so terrible if it's not done right."

"Well, it was all right."

232

"Maybe they'll have something you like better tonight. Do you want me to check the menu?"

"You know who made a really fine meat loaf was your aunt Pearl. Do you remember her?"

"Gee, no, Dad, I don't."

"Well, you wouldn't remember her meat loaf then. Mighty fine with little chunks of I think it was green pepper."

"Green pepper?"

And on and on. I think those must have been the days we were most afraid. Death would not cross my mind as we talked and I moved through those conversations playing out my words like a lifeline as if I were holding him in this world by the meandering thread of our aimless talk.

In the waiting room, Darcy and I talked of little things too: Jeff's flashy new girlfriend from Baltimore, the new snow tires Darcy had bought for his car, a song he'd heard on the way over to the hospital. How heartened I was by Darcy's small news as if the world going about its business beyond the hospital walls suddenly needed the proof of his telling. Often I didn't talk at all but only sat resting, listening to Darcy. It is exhausting attending illness. And it wasn't only the worry that tired me; it was anger too. Anger at a world in which my father's kindness seemed to count for so little, and deeply, secretly, guiltily I was angry with my father who lay so docilely under the threat of death. I knew that being Dad, he would accept it as he had accepted life . . . as it came to him. Without a struggle he would leave me, retreat from me forever behind the impervious delicacy of his eyelids. Although Darcy and I never discussed it . . . I would hardly have known how to tell him . . . being with him made me able to contain the anger, catch it, hold it away from Dad. I never laid an ungentle hand on my father.

One Friday morning, they called me from the hospital. "You must come quickly," they said. As I drove to the hospital, the sky was thick with gray woolly clouds. The stillness of the winter morning made it seem as if I had gone half deaf at the words, "You must come quickly," or that the billowing press of low hanging clouds had muffled the sounds of the earth.

The doctor met me as I walked on the ward. "We tried to call you, Jessie," he said, "but you'd already left the house." My breath caught in a burning lump in my chest. "Has he passed over?" I asked, surprised by the phrase. Passed over? It was an expression a great-aunt of mine had used. And whenever she'd said it, I had thought of a big, dark blimp going down over a hill.

"No," said the doctor, "but his heart stopped beating not half an hour ago. We brought him back, thank God, but it's going to be touch and go for a few days."

"I want to see him," I said.

In the eerie green light of the room, he looked no different than any other day when I had come in the morning to find him still sleeping. His long body seemed no more still, his breath no more lightly drawn. And for me, there was the same relief I'd felt any other day to see he had survived the night. I told myself as I might have explained to a child, "Half an hour ago he was dead." But instead of the fear I would have expected, there was a surge of joy at the sight of him. How desperately ill he was and yet he had beaten death. My eyes moved down the length of his body and I will swear that I could see the power of his resistance enclosed in the deep blue shadows under his eyes, in the rough knotty knuckles of his limp hands, in the steep rise of the sheet over his feet.

I sat by his bed, hardly daring to move as if I could fool some fate into overlooking my father. If I didn't call attention to us, Dad would be spared. I was rigid, not wanting to upset, with my body or my mind, the delicate balance between life and death that my father had struck.

In the undersea light of the room, Dad and I were out of time. Outside, perhaps, winter was over and spring had begun. Outside, perhaps, it was last winter still and

Dad was going about his life oblivious to the beat of his weakening heart.

I sat by his bed all that day and through the following night. I didn't think I had slept at all but there is a dream I remember and I know I dreamt it by my father's bedside. In the dream, I look toward the sky which is cloudless and the pale cottony blue of winter. Two geese fly into view. They are the Canada geese we see in late fall around Hooke's Crossing. Sometimes they light on Bright River by the hundreds. They're big-winged birds with sleek long necks and they cut through the air so effortlessly when they fly that they seem to be moved by the turn of the earth. In the dream, it struck me as very sad to see just the two of them. Suddenly there was a gunshot and one of the birds fell out of the sky. When I turned in horror, I could see a still-smoking gun barrel trained on the second bird. And then I watched this bird, wild and unwitting, move through the purity of the open air toward death. The silence in the dream was charged, ringing just as if the second shot had sounded before I woke. But as I opened my eyes the bird's great wings still beat the air in a vast and impotent grace.

Toward morning Dad opened his eyes. "Jess," he said, his voice barely rising over the self-important hum of the machines around his bed.

"Hi, Dad." He tried to smile but the wrinkles around his eyes hardly deepened and his jaw was slack.

"I dreamed I died," he whispered.

"You nearly did."

"No." His voice was thin, stretched tight like a violin note. "Not yet. I got to see my grandbaby." Then he closed his eyes and went back to sleep.

When he had awakened, what had he seen? Me sitting in the underwater light, my arms resting lightly on my belly. Pregnant women sit that way, cradling the unborn child as if they knew just how the baby lay. Do they feel the tiny heartbeat beneath their fingers? And does the baby press its amphibious face against the womb and drop light kisses where its mother's fingers rest? I would never know. And yet my father, with his eyes perhaps still dazzled by the image of death, clung to the sight of me as if those were the very things I knew. He touched this life again in my body that for him swelled with the same ageless promise as the lone mountain behind our house. I knew my father believed in his own immortality, reckoning it wordlessly from the endurance of the land he lived on and from any children I might bear.

And yet I harbored nothing in my womb but my father's hope. I hugged my arms hard around my belly and I was ashamed again of my blighted body and my lies. My eyes felt lidless from the sleepless hours and seemed in their dreamlessness to be straining with some futile watchfulness as if I were staring into the dark. They burned and tears coursed over my cheeks stinging my skin. Ah, when Dad was stronger I would tell him everything. I would begin with Stephan when I explained it and I wouldn't expect him to understand. I would prepare myself for the look he gets when he thinks something important has slipped by him. "Think of that, Jess," he might say, "no baby." I could just hear him say it. I might already have begun to tell him right there in the hospital. I even said, "Dad?" but my voice was no louder than his had been and he slept on.

I wiped at my tears. They must have looked green as glass in the strange light of the intensive care ward. I dried them and began again, thinking of my father again. The tie that held him to this life was only a thought in his mind. There was no baby and yet his belief that there was was strong enough to keep him struggling against death. Would I release him to death with the truth? Sometime this "pregnancy" of mine would end and I would have nothing to offer him. Wasn't that more cruel than the truth? Was it?

Dad stirred in his sleep. I smoothed his pillow and when it looked as if he might wake, I drew my hand away.

When Dad and Darcy and I had all played at the dream of the baby, those were some of the happiest days of my life. And this dream baby, this child of the heart and the mind, had probably saved my father's life. In the hospital, listening to the uneasy flutter of my father's breathing, I was afraid that the tenderest moments of my life had passed, bound up in Darcy's and Dad's belief.

I would lose more with this baby than I ever imagined. This baby. This baby. Once again so easily, the deception took on a life of its own. What had been so firmly in my father's and Darcy's minds because they had no reason to doubt had lodged just as firmly, in the end, in mine. And I could feel it as a reality. A spirit? A ghost? A bodiless soul just out of reach of our wishes? This creature we had all loved unseen called to my father in his death, called to him with a sweeter urgency than any plea of need that I, with hands to touch and lips to speak, could bring to him.

And in that moment of gratitude, I knew that I would never tell my father that there never had been a baby. I promised, crossed my heart and hoped to die, as if to call the child imaginary again would be a dangerous admission, a trick played on vengeful death. I planned in a most unreasoned calm to tell Dad when the operation was over that the baby had been stillborn. In his countryman's respect for order, my father would understand a child withdrawn from the world. "Too weak for this life, looks like," I had heard him say cradling the silent limp form of some pup born dead, cradling it against his chest as if his own heartbeat could remind the lifeless animal to breathe. A stillborn child would be something to grieve but nothing to question. But where would the mourning end for a child that my father imagined alive and forever lost to him?

Sitting there submerged in the sea-green light, feeling as if I were breathing some substance other than air, I was cool-headed, sure of my resolve. My father turned his head on the pillow. His cheek sank into cavernous shadow, and from deep in its socket one eyelid, bowed by the hidden eye beneath, gleamed smooth and elliptical as a bird's egg.

Toward evening, the doctor came. He examined Dad who barely stirred. "Your father seems fine for now," he said. "You go home and get some rest. We'll call you if anything happens."

I hated to leave him and lifted each of his hands to smooth the blanket underneath. I brought him water that I knew he wouldn't drink. And when at last I walked past the waiting room, Darcy was there.

"I'm going home to sleep," I told him.

"The nurses told me it was a close one, Jessie," he said. I could smell the liquor on his breath.

"I have to sleep," I said, annoyed by the sob that found its way into my voice.

"Sure thing," said Darcy. "I'll just see you home."

On the way home, Darcy's headlights shone behind me. The wind was rushing over the fields and old snow blown loose from the ground undulated like ghosts over the road. I was so cold. Even when I got into the house, chills rippled over me in icy waves, shaking my body, leaving me breathless. Darcy led me upstairs to my room and after taking my shoes off, he put me into bed with all my clothes on. "Wait right here," he said and was gone. I lay shivering under the covers, my head beginning to throb. In a moment, Darcy was back, carrying a bottle of whiskey. Pulling his boots off, he climbed into bed beside me.

We sat for a while bundled in the covers and passing the bottle of whiskey back and forth. We talked and as I began to warm with the whiskey and the warmth of Darcy's body, Dad seemed close by as if he'd never been sick. If Darcy had accepted the night I'd asked him to bed with me, I imagined that it would have been much like this night. We would have been lying in bed together just as now, whispering and giggling over a bottle of whiskey and Dad would have been sleeping nearby.

I took a drink from the bottle. Outside, the wind rattled at the windows and pried at the shutters. "Rain, rain, go away," I laughed.

"It's not raining, Jessie. I think you're drunk," said Darcy.

"That's possible," I said and indeed the bed was very warm now and seemed to buoy me up lightly like a pool of water.

"Well, it'll help you relax. You been through a lot," he said. "You warm now? You want another blanket?" Clumsily he rearranged the covers over us, upsetting the bottle of whiskey that had been sitting between us. "Oh oh," he said, dabbing anxiously at the stain with his shirt-sleeve.

"It doesn't matter, Darcy," I said. "Listen. Listen. I kept my father alive, Darcy," I said. "If I hadn't wanted him alive so bad, he would have died."

"That's not true, Jessie," Darcy said sternly. "You know better than that."

"Yes, it is true." I settled back into a pillow propped against the headboard and folded my arms. It was a calm truth I was telling.

"No, no listen," said Darcy sitting straight up in bed, "if that's so, then I killed my father."

"How do you figure that?"

"Because I wished him dead until he died."

"Then it's true, you killed him," I said and began to cry. I lay down and Darcy lay down beside me, putting his arms around me. His face was wet with tears. We lay holding each other and weeping. I turned out the light and soon Darcy was asleep. We lay on our sides and his body followed the contours of mine, his back was a bulwark between me and the wind that moaned and shook the house. The odor of whiskey was sharp in the room and it reminded me of the smell of an apple orchard in the heat. Brown, rotting apples, pulpy and seductive, feeding the bees. Apples liquefying under the sun until they seep like sweet blood into the ground to feed the earth and their own seed. I fell asleep in the warm bed dreaming of summertime.

Lilly

I have come home from work for lunch and I have just set a sandwich out on the table for myself. I glance out the window and the sky is bright blue, the clouds white as sheets spanking in the wind. Such a clear winter day and such a clear head I have as I walk to the front door at the sound of a knock. When I open the door, it's the clear bright sky that holds my attention, not the big awkward sheriff standing in his thick muddy boots on my porch. I know why he is here and yet still I stare into the sky. Will God tell me? Will God appear in the sky in a silver streak of winter sunlight to tell me where my Darcy is?

"Afternoon, Mrs. Blunt. I hoped to catch you home for lunch," says Jim.

"Yes, won't you come in?" I say.

"Oh, no thank you, ma'am. I'm awful muddy." He shifts unhappily from one foot to another and the snow on the ground is so brilliant it seems to light the sky to its pained blue clarity.

"Mrs. Blunt," Jim says, "I'm just awful sorry to tell you this"—his hat goes round and round in his hands—"but we found Darcy this morning."

"Is he . . ." I ask God looking into the shining blue above Jim's head.

"Yes, ma'am. I'm awful sorry. He was dead when we found him."

"Yes, dead."

"Froze he was, Mrs. Blunt. I'm just sorrier than I can say." And the blue skies are silent, rushing away from me into cool still regions where no human breath could raise a cloud of steam, no human voice a shout.

"Yes, yes, I know, Jim," I say, comforting in an automatic way. "I know, I know."

"He was coming home from the Blue Moon is what we figure."

"Yes," I say, "he often went there."

"He passed out in some brush along the river and we just never saw him till this morning." Jim's big boots are slimy with river mud. There's a special odor to the earth by the water and for me it stirs memories of Ivy and me digging for crayfish with old kitchen spoons. We were digging to China, through the black alluvial silt, down into the ooze of mud below. And I fancied then that the smell that came up under the clack of those old scarred spoons was ancient, released from the time of the Indians as if they had buried not just their pots and arrowheads, but the very memories of their lives on the riverbank.

"He died by the river," I say.

"Yes, ma'am," Jim says, and there is a rhythm to the way he passes his hat through his fingers, like someone saying rosary beads.

"Jim," I say . . .

"I always tried to look out after Darcy. I always thought of Darcy as my friend."

"I know you did, Jim," I say, formal now, my hands clasped before me. "Don't you hold yourself responsible."

"Thank you, ma'am. That's kind of you to say but I don't believe it will ever be off my conscience."

"I don't hold you in any way accountable," I say.

"Well," he says shaking his head. "Could I call your sister for you?"

"No, thank you, Jim, I'll call her. Thank you for coming. I'll be all right."

"I'm awful sorry, Mrs. Blunt. That's all I can say."

"I know."

"The county has him now," says Jim. He has turned and stands with one foot on the porch and one foot on the first step. "You might want Henry French to call for him."

"Yes, thank you, Jim," I say and begin to close the door. The last thing I see as the door clicks shut is a ribbon of bright quiet sky.

There's another person who walks through your grief for you for a while. This other person moves your mouth and words come out, lifts your feet up and you walk. But somewhere you are far away, listening and watching in astonishment at all this other person does. I don't call Ivy. Otis has taken her to Washington for the day, a trip he has promised her for a long time. I stand at the window for a moment as if I were making plans, but when I go to the phone to call Henry French, the undertaker, I don't remember thinking of doing it at all. Henry says he will go to the county seat within the hour to fetch Darcy home to Hooke's Crossing.

I make another call to Mr. Enderly at the store to tell him I won't be back in for the day. "Are you ill, Mrs. Blunt?" he asks worriedly. Yes, yes, ill. After I hang up the phone, I make myself a pot of tea, brewing it with a care I used to reserve for guests. Then I sit in the front room, the cup of tea poised on my knees. I lift the cup to my lips and admire the delicate, floral taste of the tea . . . Earl Grey it is, my very best, as if I deserve a reward for my suffering. I wait for Tim to come home from school and hours pass very slowly as I think only of lifting the cup and setting it down precisely again into its saucer.

Jingles lies near my chair. He raises his head from time to time to look at me. He knows in some dog way, not that Darcy is gone, but that something important is afoot.

"Jingles, Darcy froze to death by the river." I try the words out but they are remote from the picture I carry in my mind of my son. It is as if the image of him that I have holds him fast in this world and has nothing to do with the Darcy Jim Atherton came to see me about. No tears come at the sound of the words in the empty room. After I tell Tim and Ivy, I promise myself, I won't say the terrible words again. There's time enough for the belief that comes to you with the reluctant undeniability of tears dropped in secret. I take whatever shelter I can find.

In the front room where I sit, the clock ticks and I lift the cup to my lips again and again, lift it, I think, a few times more before I realize it's empty. The door bangs open just at three thirty and I call, "Tim." It seems as if I can feel just the way my voice falls upon his ear, as a pleasant surprise. And he is unsuspecting as he comes toward me, dropping his books into a chair and sitting down across from me.

"Tim," I say again and he says, "How come you're home so early, Gran?" He pulls at a thread on one of his shirt buttons. The thread unravels, sending the button bobbling across the floor. He is grinning foolishly as he raises his eyes to mine.

"What?" he says and I see the first glimmer of fear in his face.

Quickly I tell him, calmly, flatly, perfect pitch of dead-earnest news. "Tim, honey, they found your daddy today and he was dead."

A small laugh seems to catch halfway up his throat. "What do you mean 'was'? You mean he isn't any-more?" Oh, grief is no foreign country to my Tim but he's such a poor traveler.

"You know what I mean, honey."

"Uh," he says. The sound is like an ax on the first strike into a tree. "Uh," like the thunk of a baseball bat hitting something solid. "Uh," like a bucket hitting the distant, pitiless bottom of a dry well.

"God called him home, Gran," he says.

"Yes," I say but the word is dry as ash on my tongue.

"No," he cries and leaps to his feet. He runs toward the steps and takes them two at a time. The house shudders like a convulsive heartbeat under his feet.

I walk to the bottom of the steps and I can see him in his room. He is caroming around the room, pitting his body against the strength of the walls as if he could break the barrier that presses his grief upon him. "Uh. Uh." If I could cry I would go to him. Without tears it seems indecent to intrude.

"Tim," I call to him, knowing he won't come, knowing he can't even hear me.

"God!" he sobs from above and I hear the springs of the bed squeak under his weight. Now I climb the stairs and go to him.

He lies full-length on the bed, big and gawky, the toes of his shoes pointing outward. There are no tear tracks on his face. The skin is thoroughly wet as if he has washed himself in tears.

"Tim," I say from the doorway.

"Why, Gran?" he asks in a constricted voice.

"I want to give you an easy answer, dear," I say crossing the room and sitting on the edge of the bed. "But something about your daddy and the way he was won't let me."

"Do you think God punished him? Do you think that's what happened?"

"No!" I say and tears of anger leap into my eyes. If God is as simple as silent blue skies, then why is death the merciful judgment and life the trial? Why am I alone with no answers and only strength enough to clasp this child and rock him in the remorseless brightness of a winter afternoon? In tears, Tim and I together, the two ends of Darcy's life with our center missing, rocking together on the edge of the bed, rocking and rocking as if we could sail away.

And for the rest of the day we are dazed, nearly silent. I make Tim a big dinner, all his favorites and he, almost shamefaced, eats it all. I stand leaning on the sink watching him eat, not able to think of anything else to do. I am a clock run down, my function forgotten, my face immobile. And then suddenly it seems the front door flies open and Ivy comes to us, enfolds us in a confused flurry of her spicy perfume and the white smell of winter air in her coat. Ivy, my most intimate witness to my son's life, mingles her tears with mine and I am set in motion once again.

In the next two days, my sister and I make funeral arrangements. Tim and I are delivered into a state of suspension where it seems as if nothing is decided, not even Darcy's death. Tim says he feels as though we are all people in a dream, either that or everyone else is in a movie except us. He plays his rock and roll very loud but I hardly mind. I wonder if it keeps him from thinking. I hope it does.

The night before the funeral, Ivy brings us a dinner she has made for us. I send her home telling her Tim and I are tired and will go to bed soon after dinner. I stand in the kitchen heating the food. The odors rise quickly as I stir the pots. Even now, I know I won't have to call Tim to dinner; the smells will call him down. As I'm dishing the food onto plates, I hear his radio stop and then I hear his footsteps on the stairs. He walks with a tentative, careful step as if he were made of glass. Indeed, I think of him as being poised to shatter at the first rough touch.

As he enters the downstairs hall, the phone rings and he answers it. "Hello, Mama," he says and as I step into the doorway of the kitchen, he rolls his eyes.

"Yes, everything's fine. How are you?" he asks, then covers the receiver with his hand. "I can't tell her," he whispers. "I don't know how she'd take it."

"Yes, Mama, I remember what you told me. I check it every day. I swear." When I look at him questioningly, he whispers again, "My horoscope."

I throw up my hands at that nonsense and retreat to the kitchen. I can still hear Tim in the hall.

"Yesterday it said you should buy property and I wondered if you did."

"A ranch, really? Are you out west then?"

"No, nobody but me wants to know. Mama, no, I swear, Gran didn't ask. Not Daddy either."

"She does not. I told you before."

"Okay, okay, Mama. Listen, are there horses on your ranch?" I can hear a catch in Tim's voice.

"Yeah?"

"Huh!"

"Well, I swear."

Setting the table, I steal a glance at Tim through the kitchen door.

"No, I do," he says into the phone and swallows hard, squeezing his eyes shut for a moment. "I've heard of blue dogs. No kidding. Bluetick hounds, you know. People around here use them for hunting."

"Yes, they are kind of blue. I can believe it, I swear." His voice is husky now and in the light from the kitchen, tears glisten in his eyelashes.

Damn Evelyn. Tim doesn't need her crazy prattle right now. It almost seems spiteful the way she burdens him with her peculiar notions. I suppose it's what Ivy calls my lack of imagination but I can't stretch my mind or my tolerance to encompass the astounding depths of Evelyn's madness. It's as though she makes it up, knowing full well how it frightens and disconcerts people. When I am forced to talk to her, I want to tell her, "Evelyn, there's just no sense wallowing in that craziness. Stop it this minute and come to your senses."

But I don't guess that would faze her any more than anything else I might say to her. Evelyn is closed against me, crazy or not.

I turn away from Tim. I try not to disturb him when he talks to his mother but tonight I nearly hate her. I stay busy in the kitchen to keep myself from rushing out into the hall and putting an end to the call. I am setting our teacups by the plates when Tim hangs up the phone. His eyes are dry when he enters the kitchen.

"Mama sounded pretty good tonight. She says she bought a ranch in Montana," he says with a great show of cheer.

"Montana? Well, I never."

"She seemed awful happy about it. It almost made me believe her."

"Well, I guess even crazy people could have money."

"You just never know, do you?" says Tim sitting down at his plate.

"No, you surely don't."

Tim eats with concentration for a while. Our knives and forks clink against our plates in the silent kitchen. The only other sound is that of the furnace downstairs. It thunders heroically, then sputters to a stop with a polite cough. It is anybody's guess when it will start. Sometimes it doesn't start up again until the house is thoroughly cold and Tim and I are in our coats. Maybe when there is money to fix it, I won't hear its every fit and start.

There's no ease in the silence between Tim and me. Since the news of Darcy, I've had this constant feeling of having something that I must say to Tim and yet I can't imagine what it is. It is as though I have a message of great importance for him that just won't come to mind. And in his silence I think of him as burrowing down into some dark idea that needs me to turn it right side out. A sharp wind starts up from the direction of the river and sets the shutters of our house to clattering.

I think of the funeral to come tomorrow. It will be Saturday. We made arrangements with a young priest at Saint Matthew's. He's a young man I don't know and he doesn't know me or my family. I haven't set foot in the church since Aaron died. This young priest . . . Father Michael, Father Mitchell, I don't remember . . . says that Father Brennan, who surely must be the oldest man in Hooke's Crossing, is ill and can't perform the funeral Mass. I wonder if the old priest is truly ailing or if he knows as well as I do that Darcy took his life with liquor as surely as his father took his with a rope.

"Gran." Tim startles me when he speaks.

"Yes?"

"Don't you feel like Daddy's still here or like he's

250

going to come in any minute?'' We both regard Darcy's empty chair.

"Yes, Tim, I do. That's the way it is for a while.''

"It's like they just go away gradual-like, you know,'' he says and lays a caressing hand on the back of Darcy's chair.

"I don't know. Somehow, it doesn't seem as peaceful as that.''

"No,'' he says, "I don't guess. How long do you suppose it goes on like that, thinking they're here.''

"Let me think about your grandpa. Oh, my, it's been a long time ago now. Ummm. Maybe a year. I'd have to remind myself all the time he was gone. Sometimes I'd just plain forget why I felt so bad.''

"A year?'' he asks distressed and I nod. We sit in silence for a while until Tim says, "Remember the time he put his hat on your broom and danced around the room with it?''

He asks this uncertainly, testing the wound under a wary touch. We've barely spoken of Darcy since his death.

"Yes,'' I smile, "and he named the broom Matilda.''

"That's right, that's right,'' Tim nods enthusiastically, "Matilda. 'Waltzing Matilda, waltzing Matilda, you'll come awaltzing Matilda with me . . .' '' Tim sings in his uneven adolescent voice.

"I remember,'' I say.

"Then he leaned her against the chair and invited her to dinner,'' says Tim.

"Yes, I remember it. We all laughed so hard.''

Oh, we don't really laugh now but both of us are eager all at once to talk about Darcy. The furnace clanks into operation and we are given heat awhile longer as we sit over the uncleared dishes at the table.

Tim's tense young face softens with the sweet surge of memory of his father. And Tim and I . . . and didn't we love him best of anybody? . . . talk about Darcy and all the good times. Darcy teasing Tim into laughter on the riverbank the summer before. Darcy singing the old songs I loved in a sweet rich tenor. Darcy holding a younger Tim and warming him against the chill of our temperamental furnace. The wind beats a steady rackety-rackety against the house but Tim and I barely hear.

It's late now, after midnight, and the dishes still clutter the table, but neither Tim nor I mention going to bed. He begs me for stories of Darcy when he was a boy. Some of the stories make us cry. And when I tell Tim the story of Bo, he shakes his head incredulously. "How long did Daddy have that dog?"

"All his life."

"All his life?" Tim gives a short laugh. "And Grandpa wanted him to shoot that old dog just like that?"

"Well, he thought it was the best thing to do, you know."

"Shoot his own dog?"

"He was old and sick, Tim, don't forget that," I say.

"That's just like Daddy though, isn't it? He wasn't going to kill his dog, no, sir, no matter what."

"That's pretty much the way it was."

Tim sits back in his chair, folding his arms in satisfaction. "I wouldn't have done it either," he says. "I mean it. I wouldn't have done it."

"I don't imagine you would have, honey."

Tim leans forward. "I wouldn't have," he says as if I needed more convincing. "And I would have made a nice place for him in the woods and everything."

"I'm sure of it," I say patting his hand.

The sun is rising on a cloudy day when we go to bed. As I pass Darcy's room, I can see that the pale light from his window has stolen still and gray as dust over his bed.

Ellen

RED Rooster. Red Rooster. The road slips away under my wheels. I'm on my way to Danielsburg, fifty-five miles away. I've told my parents I'm spending the night with a friend from work and I am free for the night—free from David, free from the silence I have had to fill at home since the night that Bip spoke his three words under the wounded red of that summer sky. I pull another beer out of the six-pack on the seat next to me. As I take a sip, its metallic iciness reminds me of a hundred other winter nights when I've been riding with the windows of the car rolled up against the cold. Riding through the night with the radio turned up loud and the heat from the heater gathering up my perfume and the smell of beer like a bouquet. I breathe deeply and memories draw together as if I have been rolling rolling down the road to the Red Rooster forever, as if this night and the first night I ever went there were no further apart than the hour's drive it takes to get there.

And just for a moment, words stir deep in my mind like conversation heard at a great distance. . . . Darcy dead by the river. I heard it in town yesterday and the world just at that instant of hearing became a very bright place where the sounds were cut from a hard new clarity and colors flashed with a painful vibrancy that permitted no grief. I was filled with a frantic energy that hasn't let me sit still for a moment. I've worked and laughed and

255

talked in the hours since I heard the news. People at work even commented on how vivacious "our quiet little Ellen" was. Last night I went for drinks with friends and drank until I knew I could sleep. And for this little while I've kept one step ahead of the sorrow but I hear it behind me, eerie as the river is sometimes on summer nights when you would swear to hearing voices in the water. "Ooh, Ellen," it moans, "ooh, Ellen," like a shiver.

I press on the accelerator and turn the radio up. The music churns out and moves me along on the power of its yearning. The drums pound like the engine pumping in the car. The guitars press into the momentum of the music like the shrill thrum of the wheels skimming over the road. The singer cries out, rakes my soul with the raw edge of his voice, draws blood and would draw tears but I am racing, racing . . . "oh, the pain of love. . . ."

And it's like any other night driving toward the Red Rooster to find a man to be with for one night. One night. The time must be compressed, my motives clear to me. And then I am rushing toward the one sure focus of concentrated purpose, that brief space of time when I shed the context of my life, when I rise inside my own mind brave and light as air as if I will never again spend the time I do explaining myself to myself, defining my feelings, worrying whatever wisdom I possess into skeins of words ready always to be wrapped around the men I love.

I'm near the Red Rooster and the six-pack next to me holds three more beers. I check myself, probing for guilt . . . an almost married woman at the Red Rooster. Yet David has so little to do with why I'm speeding down the interstate, drinking beer on the way to Danielsburg. No, wheeling into the bar's parking lot, I'm revved up and wild . . . I could howl like a wolf. I'm no Ellen David knows. I'm not sure why I'm here alone, looking for some long-legged, happy-eyed man to be with me. When Darcy was with me, I never came here. It was quiet in his arms and memories of him tick in the back of

my brain and I think backward before . . . before I loved
Darcy. A hundred beery nights that drained to pearly
gray beyond my bedroom window began with me bumping over the gravel outside the Red Rooster.

I park the car, brush my hair and smile into the
mirror. Pretty girl, pretty woman, and the band will be
thumping, wailing away inside. When I step out of the
car all I can hear is the hollow thud of the drumbeat.
Boom boom boom. The beer is a golden buzz inside my
head and I'm already stepping in time to the music.
Stepping out, stepping out. . . .

I smile at the man at the door who checks my ID card.
He's a big man and smiles back. But he's too bold and I
don't look back at him. From the head of the bar, I start
toward the tables in the back near the band. I step down
firmly, no apologies for being alone, but I look around
as if I'm meeting someone. As I walk down the length of
the bar, the men there turn to look at me, the shyer ones
glancing over their shoulders as if they just happened to
look around. They all look even if it's only for a second.
A faint trembling plays lightly over my wrists and quick
and cold as a draft, passes over my heart. "Hey, baby."
I hear but I don't look back.

I sit down at a table for two by the bandstand. I order
a beer and sit swinging my foot in time to the music. The
smoke, turned pink and blue from the lights around the
bar, rises toward the ceiling in lazily swirling clouds.
The singer in the band taps his foot and sings mourn-
fully, " 'I'm still missing you, honey/ although you were
never true/ I'm still missing you, honey . . .' " The beer
is warm and stings my tongue. The man playing the bass
guitar is looking my way. He's bearded and it's hard to
tell his age. But I like the way he shifts his weight from
foot to foot while he plays. He hunches slightly over his
guitar and it's the concentration in his face that attracts
me.

Look at me again, Mr. Musician, move your eyes
over my body the way your fingers move over your

guitar. Look at me. And he does. He looks and smiles slowly.

If he would sing to me. If he would walk to the edge of the bandstand and looking down at me, sing me a love song, I could begin to believe that I'd love him. I might believe with another beer or two that I was the first girl that ever made him do that. And then I might dream further that he would sit up in bed after we had made love and sing to me.

"Hey, honey, you want to dance?" The man stumbles as he steps toward me. I know he's very drunk and will maul me on the dance floor. But I'm afraid he'll be belligerent if I turn him down. I must be careful.

"No, thanks," I say with a bright smile. "I'm waiting for someone."

His eyes harden for a moment but then he walks away. The guitar player watches, smiles. He's sure of me already and that's never good. Make it interesting, play it out and dream a new dream of him standing by the window, his bare back, a white shimmer in the moonlight.

Dreaming in the raucous, charged air of the Red Rooster. And I am dreaming always, sometimes not certain what arises from my daydreams, what arises from my life, what arises from my dreams in sleep. Somewhere I've loved a man who has stood just so by a window and I have seen this man so many times in dreams that have lulled me while David holds me in his awkward embraces. And I do not know if I am awake or asleep when I have closed my eyes and seen the man by the window. How fast he has held my attention through all the dry disjointed bumpings of David's body on mine. Tonight in my mind the man still stands by the window, his face averted, and folds his arms across his chest as if he were cold.

I order another beer. When the waitress brings it, she says someone has paid for it. She points the man out when I ask who he is. He is a thin man with a mournful mouth. I raise my glass politely and turn away. I want a laughing man tonight, an I-don't-give-a-damn man to make me laugh. I don't want to hear about somebody's ex-wife or lost job.

"You want to dance?" I turn. This man is smiling, good-looking. I saw him come through the door and stand at the bar for a while. He has a swagger to his walk but his smile is shy. Maybe . . . "Yes," I say.

The dance floor is crowded. Even though the music is fast, we can barely move with all the other couples around us. " ' . . . you're the best I ever knew . . .' " the singers on the bandstand wail. My partner is well-built but not easy with his body when he dances. But I step out, strut and whirl around him. I love to dance and already this man loves to watch me. The guitar player watches too. " . . . 'there's nobody quite like you' . . ."

When the song is over, the man walks me back to my table. "Mind if I sit down?" he asks.

"If you want to."

When he is seated, he says, "Let me buy you a drink."

"No, thanks, I'll buy my own."

"You're real independent, aren't you?" he says.

I smile teasingly.

"I could tell that," he says, "the minute I saw you."

"Oh, yeah?"

"Yeah, I could see you were in here by yourself. Now that takes guts."

"You're in here by yourself," I say. He laughs and I like his grin. It is wide and honest.

"Yeah, but you aren't coming after me like I'm coming after you."

"How can you be so sure?"

"Because I'm only about half as pretty as you are."

"You're doing all right."

"You think so?" he says. "It's hard to tell with you women. The ugliest man I ever knew was a guy had his nose bit off in a fight. The women couldn't get enough of him."

"Oh," I say, "I know that man. He'd never come near me though."

"He'd be crazy not to."

"He has his reasons. Who do you think bit his nose off?"

He throws his head back and laughs, then says, "What's your name?"

"Ellen."

"My name's Bob. Ellen, you're all right."

He reaches across the table to shake my hand. It's the first opportunity he takes to touch me. There are others. He bumps his knees against mine under the table. He fills my beer glass from a bottle and gives it back to me wrapping his hand around mine. And of course we dance. In the slow songs his arm circles my waist. I feel his breath even and smooth on my cheek. He's not a dance floor mauler and I like the way he touches me when we sit at the table, his fingers playing over my wrist gentle and insistent as the pulse there. He walks his long fingers over the pale blue veins, presses the thinly covered nerves, gauging how I like him, I suppose.

The band plays on and on. The guitar player sings to a blonde near the bandstand. The beer has brought me to an absolute clarity where the sounds that make the music are woven separate and unified as the threads of a tapestry. Bob's face looms out of the darkness of the bar with the sharp lines of a skull. Sometimes when I am drunk like this, I feel I'm at the center of time and that I am suspended, able to examine all the time I've ever known before it moves on again and understand at last all my life through this one moment. If I could concentrate, if I were not distracted by the man across from me at the table. . . .

Oh, but I like the way he wears his jeans. I like the way they've worn to lighter blue over his thighs.

"Last call," the waitress says and we each order one more beer. When the beer comes he says, "Well, I guess I'll be going on home." He tilts his head and smiles at me.

260

"Do you have to?" I ask.

"No. How about a little party at your place?"

"That would be very difficult."

He nods and smiles. He thinks I'm married. "Well, we could go to my place, then. It's just that I got nosy neighbors."

"Who says there's anything for them to be nosy about?"

"Not me. I didn't mean that. No strings attached, I promise."

"Okay," I say and we both sit back.

Easy to have someone for the night, someone to cradle while he sighs against your ear, someone to pretend that every time is the first time again, someone to hold until the urgency goes away.

After a short ride, we are in Bob's room. I've watched him undress. And there is a fond recognition in the familiarity of his naked body . . . the broad male shoulders, the indentations in his buttocks along the tight curve of his hips deep as if loving hands had pressed there. In the dim light of his disheveled bedroom, he lies down on his bed and turns on his side to watch me. When I have undressed, I lie down at the opposite end of the bed, my head at his feet. His erect penis casts a crooked shadow on the wrinkled sheet between us.

"Just give me a minute to get used to being here," I say.

"Honey, you take all the time you want," he says and pulls the sheet up to his waist.

"I just need a minute," I say. The beer rolls queasily in my stomach now that we are here. Maybe I will just get up and go home.

"You're awful pretty," he says. His eyes are glistening in the half-light. A sudden surge of desire burns through me at the thickness in his voice. "You're awful pretty."

I press my foot gently on his chest and wish that he would kiss my ankle there by the bone, kiss the arch of my foot, the back of my knee. A memory makes a slit thin as a knife point in the back of my mind, then closes up again. Bob takes my hand and pulls me up until we are face-to-face. His hands move over my body with a predictable progress, from my breasts to my thighs. Just for a flash I am frightened by disappointment. But when he turns out the light, that part of my mind goes dark too and I move over and under him as silkily as if our bodies liquefy and blend. We are whole and alone in these moments, falling fearlessly down, down, down until he explodes in a gasp and a quick contortion of his body. I am not nearly there but if I lie quietly beneath him, this heated demand will ebb away.

In a moment his breath is even and he rolls away from me. When he retires into himself again, it is as clear as if a door has slammed shut in the room. The air is chilling now to my damp skin and I pull the sheet, thin protection, up over me. I lie away from him, redraw the borders of my vulnerability. There's nothing this man can do to hurt me because soon I will be married. I begin to feel nearly cozy under the covers and think of Mama and me last week cutting the lace for my bridal veil from my grandmother's wedding dress. The lace was yellowed, finely wrought as spiderweb. We were in Mama's bedroom. In a rare mood of teasing, Mama stood before a mirror and draped the lace over her head. As she stood regarding her reflection, she smiled, nearly preening.

"You look pretty, Mama," I said.

"Ach," she said, "don't be silly. I was only thinking of my own wedding day."

"Were you nervous?"

"Hmmm," she said tilting her head and considering. "I was nervous a little bit. Then I saw your father at the front of the church."

"And then what?"

"And then I was nervous a lot. He cried when he saw me. You know your father."

"I think that's beautiful."

"Beautiful! He cried and I smiled. Imagine."

She looked again into the mirror and gave a soft smile. Then she pulled the lace from her head and folded it in precise quarters.

I wonder if David will cry to see me walking toward him down the aisle. I doubt it. David's feelings always seem to come from the long remove of much consideration. Oh, but it doesn't matter. I think of my marriage to David as a slow accumulation of devotion and respect. A life that would work soothingly over my heart until I would hardly remember lying here by this stranger in the ragged gloom of this winter Saturday dawn. I shiver beneath the sheet. If this man in bed with me should draw me to him by a word or touch, if he would talk about anything, the weather, something we could agree on . . .

He moves now and lights a cigarette. "Not a bad band at the Red Rooster. I kind of liked them," he says.

"Oh, yeah, me too."

"I hope I'll see you there again."

"I don't know."

"You want to sleep for a while?" he asks.

"No, I've got to go."

He heaves himself up on the side of the bed and reaches for his pants on the floor. After he pulls them on, he sits on the edge of the bed rubbing his head. I turn my back to him while I dress. The room is silent except for the sound of my dressing, clothes slipping in whispers against my skin. Can he hear my breathing? Is he listening?

At the door of his room, he says, "You like motorcycles? Maybe we could go riding sometime."

"I hate motorcycles," I say. "My brother was killed on one last summer." There are no tears left and the words are smooth as worry stones on my tongue. And I can even think straight on of Bip standing under a red sky telling my father he hated him. That's the way he left us, those terrible words the last we knew of him so that all our memories of his life must always come to

263

rest at that moment and the wound is freshly struck each time.

"Okay," says the man in the doorway, "something else, then. Why don't you give me your number?" He yawns unwillingly. "Sorry," he says.

"No, I'll take your number," I say and write it down on a scrap of paper from my purse.

Later, as I turn out onto the highway toward Hooke's Crossing, I flip the piece of paper out of the window and it flutters away behind the car. And when I get home, I'll put Bob down on The List, imprint his name, my fiftieth, my last lover.

I am on the river road now. The trees are ghostly, the river masked by the mists of the cloudy dawn. Nothing but the road is definite enough to claim my attention and I have only to hold the car steady on the road, hit a straight course for Hooke's Crossing. When I look at my speedometer, I see I'm going too fast. My foot trembles on the accelerator . . . my body shaking loose from last night's beer. My mouth is dry and suddenly tears are spilling from my eyes without a sound. There is a tingling in my fingers that rushes along the pathways of my nerves toward my brain, hurtling anxious and duty-bound to tell the news: Darcy dead . . . as though the dawning of his funeral day makes it at last imperative to know.

I move my foot to the brake and pull off onto a side road. The woods are close on either side of this road but I find a small clearing to pull the car into. The leafless trees are closely grown and they hold the darkness against the thin gray dawn. When I turn out my headlights I am blinded. I close my eyes and in the darkness the man at the moonlit window turns and flips the pages of The List he holds in his hand. Little red leather book bound by a spiral of gold. He thumbs the pages and they flutter in his fingers like birds that would take flight. "It's a lot to go through just to fuck," he says. "Whew!"

I laugh out loud from the bed. Moving out of the moonlight and through the shadow, Darcy enters the sudden secret circle of light from my small bedside lamp.

Naked, I sit at the head of the bed, my legs stretched out and crossed at the ankle. We are in my bedroom, with the freedom of having the house to ourselves. My parents have gone to spend the night with my mother's ailing great-aunt. I have to remind myself that we're alone, as I push the blanket to the foot of the bed. Mama's starched sheets flow like tidy white rivers where they are smooth and sit up in sharp peaks like mountains where they are rumpled. Darcy comes to sit on the side of the bed and strokes my leg.

"How long now until the wedding?" he asks.

"About five weeks."

"Huh," he says gazing down at The List. "Are you going to let me read what you write about me?" He taps the cover of the book.

"I might not write anything about you."

"Why not?"

"I only write about them when it's all over." I pull a light robe on, crisscross it over my breasts and settle the hem over my knees.

"Say what you mean, Ellen," says Darcy.

"We don't have to stop seeing each other when I get married."

Darcy puts his hand to the side of my face and pushes my hair behind my ear. "You know the way your hair grows all yellow and curly there right alongside your ear, it reminds me of baby birds. It just about kills me," he says so softly.

"We could, Darcy. We could just go on seeing each other," I say.

Shaking his head, he leans back on the bed, careless of his nakedness. "Nope, nope," he says as if he were talking to himself, "then I'd be the only thing between you and respectability and you'd get to hate me."

"Darcy," I say, "I don't care about that."

"Ellen," he says brandishing the book, "it's all here in black and white."

"No," I say faintly.

"Yes," he whispers and he holds me. My tears spilling over his shoulder are chilled when they meet my breast.

"Look here," he says in a minute, sitting away from me, "I'll write my own in your book. Okay? Okay?"

I nod, dabbing at my eyes. I hand him a pen from the bedside table. He bites at the end of the pen and stares off, then he writes rapidly in the book. He makes a great show of covering the page while he writes. When he finishes, he hands me the book.

Four lines in the middle of the page are written in his jumbled schoolboy handwriting:

> Roses are red,
> Violets are blue,
> If one of us was different,
> I'd be married to you.

"Which one of us, Darcy? Which one of us would have to be different?"

"It'd have to be me, I guess. I'd have to be some guy with my initials on my boxer shorts." We both laugh.

"I might not love you, then," I say taking his hand, "or you might not love me. Maybe it's me that should change."

"The only way for you to be married to me is for you not to expect anything, not to want anything. Then there'd be nothing to hold us together at all. Ellen, we've talked about this before. You know it's not possible."

"I guess."

"No, honey," he says closing the book and smoothing the cover with his hand, "there's no way out of this one. Every time you turn a corner, it's the same old scenery."

My tears are silent now and Darcy, humming sadly, rubs my hand. Toward morning he lies sleeping on his stomach, his arms above his head. It is a sunlit dawn and the rosy light skims along his body, passing smooth and golden over his skin and crackling into electric points of light in the hair of his legs. I sit naked on the edge of the bed, one leg tucked under me, one toe touching the floor and I bend to him, kissing the side of his neck where his heartbeat pulses, kissing the cleft of muscle between his shoulder blades, kissing the base of his spine, the inside of his thigh as he begins to stir and I awake. Ah, ah, ah. . . .

If I could hold him in my arms just one more time perhaps my life would begin again. This sorrow is too much for me to hold, as if I had run out into the night, my arms stretched wide, and I in begging for comfort would find the whole great emptiness of the sky, all the vast space that spins away beyond the eye, beyond the imagination, would come to rest in all its starry longing in my arms.

I stumble from the car. Outside it is very still and the tang of snow is sharp in the air. A granular gray light shyly touches the bare limbs of the trees, sifts soundlessly down the trunks and hesitates above the still-darkened ground. I walk a few steps toward the river, trip and catch at a tree to steady myself. I cling to the tree, its bark cold and rough against my cheek. And I scream, scream until my throat aches, until I am light-headed, scream until I know my grief echoes up and down the river. When I stop I am as empty as if I have poured myself out in the sound that seems to me still to vibrate in the air, shaking the trees and piercing the water in fiery jagged strokes.

Oh, I'm shivering now in the morning damp and I go to sit in the car again. I turn on the engine to get warm. The light of morning creeps over the underbrush now and a few wan flakes of snow lick my windshield. I press my fingers to my temples. My head aches and I stare blankly through the trees as the sky lights to silver. When the sun is up, my head will be clearer. My father always says he does his best thinking in the morning.

Daddy would be up now watching for me at the window, worrying about the weather. "Who is this girl she's gone to see, Gret?" he might be calling over his shoulder to my mother. When I'm at home he watches me all the time as if I, like Bip, will disappear. Yet for all his attention, until the wedding plans we still had no more to say to each other than before. But now the three of us, Mama, Daddy and I, sit nearly every evening around the kitchen table before David comes and talk about the wedding. I'll admit I'm beguiled by the coziness of those evenings. Love seems to me to be described in the very curves of our bodies as we lean toward each other. And there is a feeling I have when we all sit together like that, when I can see the happiness that the wedding makes for my parents and the feeling is almost like the love I wish I felt for David. It's not that the doubts disappear, they only lose importance. Those evenings have seemed the first proof of our endurance in the face of our grief for Bip.

How badly we have needed them. We are so fragile without Bip, a house of three walls all leaning crazily without the fourth. At the news of Bip's death last summer, my father had taken charge of all the arrangements. He had driven out to the county hospital to talk to the doctors about the drugs they had found in my brother's body. He told me . . . because my mother wouldn't listen . . . what he had learned. He explained it all to me with great care as if he had memorized the information to pass some test that might prove him innocent of the blame he felt for Bip's death.

For some time after the funeral, he stayed very busy, checking on this, checking on that . . . Bip's insurance, the disposal of the twisted bike. But suddenly, as if he had just realized there was nothing more he could do for Bip he seemed to go gray with grief. And in the hours when he was away from the store he sat in the living room, tears crystallizing like ice on his cheeks in the blue light of the television. He was thin by then with wattles of loose skin gathered at his chin and throat as if a cruel hand had yanked at his face in some brutal redress. And my mother, God, she would lie on her bed for hours after Bip died, staring stony and still, at nothing. She was dry-eyed. If she cried I never saw her. But her mourning was more terrible than tears. I was so afraid to see her lying there and amazed by the extravagance of her mother love. Could she, remote and stern as she was, have loved my brother so? Would my own death sound the depths of her grief? How could we ever think we knew her now?

I was powerless before my parents' grief and my own. If we had been able to comfort each other at the start, would our sorrow have taken on such a commanding presence? Would it have lived in our house growing bigger and bigger, absorbing the substance from our family and all the familiar things around us? Thinning the very gravity of our lives that seemed drawn on toward some time when we would, from sheer helplessness, float free of the earth entirely? I was desperate to comfort them and spent most of my time at home, seeing little of Darcy.

It was in those days that I began to see more of David. He often came to the house and his visits seemed to cheer my parents. My mother would be up and moving around the kitchen with some of her old purpose if I invited him to dinner. And my father would turn off the television to talk to him. It was when I saw David talking to my father that I thought I could love him. David would sit forward in his chair, his face serious, his hands chopping horizontal slices in the air as he explained import quotas to Daddy. And my father with a tentative enthusiasm that heartened me would pull himself up in his chair and say, "Well, David, this is the way I see it. . . ."

One night at dinner with my parents, David asked me again to marry him. "Oh," I said, embarrassed by my parents' presence, "maybe."

"David," Daddy hooted, "I believe she means yes."

I said nothing, smiling, allowing the moment to pass when I could have protested. I was so grateful for my father's laughter. I thought perhaps this was enough for love after all, the gratitude, the quietness that David had brought to our house. I sat silently, the tremor of fear and anger in my throat growing fainter and fainter as they all smiled my way. And the wedding plans have piled one on top of the other in the blessed comfort of those evenings around the table.

The car is very warm now and my cheeks are flushed from the heat. I turn the engine off. The sky is nearly as bright as it will be on this snowy day. I look into the rearview mirror and brush my hair. I dab at my eyes to wipe away the smeared makeup. It's a good thing, this marriage, I decide. There'll be no mornings like this one having to warm myself from the chill of some stranger's bed. If I hadn't stayed my father's little girl so long, perhaps I wouldn't have had to re-create myself as a woman time after time in nights like last night. How I've hated it, this heated force that would shame my father, shock David. It has created The List, made me deceitful, disjoined the continuity of my life like the cracks in a mirror. A good thing, to put this yearning to rest, like closing the door against the night.

I put my palms together and my fingertips tremble one against the other. Then again without warning I am crying, sobbing. The tears leap into my eyes as if they are eager to be there. Washing down over my face, they tell truths I cannot bear to know. I haven't always hated the power that has sent me out into a bar looking for a new man. No, sometimes I've felt it singing in me like a full-blooded chamber of my heart and I have understood that there was more to it than just the men I've known. I've felt the vital connection it has made in me in times when I believe I have heard some vast blessing of my femaleness stirring in the earth in womanish whispers. The night I sat astride the truck above Darcy, I was suffused by the generosity of this female power, opulent and abundant as the moonlight flowing milky over my bare breasts. In that moment when I held my arms out to him, I revealed all the danger and secrecy of my joy in being a woman. And he had smiled as though his heart ached at such wide audacious beauty. Later when he held me in his arms murmuring, "I love you, Ellen, I love you," I thought I would never again feel shame. Darcy, my darling, there is such gravity in love begun in moonlight, as if the moon pressing its bright coins upon our lids brings us deeper dreams.

The tears slip down my face and break like stars onto my coat. The cold has begun to insinuate itself into the car again and I put my hands in my pockets. Will I always dream of Darcy? What if his face that night in the moonlight should come to be the beginning of any measure I shall ever take of love? What will happen to me when I am married to a man whose face I can barely call to mind at all? I wipe my eyes. Could I ever tell my father the truth?

Bip was the truth teller in our family even though they were no truths that Daddy knew. We all concoct the truth in different ways, construct it like a country of the mind. And it has seemed to me that the integrity of honesty lies in describing that country as precisely and purely as you see it. Bip's truths were ferocious and he gave me hope that one day I might stand up and introduce myself to my father with some small degree of honesty.

Darcy said one time that it didn't matter what you told other people so long as you told yourself the truth. But he didn't tell me that sometimes once you've told the truth to yourself, it can gain a power of its own that grows larger than your heart, beats reason out of your brain, rings in your ears until you have to say it.

The sun rises behind the heavy clouds. The sky is gray and gauzy like dirty curtains. I can see the river through the trees. The water is a dull silver tarnished here and there by the slowly moving current. The snow is icier now and falls faster. I start the car and turn toward home.

Jessie

DARCY will be buried today. The morning has dawned cold and snowy. The land is dead, buried under the snow, the fields infertile in their sterile white. Darcy will be laid away in the ground, below the freeze line, among the roots there waiting for spring. But when the roots push their long, long way up to the sun, Darcy will remain in his silent, horizontal darkness underground.

It's too soon to believe the end of him. He doesn't seem dead, not dead like my mother . . . for all time. I think of him as he must have died, and I try very hard to believe he was warm and sleeping just as he had been that last night I had held him under the covers of my bed. It doesn't seem as if someone could die so quickly, go from warm to cold in a few days' time. And I think if I just get up and walk to the window, I might see him coaxing his laboring old convertible up our long driveway.

But I stay seated at the yellow kitchen table, a cup of cold coffee before me. I had tried to drink it, but somehow I can't swallow. I stir the spoon around in the cup but the clink of it on the rim sounds lonely and I stop. It's nine o'clock. I sit at the table, my hands resting on the top. They feel useless this morning, too heavy to lift. I can't go to see Dad today. I have called the hospital and used the weather as an excuse. Thoughts of Darcy are too pressing to hide and I can't tell Dad yet. In the past few days he has seemed so much stronger. The doctor is very hopeful and has talked of Dad going home in another month perhaps. Last night he sat up in bed and ate his dinner with some of his old enthusiasm. But still I think he is not well enough to hear the news. I heard about Darcy on the radio yesterday. I was riding home from the hospital. The news was already a day old. "Hooke's Crossing man found frozen by Bright River." After the news they played a love song that used to make me cry. It just touched around the edges of the loss of death.

Slowly I rise from the table, smoothing my shirt down over my protruding belly. I walk to the telephone, but I have to look up the number. I've never called Darcy's house before.

"Mrs. Blunt?" I say when a woman answers.

"Yes."

"This is Jessica Talbot."

"Yes, how are you, Miss Talbot?"

"Well, under the circumstances, I'm all right."

"And your father. I understand he's ill."

"Yes, but he's getting better, thank you."

A short silence falls and for a moment I've forgotten why I called. Mrs. Blunt is silent at the other end.

"Mrs. Blunt, the reason I called is I'd like to come to the funeral today but . . ."

Another silence until Darcy's mother says, "But what?"

"Well, I'm pregnant," I rush to say. Oh, it isn't at all what I wanted to tell her. "And I was afraid people would think it was Darcy's."

"Is it Darcy's?"

"No, ma'am, it's not. But Darcy has been very kind to me and my father."

"Yes, dear, he spoke very highly of both of you." I try to imagine Darcy sitting at dinner with his mother and son talking about Dad and me. I couldn't think of a thing he might have had to say about us.

"Thank you. My father would have been at the funeral today but he's still quite ill. And I was worried that

276

if I came it would embarrass you and your family. I'm not married, you know."

"Good Lord, Miss Talbot," laughs Mrs. Blunt, "you won't embarrass me. You come if you want."

"Well, I don't know," I say. "I hope you understand."

"Yes, of course."

There doesn't seem to be any more to talk about but still I feel as if I haven't told her anything at all I set out to say. Then words spill again into the strained silence.

"Why I called you, I guess, Mrs. Blunt, is just to say that I'm going to miss Darcy very much and so will my father. And I wanted you to know how sorry I am for you and your family."

"Thank you, dear," she says and then there really is no more to say.

"Well, if you do decide to come," says Mrs. Blunt, "the Mass is at Saint Matthew's at eleven this morning."

"Thank you. I'll keep that in mind. Thank you very much." I hang up the phone.

I picture myself at the funeral. No one in Hooke's Crossing has seen me all these months. No one knows unless rumors have traveled as far as from the county hospital. I could walk into Saint Matthew's with my belly thrust ahead of me like an offering in Darcy's behalf to Hooke's Crossing. He liked the whispers behind his back. He liked the stories that over the years had accumulated to make him the town's laughing bad boy. He could be Huck Finn at his own funeral with me coming on as the final outrage. There's a strength that lights my heart for a moment and Darcy seems invincible in his incorrigibility.

But when I think of him on this snowy morning, when I draw his face to mind, I don't see him as he was at the Blue Moon, laughing and daring me on to the long moonlit ride of that night. I don't see him, his smile impertinent, his logic quixotic and maddening, as he was when we disagreed over the rocking horse. I see his face the way it was the night he told me he loved Ellen Gibbs. The tenderness in his eyes was pained, poignant with regrets that I could only guess at. And when he had refused to hear anything against her, he seemed to close himself all around her like a flower closing up over its heart at evening. It was as if he wanted not only to protect her from any new slight but even more he yearned to undo whatever hurt she had been done in the past. How angry and betrayed I'd felt that night. And yet remembering his face now, I could imagine how he must have loved her. He would have, I am sure, sheltered in her flesh, spoken to her in whispers, saying he loved her. He would have soothed her when she was sad, talking softly to her and stroking her small nervous hands. He was her lover and on the morning of the funeral I felt myself to be Darcy's secret ally still in knowing not to hurt her. I wouldn't go to the funeral, I decided. I wouldn't risk her thinking that Darcy had fathered another woman's child.

Her grief must be so much more than mine—and mine, as I stand in the kitchen in the house shut away by the storm, is so huge, a great darkness spreading out before me. Death. The word strikes with the power of a blow and for the first time in my life, I feel the inevitability of my own. I don't feel it in the way that makes us say, "Well, we've all got to go sometime," laughing and not believing at all that we will ever die, not able to believe the end of sensing this one self. No, I feel it at the very center of me in some organic recognition of the truth. And I am afraid. There is an iciness in my fingers as I reach for the phone again and dial.

"Hello," I say when the voice at the other end says, "Doctor's office." "This is Jessica Talbot. I'd like to make an appointment for surgery. Can you schedule me in about six weeks?"

"Oh, yes, I remember you, Miss Talbot," says the nurse. "Six weeks, my that's a long time. We thought we would hear from you sooner."

"Six weeks," I say, "it really must be six weeks."

The doctor comes on the phone but I am calm and firm. I pretend that I don't hear the bewilderment . . . is it even disgust? . . . in his voice. "It's been months Miss Talbot and now you want to put it off further?"

"Yes, the delay has been necessary." He sighs and the appointment is set. I hang up.

I sit down at the table again and lay my hands tenderly over the girth of my belly. My womb is filled. I can picture it, dark and tangled. No baby, Jessie, I say once again to myself, no baby. There would be a lightness to a real pregnancy. The baby would float free in the womb buoyed on its amniotic sea. No baby, Jessie.

But it's time now to put my life in order once again. It's time to restore my health in a sensible way and apply for a job at the county high school. That way I can stay home and look after Dad. I will go up to the attic right away to get a small suitcase for my stay in the hospital. I shall be prepared and I will know myself again, practical and clearheaded. I rise resolutely. I try to remember how my body felt before the strange growth began. It was a girlish body, it seems to me, slender and insubstantial without the ballast of my false motherhood. How did I move through my life so weightless, in thrall like a dust mote to every draft? It should feel like freedom to me to know I'm getting rid of this unseemly bulk. And yet just the thought of it creates an ache of emptiness just below my heart. The baby gone. All my babies gone before they were ever mine. Darcy gone and the little pocket of sorrow burgeons slowly. If it goes on, if there is nothing I can do to stop it, soon I'll be hollow as a reed.

I will my feet to carry me toward the attic. On my way I pass the rocking horse. It sits by the dining-room door where we left it when Dad had finished affixing its rockers. I touch its sleek nose and it begins to rock slowly. One blind painted eye blinks blue to white in the light of the window.

The house is dark as I climb both sets of stairs to the attic. When I open the door, the attic has a compressed silence to it as if it has kept the sounds of our house in the same airless abeyance as the old furniture and clothes we've stored up there for years. A bare light bulb splashes a cheerless yellow over the dusty jumble when I pull the light chain. There is an odor, light and dry, like old leaves. When I was a child I was frightened to be in the attic. I thought there must be ghosts in a place so full of old things. And the memories that rise up out of the shadows are startling as ghosts.

There is the mahogany sleigh bed that my mother and father shared for as long as she lived. The mattress is propped against the wall and its ticking trickles from small holes gnawed by mice. I run my finger through the dust on the long curve of the headboard. The wood shone a rich red, a color like ripe black cherries, when she was alive. And when she was dying, I remember how odd it seemed to see her sitting in the bed in the middle of the day, her hair down over her shoulder like she wore it at night, her skin pale as moonlight against the dark wood of the bed. I thought that no queen, no matter how grand, could be more regal or more beautiful than my mother when she sat in the big bed. When she was sick, I would sometimes sit on the bed with her and play cards. Later, she was too weak even for that.

I cling to every small memory I have of her. There are so few of them and I have always been afraid that I would forget her and it would be as if I'd never had a mother at all. Like Athena, I might have been born from my father's head, my femaleness arising from the moon, or the earth or, worst of all, no place in particular. Suddenly I am aware of the cool weightless fragrance of violets. My mother's cologne. It dances in the musty attic air for a moment and vanishes.

I fall to my knees beside my parents' bed. The winter chill seeps into the house from under the eaves. It creeps quiet as spiders over the cobwebs and cast-off clutter of my parents' lives. But I don't mind. I'm oddly comforted by the easy way all these old things rest here as if they know their time has come and gone.

Behind the bed is a stack of old photographs propped carelessly against the wall. I pick up the one on top. The frame is wooden, ornately carved with leaves and birds. My father's face smiles through the dust of the years. I wipe the glass with the side of my hand. My father is a young man in the picture, his neck too thin for the collar of his army uniform. His hair is very dark and slick. His teeth are the same as now, long, square, very white . . . good Talbot teeth. Oh, no, he's not handsome. His face is too long, his nose and ears too big. It's not even a strong face. I suppose Dad is too gentle for that. But it is a kind face. And there is something else about the face smiling out from the picture. It's an expectancy in the eyes, an inquisitive set to the wide thin mouth. And it's still in his face after all these years, a faith that he feeds on the ordinary, a good meal, a new pup, a long planting season. My father tenders his joy in these things as though it is part of a deal he has with life, as if his love were necessary to drive the process of the world.

I think of him as I've often seen him, staring out over the fields behind the house. He looks toward the mountain and he is still then, motionless and blind as blue sky. I've asked him what he thinks of at times like that and he says, "Nothing, nothing at all."

And I know that if you stare away, thinking of nothing and listening to the silence of your mind, the edges in the scene before you begin to blur and every object there seems to lose its shape and become indefinite and diluted by the withdrawal of your attention. And I know that when this has happened to me I snap to and organize everything as it was before, as though my perceptions were all that kept the whole world from disassembling before my eyes and disappearing or turning into something else entirely. It's an Alice-in-Wonderland kind of feeling in which the only order in life is what I can impose from my own mind. After all, I've seen at first-hand what happens when you look away too long, when you slip between the moment of certainty and dreams.

Yet I imagine that Dad allows the colors of the scene to run and merge in any way they might as he stands there disengaged. He allows it humbly just the way he is, trusting always in an imperturbable identity and design.

It's not that his faith is mine to have, but somehow its influence has become such a part of me that I believe it skips along with the electrical impulses that jump from nerve to nerve in my brain to shape a gesture of my hand or to banish a thought of surrender that passes quickly through my mind. Cecil Talbot's daughter would not lie down here where the winter hovers in the house, would not lie down and die like Darcy in the cold.

I set the picture back down, turning it until it faces the wall. My knees are stiff from kneeling on the floor and they creak like tree limbs in the cold when I rise. I pick up the small overnight bag I came for and start down the stairs. I turn the light off without looking back. The attic door sighs shut behind me.

On my way downstairs I put the overnight bag in my bedroom. When I return to the kitchen, I rub my hands together, warming them. I put the teakettle on the stove and light the flame. While I wait for the water to boil, I walk into the dining room and look out the window. The snow is falling faster now. The flakes don't spin languidly out of the sky as they did awhile ago. They are compact and fall fast and straight. Most of the dogs are in their shelters. Their paw prints are tiny dusky valleys in the runs. Only Ginger, the breech pup, is stirring. Kicking up plumes of snow behind her, she runs and leaps. I can feel a chill through the glass of the window. I wonder that Queenie doesn't come out of her shelter to chastise her nearly grown pup.

But I realize that Ginger doesn't need her mother now. Queenie has taught her all she knows. How did Queenie know so well what her pup would need to know? In dogs we call it instinct and say it springs from the womb. In people we call it love and say it springs from the heart. But neither love nor maternal instinct is so automatic as we like to pretend. I've seen dogs who couldn't mother and I've seen people who wouldn't. I myself have loved a baby that wasn't even there!

282

Ginger flings herself against the kennel fence and barks at three big crows hunched in a tree nearby. The birds, huddled close together, don't even look her way and the branch they perch on rocks in the winter wind.

Darcy was right. Love is no trick of the blood. Surely my strange love for this baby that never was holds the promise that in some future circumstance I could love a child that wasn't my own.

Ginger dashes once more to the fence. The crows fan their wings out behind them like long black capes and fly away into the snow. Behind me the whistle on the tea-kettle shrills. When I pour the tea, a warm leafy odor rises. It smells like a wet spring day. I carry the cup on its saucer and stand leaning in the doorway sipping my tea.

The rocking horse seems to stare out the window. Even in the heavy gray light of the storm, its colors are bright. Darcy would have loved to see it there. A long slow wave of longing for him reaches through me. It's a distant stirring, a warning of all the time to come when I'll miss him.

If Darcy had lived, would he have kept on coming to see us? I think he would have. I can picture him coming year after year until I am an old woman alone. And when I think of being alone, I imagine it always alone without a man or a child. It's a funny thing about women like that. A man alone can seem romantic, irrepressible. "Oh, nobody'll ever tame that one," people will say with a smile. But a woman alone only seems unused, superfluous. At the very best, she seems the pitiable end cipher of a subtraction of her loved ones.

I try to picture myself old and alone, a crone on this farm slowly going to seed around me. The weeds high in the garden, the barn slope-roofed and sinking toward the ground. Maybe the children around here would be afraid of me and call me a witch. In the old days, it was mostly women alone who were burned as witches, as if a woman's power must necessarily go for evil if she has no one on whom to spend it.

How do women come to it, this being alone? It seems to me if it's to be anything but a shame to them, they must become one of Darcy's renegades. They have to measure themselves by their own conventions. But where do they begin not to care whether they're pretty or not? Where do they build their self-respect when they are necessary to no one?

The aloneness itself perhaps becomes the seed of pride. If I imagine myself at the end of my life alone, I like to think that I will be a fierce old woman, unapologetic and bound to my own importance. I will dress in rags that fly like flags in the wind and let my hair grow wild. Oh, Hooke's Crossing can all be damned.

I smile to think of it. Darcy would have been my friend forever. We could have been old, two old renegades together.

I set the teacup down and walk into the dining room. The snow is dense now and the wind is still. In this quiet place in this terrible winter, there is a calm as if Darcy left this world gently, as if dreams were forever, as if there are no ends and no beginnings.

I pick up the rocking horse. "Hello," I whisper. Its weight is balanced and delicate in my arms. The odors of cut wood and fresh paint are still strong. Cradling it against my body, I carry it upstairs. At the top of the first flight of steps I set it down to catch my breath. Then I lift the little horse again and take it up to the attic. I pull the light chain and the light swings overhead. I set the rocking horse down.

My breath makes a puff of steam in the air. It's strange, it didn't seem so cold awhile ago. I'm anxious to be gone. Turning quickly, I turn out the light. The last thing I see as I close the door is the little rocking horse, a riderless mount, a steed for Darcy, who would sit astride no doubt, winking and wobbly, a flawed white knight, riding the horse to the moon.

Lilly

TIM is fragile, solemn in a new black suit. Standing at the window in the front room, he pulls aside the curtain. Through the frosty glass, I can see Henry French throw open the door of his undertaker's limousine and advance smartly up our walk. I take a last look into the mirror to adjust this hat I can't imagine ever liking. I've had it since before Aaron died. What a silly woman I must have been to have bought such a fussy hat. Tim looks as though he were standing at attention while he waits for Henry's knock. I step toward him and brush the stiff lapels of his jacket with a gloved hand. His eyes are faraway, the way they are when he daydreams, and I am reluctant to bring him back to the day of his father's funeral.

"It's going to be all right," I say automatically. He nods hardly aware, I think, of the sound of my voice.

There is a sharp rap on the door. "Morning, Lilly," says Henry, soft-voiced and woeful when I open the door, "deepest condolences for your . . ."

"For our loss. Yes, I know, Henry. Thank you. We're ready to go."

As we pass through the door Tim seems to shake himself as though from sleep and comes to walk behind me onto the porch. The sky is leaden, heavy with the snow that must have begun falling soon after Tim and I went to bed. The floor of the porch is slick. Henry, in a surefooted stride, leads the way to the car while Tim and I mince timidly across the wet porch. As we edge along the sidewalk, Jingles runs, barking, from under the porch. His leaps of greeting spatter mud on the hem of my coat and scuff Tim's shined shoes. When the dog catches sight of Henry waiting at the curb, he slinks out of sight under the steps.

"Careful, Gran," Tim cautions, taking my elbow.

When Tim and I step into the limousine, Henry takes his place behind the wheel and the car pulls away from the curb with a self-satisfied surge. Soon we're on the river road headed toward Saint Matthew's. The winter river shines with the dull sheen of wet slate. Moving sluggishly it will be frozen in some of the shallow places near the shore. Snow along the banks from an earlier storm wavers milky and uncertain on the still surface. The naked trees, too much the same gray as the river, barely reflect in the water.

The snow is falling in fat flakes as we round the corner to the church. I almost expect it to make a sound in its heavy wetness. It quivers in a thin layer on the pavement, dusts the graying hills of snow left by the snowplows and smudges the people, the church, the road into vague outlines. Only the hearse parked in front of the church is knife-edged in its implacable blackness.

Tim and I step from the limousine. By an unspoken agreement, we become bolder on the treacherous footing and outdistance Henry who must come from the other side of the car. As we pass the hearse, Tim determinedly avoids looking at it. Yet I . . . I can't take my eyes from it. Darcy, Darcy, my son, my heart. Your life bound me to the future, to the stars. Oh, you dream for your children, not even wanting to . . . almost as an afterthought when they're grown. Dream for them from the first flutter of life you feel in your womb. Dream for them, not knowing them, dreams of success, not knowing them. How often we account for the enormity of our love for our children by some singularity in them. And when they're young, our dreams grow wings that would take them to the sky. In the end, my dreams for Darcy were modest, little more than finger-crossed wishes, not even so grand a dream as I might have had yearning for his happiness. In the end, it was only this . . . some small compromise with his rage to allow him a measure of peace with himself. It never happened, of course, and it would seem that my dreams for my son sustained me better than they did him.

The snow has powdered the roof of the hearse, but the flakes are defeated by the warmth of the hood and bead into small trembling globes on the shiny metal. The pallbearers have come to stand at the rear of the hearse. Three of them are men I do not know from the funeral home. The other three are Jim Atherton, Jeff Maynes, and Ivy's Otis. "Has Ivy mentioned my back problems?" he had said when I asked him to serve as pallbearer. "Why, no, Otis, I don't believe she has," I said, and in the small silence that followed, Otis glanced at Ivy. She sat with her hands folded in her lap, her ankles crossed primly, and she wore an expression I hadn't seen since our childhood arguments. "Oh, well," said Otis, "if you need me, then."

Now Otis separates himself from the pallbearers and comes toward Tim and me. "Ivy will be along shortly," he says and immediately steps back into the company of the other men who all nod briefly in our direction. I shiver in the damp cold and soon feel Tim's hand beneath my arm.

We turn to see the priest standing on the steps of the church. He is a slight man and seems barely older than Tim. The wind catches the skirt of his cassock and presses it around his thin body like a tightly wrapped umbrella.

"Mrs. Blunt, Tim," he says, extending his hand and drawing us through the heavy oak doors of the church. These doors open into a vestibule where we pause. It is a small room, drafty and stuffy at the same time when the doors to the body of the church are closed as they are now. To one side of this room stands a wheeled, metal cart, which I assume will hold the casket.

"God is with you in your sorrow, Tim," says the priest and takes Tim's hand.

"Yes, Father," Tim croaks, and suddenly the room grows smaller as he tries to back away from the priest while keeping a manly grip on his hand.

"Yes, Tim," he says smiling and nodding. Tim nods too. The priest releases his hand.

"Shall we begin?" he asks, turning to me.

"Well, my sister isn't here yet," I say.

"Oh, dear," says the priest glancing at his watch, "I'm so terribly sorry, but we do have a wedding scheduled for noon."

Where is Ivy? I fume. She's always late. We'll begin without her. We must begin. This small room has begun to feel like a jail cell. Raising my hands to my head, I discover my hat knocked askew by the wind. Straightening it with a firm hand, I say, "We'll start then. She can't be long away."

"Just as you wish," says the priest. He sticks his head out the front door.

"We'll begin now," he calls quietly, but his words are carried away by the wind that eddies through the open door. He raises his voice. "We'll begin now." Then he steps back inside. He wheels the strange cart over to stand in front of the doors into the church.

"If you stand there to the side, I think you'll stay warm," he says. "I have to prop these outside doors open."

We can hear shuffling on the steps and through the door, then the head of the coffin emerges shouldered on each side by Jim Atherton and Jeff Maynes. The other men follow with Otis supporting one side of the end.

Jim Atherton glances over at me. His bulldog face has the same look of pained apology he wore the day he came to the house with news of Darcy's death. Jeff, in an ill-fitting suit, walks stiffly. His neck has the raw look of a recent haircut. Otis, struggling with his end of the burden, walks with one oddly crooked hip and he reminds me of a picture in an old nursery rhyme book I had of a man with stovepipe legs. He straightens with a grimace as the casket is slid onto the cart.

The priest opens the door into the church and takes his place behind the casket. Tim and I fall in behind him. As our little procession begins to move up the aisle I look everywhere but at the coffin that seems now to glide by itself on its quiet rubber wheels.

It's been a long time since I've been in Saint Matthew's. The candles on the altar falter and leap, their light dashing up the face of the cross and falling away again. The altar table is hung with the purple of Epiphany. Incense breathes its spicy fragrance in the air and settles over the old church like smoke from ancient fires.

Tim and I hesitate at the end of the aisle. I'm surprised by the number of people here. I hadn't thought there would be anyone but us. Some, like the five old women ranged along the back pew, I might have expected to see. Miss Liza Munson and her friends haven't missed a funeral in town for years. But what about Rudd Burnes, nodding from an aisle seat? I haven't seen him except to say hello to since that last dinner at his house long ago. Cora Carey is here too, but I might have counted on that. She looks more bereaved than I do. That woman enjoys tragedy and that's a fact. Ellen Gibbs is here, looking pale and small in a pew to herself. She turns and lifts one little white-gloved hand to me. Her eyes are swollen and red.

As we pass down the aisle, I hear a faint rustling behind us, people shifting in their seats to stare at us. My face burns and Tim presses against me. I feel him trembling and the cheap serge of his suit is slippery under the pressure of my fingers. The priest has climbed the few steps before the altar and the pallbearers arrange the casket in front of him. Tim and I slide quickly into the middle of the first pew and shrink down a little. The pallbearers take seats across the aisle from us, except Otis who limps over to our pew and sits, with a great distance between us, at the very end. That will give some of those behind us something to talk about.

It's strange that Tim and I even feel those appraising eyes anymore. But I do feel them and I can see Tim drawing into himself, his shoulders hunched, his hands clenched before him. Today those eyes are a rude intrusion into our grief. The memories that some of the others have of Darcy must stain our own, and I turn with a heartening anger to confront the stares. When I turn, I see Ivy standing at the door of the church.

Even in the dull light of the snowy day, her hair flames. With a girlish nimbleness, she kneels deeply and crosses herself. Then she is erect again and moving toward us hurriedly down the aisle. She squeezes past Otis without a word. When she settles into the pew beside me she reaches over me to pat Tim's face. She kisses me wetly on the cheek, whispering, "Are you all right, Lilly?"

I nod. She takes my hand. Her hand is soft and warm and it closes firmly over my own chilled fingers.

The priest stands behind the casket. He seems so eager it looks as if he may clap his hands in anticipation of the Mass. Perhaps this is his first funeral.

We all kneel to pray. I barely hear the words but Tim bows his head earnestly. When we sit back again, he cocks his head attentively, listening, I suppose, for the one sure phrase that will explain the pain of his young life. What will this priest give my young grandson and me to cast into the grave behind Darcy? How can the Church lay him to rest any more honorably than Tim and I did last night sitting at the kitchen table? I don't accept my son's death as a Christian act of faith as the priest instructs. I accept it because I have no choice. And I don't lie down under my loss without anger. Oh, no, I won't call my son's death godly justice as the Church does. I'll only admit my impotence in the face of it.

I rise when Ivy does, or kneel or sit, without listening at all. I lay a hand on Tim's arm. His face is tense and watchful. The enthusiastic young priest places a cloth over the communion box, signs the cross in the air and whips the cloth from the box with such a flourish I half expect a rabbit to pop into view.

The old ladies at the back of the church march single file toward the altar. They fan out along the Communion rail. This Communion at the funeral will substitute for the Communion they take each day at morning Mass. I wonder what great stains on their souls require this daily cleansing.

Communion done, the ladies resume their seats. The priest regards us solemnly, folding his arms across his lean middle as though he fancies himself a larger man. He advises us that Darcy is in God's hands and we mustn't mourn him. His voice is confident when he says this, as though mourning were truly for the dead and not for the living. We all wait expectantly through a short pause while the priest glances at some papers he holds. Then he tells us Darcy is a space traveler embarked on a new adventure. Several people shift uneasily. His voice loses some of its command as he brings Darcy home to God in a rocket ship. Red-faced, he casts about for a suitable ending. At last, "Darcy Emmet Blunt, respected and beloved by all."

Perhaps because we slept so little last night, a surge of giddiness runs through me. Darcy, respected? Well, I suppose so. For those who might take such things into account, he could drink any man in town under the table.

And beloved by all? Yes, that too. Certainly as the favorite specter raised by many an enraged woman in Hooke's Crossing when her husband or son stumbled home late from work or a lodge meeting: "You're going to end up just like Darcy Blunt, mark my words." That's not likely to stop even now.

Respected and beloved by all! How Darcy would have laughed. I steal a glance at Tim. He's bowed stiff-necked in prayer, his clenched hands pressed to his lips. I nudge him, giving him a small secret smile. At the sight of his puzzled face the giddiness overtakes me altogether.

My first muffled giggles could be mistaken for sounds

of grief. Ivy, eyes closed, squeezes my hand. The priest opens one eye that fixes on me soberly. I press my knuckles to my lips, but from somewhere very deep laughter bubbles up. Now there can be no mistake that I am laughing. Ivy looks at me in great concern and Tim seems stunned. The priest stops in midprayer. "I can't stop," I tell Tim desperately. "I have to get out of here." Tim rises, his ears a ferocious red. As I edge past Ivy, I see Otis sitting ramrod straight, his eyes squeezed shut as if he were deep in prayer. His bony knees graze the backs of mine as I push out of the pew.

I try so hard to compose myself for the walk back up the aisle but the laughter goes on welling up and out of my mouth in the dazed silence of the church.

Jim Atherton looks dumbfounded while Jeff Maynes leans around him to catch my eye in a wink. Ellen Gibbs watches us, the tears washing in a mighty rush down her cheeks. Rudd Burnes looks discreetly away. And Cora Carey, why, her mouth just opens and closes like a beached fish. Ivy moves in an ineffectual flutter behind us. As we pass the old ladies in the back pew, they begin to make an excited buzzing like a swarm of dislodged bees. The sound follows us through the heavy doors of the church.

I'm refreshed by the light cold wind that blows the snow in lazy arcs and tugs at the brim of my hat. I clutch my hat to my head. The snow on the sidewalk has accumulated enough for a surer footing. I'm still shaking with laughter and I stagger a few steps past Ivy and Tim.

"Oh, Lilly. Oh, Tim," says Ivy behind me.

"She's hysterical," says Tim indignantly.

"Yes, she must be," says Ivy.

"Should I slap her?" asks Tim.

"No, no," says Ivy. "Oh, dear."

I turn back toward the two of them. They stand in the slowly falling snow, eyeing me helplessly.

"I'm so sorry," I gasp, and at the sight of tears in Ivy's eyes, my laughter stops abruptly. "I want to go home," I say. "Tim, you can stay. Aunt Ivy will stay with you."

I am surprised by the words, surprised even more to know I mean them. I won't go back. I think of the coffin as it lay before the priest. It was long, much longer than my Darcy, and it was heavy, so armored against the enticements of the deep quiet earth that it takes six men to carry one man to his grave. I feel a terrible rage at the emptiness I found in the funeral Mass. The words were men's words to my ears; as if this was merely Hooke's Crossing having the final say on my son.

"Stay if you like," I say again to Tim.

He shakes his head, avoiding my eyes.

"I'm sorry," I say and he says nothing.

"Oh, Tim," Ivy says taking a quick step toward him, her arms outstretched. She loses her footing and rocks precariously like a big ship riding a storm. Tim and I are at her sides in a moment, grasping her elbows. Tim casts me a look of fatalistic terror as we struggle to steady her great bulk. Ivy, catching the look, says when she is firmly righted, "Goodness, Tim, I wouldn't fall on you, honey."

Tim's eyes are wide. He stammers apologetically.

"Don't worry now," she tells him as we begin walking up the street. Tim nods formally and begins to walk away from us. "Lilly!" a distant voice calls behind us. Without looking around, we all quicken our step. I wave whoever calls after us away over my shoulder. We decide to go home through town rather than by the windy river road we took with Henry.

Tim walks ahead of us. The snow flakes light in his hair and twinkle like stars as they melt. He shivers in his new black suit and walks head down. I stare at the slender line of his bare neck. The white flesh there, the closely clipped hair, seem a dangerous exposure, as if the shadow in the indentation just below his skull announced some deadly vulnerability. And I want to rush to him, cover him up, take off my coat perhaps and wrap him up warm as I did when he was a baby. I take a step toward him and then fall back. Oh, he seems as far from me in his latest grief as Darcy does in death. What consolation do I have to offer this child? My solace, it would seem, has been meager indeed, not enough for my husband or my son. Perhaps Tim too, bent under a pain I cannot soothe, will be lost to me in some terrible way. If only, I have thought, if only I could have set the men I loved to rights with the world. I can remember crooning to Darcy as a child, "Everything's going to be all right. It's going to be all right," and believing that I could somehow mend whatever troubled him. But that was a long time ago and the memory comes to me like a dream in which the colors, brighter than life, could break your heart.

The wind gusts and I set my hat squarely atop my head. I pick up my step and tuck my hand through Ivy's arm. She steers us up to Tim and links her other arm through his. "Well," she says to him, "what a time you've had as if you didn't have enough today. First your crazy grandmother and then your fat old aunt nearly falls on her you-know-what."

Tim, his chin sunk on his chest, doesn't look at her.

"No, Ivy," I say peeking around her to glance at Tim, "I don't know what. Tell us."

"Lilly, for heaven's sake, the boy," she says giving my hand a sharp squeeze.

"Say it, Ivy, say it," I say in a singsong voice, an echo from our childhood. "Say it, say it, say it."

Sam Mason passes us on the sidewalk, turns a moment to stare. "Good morning, Sam," I say loudly and he turns away. "Say it, Ivy, I dare you," I goad.

Ivy purses her lips irritably and glares at me. "On my fanny," she says. "There, are you satisfied?" Her cheeks flame.

I look at Tim again. There is a small reluctant smile on his lips.

"Yes," I say, hugging Ivy to me, "I'm satisfied."

"You really are awful, you know that, don't you?" she says.

296

"You really are, Gran," says Tim seriously and his brows lower again over his eyes.

The three of us walk in silence. We pass under the clock in the bank. It is nearly noon. General Hooke doffs his hat as always. I keep patting mine back in place under the light cold breeze. Its velvet brim feels furry between my fingers and I take the hat off. It is small and black and barely covers the top of my head. A poor excuse for a hat. I flip it away with a turn of my wrist like skipping a stone over water and it spins through the air to land in a pile of dirty snow on the courthouse sidewalk. It perches atop the cold mound, its flimsy veil quivering in the wind. Ivy rolls her eyes.

I have a great feeling of heaviness suddenly as though the full weight of Tim's sadness has settled over my heart. Tim and Ivy are right, I am awful to add to his pain. I suppose I had thought to lift him on my own foolish laughter, to move him beyond the gossip, beyond the unkind stares, beyond the shame of being the son of the town drunk. If I could do as I chose, I would, with every bit of bravery or faith I ever knew, will his importance into his own hands. Ah, but I am tired now, tired, spent, used up to the bone. It seems as if we have been walking for a very long time and I feel the chill of the snow through my shoes.

We turn the corner onto Broad Street. The day is dark and some of the windows of the houses are lit. The curtains must flutter, the shades lift as Tim, Ivy, and I walk by. Within hours, the whole town will have heard the story of the scene at the church. Our house, standing at a distance, is dark, its shabby face a smirk amid the tidiness of the neighborhood.

When we reach the house, we all hesitate. Then I open the door and we all step inside, inviting the dog in after us. The front hall is dark in the winter afternoon and cold. The furnace has quit again. Perhaps it is only the chill of the house, but our sadness seems to reside here with the permanence of a member of the family and I am chastened further. I long to go back to the moments outside the church when my laughter echoed against the storefronts of Hooke's Crossing, rang among the staid old houses, danced like the whirling flakes of snow. "Damned old furnace," Tim mutters peevishly at my elbow.

We go into the kitchen where Ivy begins to make a pot of coffee. I find my knees are aching from the cold walk. I light the oven and leave the door open for warmth. We all keep our coats on and the dog, searching out the warmest place in the room, lies down under the oven door. Tim goes upstairs to change his wet shoes.

"Won't you see him buried, Lilly?" Ivy says in a low voice when Tim has left. She fills the coffeepot with water.

"Of course I will," I snap, "just not now."

"We should go back right now," she says. She sets the coffeepot on the stove with a clatter and turns on the heat.

"No." I get a blue bowl out of the cupboard and begin measuring flour into it for muffins. As Ivy opens her mouth again to speak, the phone in the hall rings and she goes to answer it.

"Hello, Father" she says nervously. "Yes, just let me call Mrs. Blunt to the phone.

"I'm not, Ivy," I call to her from the kitchen. Holding the receiver out, she trains her most commanding look on me. In fact she looks a lot like Mother when she was brooking no nonsense.

"You better tell him I'm in the john or something because I'm not coming to the phone."

Ivy claps her hand over the receiver and turns her back to me. She speaks quietly to the priest. "Yes, hysteria, so sad. Really, it's been all we could do. Yes, yes, as soon as she's able."

My back is to Ivy when she returns to the kitchen. "Well, there's your dirty work done for you," she says.

"Thank you, dear," I say very pleasantly and Ivy, rubbing her arms, begins to pace around the room.

I know she's waiting for me to talk to her but I don't. She wants me to defend myself and there is some clear thinking part of my mind that decides, yes, I will turn this minute and start back to the church to finish what must be done. But I go on making the muffins, cracking the eggs into the bowl and stirring, testing the grainy bite of the batter with my finger. I go on doing these things as if my body were set only on this course and I had no choice. I press a lump out of the batter with the spoon, add a pinch more sugar and it suddenly seems to me that all of life is like this . . . going through the simplest motions while something great and terrible has gone wrong. If I had attended to grander schemes, if I had, like Evelyn, run to the top of some hill and demanded answers from the stars, would I have been prepared to bury my son? Where is the God of my last days?

There was the God of Saint Matthew's turning the sorrows of the world on the pivot of evil in the human heart. Oh, my sins are many, I know. But perhaps they have been too long confessed and that God is gone from me. And as for a sorrowing God who seeks to console us with gifts large and small, I believe I saw that God in the bright blue sky just the other day and it struck me then that all of us are lost already in the pitying glare of that great blue distant eye.

I have a sudden longing to stand by the river as if God begins there. On a cloudy day the thin gray line between the water and the sky disappears. Then the river seems to flow upward and the sky pours down into the river-bed joining the earth in a towering silver wheel. And when I was a child, I thought that God must slide down from heaven on just such a day and enter the earth through the open door of the river.

Ivy stops behind me. "This isn't right, Lilly," she frets.

"For crying out loud, Ivy," I explode, "I know plenty about laying the dead to rest. I don't need any advice from you."

Behind me, Ivy settles into a chair with a furious rustle to her skirts. Tim returns to the kitchen as I'm finishing up the muffins. Batter folds like fat yellow ribbons down into the cups of the muffin tin. Tim sits down at the table and I slip the muffins into the oven. When I push the oven door closed, it shuts with a clang and sends the dog scuttling to Tim in fright. Tim, his face drawn and pale, strokes the animal's head absently.

Soon the odor of the muffins fills the room. The coffee is brewed and we are all silent sitting at the table, warming our hands around the hot cups. The furnace announces its revival with a muffled roar, making us all smile.

When the muffins are done, we eat and make an effort at conversation.

"There's going to be a new state road," says Ivy, "right through Lester Haney's farm. That's what I heard."

"Good," says Tim, "it won't take so long to get to school."

"Or to Glen Green," I add. The room is heating rapidly. The furnace always atones for its lapses by throwing out extra gusts of hot air. We take our coats off.

"Wouldn't it just be something if they moved the county seat back to Hooke's Crossing?" Ivy muses.

"That would sure give this old town something to talk about," I say.

"There'll be plenty to talk about in town, thanks to you, Lilly. Cora Carey will see to that. Notoriety just seems to attach itself to this poor family."

"Oh, let them talk," I say impatiently. "Where do you suppose Otis got to?"

"Oh," says Ivy with a sigh, "I expect he just went on home."

We are all silent for a moment, staring down at the table. Then Tim lifts his head. "Hey, Gran, hey," he says, "if we just keep it up I bet we'll be 'respected and beloved by all' just like Daddy was."

The laughter of today returns to me. Ivy lends a fine

contralto to the chorus and Tim laughs the hardest of all. And in his laughter, I catch a glimpse of a God of the river. This is a God of no priests, no wrath. A God of no head or hands or heart. A God who lives in the world like its breath and takes my son into the earth as if there were no other way, as if the whole universe had unfurled along a thousand paths to come to the moment of his death. This is a God of no malice and no gifts. But I am not afraid, no, even if we are human only by some undesigned collision of events. For now, there's faith enough for me in finding the human heart composed in such a way that I am comforted by so small a working of the world as a boy's laugh!

"Tim, you are a rare bird," I say rising. I walk around to his chair and hold his head against my heart for a moment. The fuzz of his new beard is silky beneath my fingers.

"Are you warm now?" I ask stepping away.

"Yes."

"Then I suppose we should go back."

He nods and Ivy rises. She fusses with her dress and pinches color into her cheeks.

"I wonder what we should tell everybody," says Ivy adjusting her hat.

And Tim, drawing his coat from the back of the chair, says, "We'll think of something along the way."

Ellen

I am picking my way through the snow in my high heels. My shoes leave small pointed tracks like deer hooves. The snow blurs my vision and I can't look too far ahead. And when I turn the snow has already gathered so thickly in the air that the church has vanished behind me. What a strange day this has been, beginning in the woods this morning and leading just now into the oddity of Darcy's funeral. I had hardly cried at the church until Lilly Blunt's laughter rang out. The sound seemed to career wildly in the big vaulted room and it reminded me of birds that had gone battering about frantically in the rafters of my own church when the doors had been left open on a summer day. When I heard her laugh, I thought that Darcy must have loved her very much and that made me cry.

There was such confusion in the church after she and her sister and her grandson had left. The priest threw his hands up and his eyes were wide with apology as if their leaving were something he should have anticipated and prepared for. Henry French sat looking from the front to the back of the church as if he couldn't quite believe what he had seen.

"Well," said the priest searching our faces for some clue to his dilemma, "I guess we'll take care of this later. That would be the thing to do, I suppose." He came down from the pulpit, stepping around the casket sitting at the head of the aisle like a guest who has stayed to the point of embarrassment. When the priest was gone all the rest of us filed out one by one.

"Oh, I wonder what will happen now?" I said to Jeff as we stood for a moment outside the church.

"I don't know," said Jeff, "but I'm glad she did it."

"I wish it was me that had done it," I said, tears sliding in icy trickles over my cheeks. "I wish I'd known to send him off that way."

Jeff took my hand and tucked it into the pocket of his coat. "Did Darcy ever tell you I might be getting married?" he asked.

"No."

He had been studying my face worriedly. Then suddenly he turned his gaze upward as if the dizzy swirl of snowflakes had just caught his attention. "Yeah, I believe I might," he said squinting into the sky, "but I wanted to tell you if you ever need anything, like your car fixed or anything, you know where you can find me."

"Thank you, Jeff," I said and he released my hand. We walked silently to the end of the street where Jeff turned off with a wave.

I only have two blocks to walk after I leave Jeff but the snow is deep enough now to fill my shoes and it seems a long way to go. I can see my house now. The living-room windows are lighted against the gloom of the day. My father will be watching television. At this time of day, it will be old movies or films of men hauling man-sized fish out of the water in some warm climate. My mother will be moving around the house somewhere, straightening, cleaning.

When I am near the driveway, I stop to draw a deep breath. My heart beats quickly now. I walk around to the back door, leaving a dark trail through the fresh snow. The back steps are slippery and I climb them slowly. When I step through the back door, the sudden warmth brings a flush to my face and I hurry to take off my coat. The harsh odor of bleach is in the air and Mama stands by the sink, her hands immersed in soapy water. Some of my father's white socks lie in a wet pile on the drainboard.

"Hi, Mama," I say hanging my coat on the back of a chair.

"Hello," she says without turning. Her wrists slip quickly in and out of sight as she scrubs the socks.

"Mama, I have to talk to you," I say. "It's important."

She turns to me for a moment and then begins scrubbing again. "Don't drip on my clean floor," she says. "Put your shoes out back."

I sit down at the table to take my shoes off. "Mama, listen. . . ."

"How was the funeral?"

"It was strange. I'll tell you later."

"You look terrible," says Mama and her hands rest in the water. "Is it so serious you couldn't tell me when you came home this morning?"

"There wasn't time."

"Well."

"I don't even know how to tell you." I pull off my shoes and small chunks of snow fall wetly to the floor.

Mama purses her lips. "If you will wipe that up, please, and then you should put something warm on your feet."

"Mama, I have to talk to you."

"Well, then talk," she says scrubbing now with great energy. "Don't drive me crazy. Are you pregnant?"

I feel the blood rise in my face. "Mama!" I cry.

"Are you?" she insists and plunges more socks into the steamy water.

"No."

"What, then?"

"Mama wait. . . ."

"Just say it, will you? Don't drive me crazy. You always drive me crazy."

"If I could start in my own way, it would be easier."

"Will it be easier for me?" Mama turns and faces me squarely. She wipes her hands on a towel. There is an odd look to her face. There is a finely controlled anger and there is the sadness that has settled in her face since my brother's death. I suppose her unshed tears for Bip will slide in secret sorrow along the lines around her eyes, beside her mouth forever. But worse than the sorrow is the fear that flickers for an instant in her eyes as if she were afraid she cannot bear whatever I have to tell her. And although she draws so quickly in upon herself that I could doubt I ever saw the fear, my resolve is shaken by the lapse of will that allowed me to see it at all. Would I dare to hurt her at all knowing that she could even imagine some failure of strength in herself? The words I have to tell her catch in a tight knot in my throat.

"Well?" she says and now she seems fully recovered, standing with her hands on her hips.

I can't look at her and stare down at the floor where my shoes sit primly side by side, the toes pointing straight ahead. The snow I brought in has melted into tiny gray puddles on the shiny linoleum.

"I'm not going to marry David," I whisper.

"What?" she says not hearing me.

"I'm not going to marry David." Our eyes meet for a moment and then she wheels and plunges her hands again into the wash water. She lifts two socks from the water and examines them in the light of the window.

"They didn't come so clean," she says. "Maybe I should wash them again. What do you think?"

I am silent. She scrutinizes the socks closely and says softly, "Who will have you, then?" as if she were talking to the socks.

I think for a moment she has made a joke. So strange. Perhaps Mama's heart is light under her long silences after all.

"Who will have you, then?" she repeats turning now to look at me.

"What do you mean?" My heart is beating wildly.

"All those men, Ellen, all those men."

"Mama, I don't know what you're talking about."

"All those men in your bed."

308

My ears are buzzing now and I hear my own voice at a distance. "How did you find out?"

"Oh, people are always glad to tell you such things. I figured it out from hints," she says.

"Does Daddy know?" I ask in a whisper.

"No," she says and leans toward me conspiratorially as if it has been she and I together all along who have guarded Daddy from the terrible secret. "If anyone says anything to him, he would never put things together. You know how it is, nobody ever says it right out."

"How long have you known, Mama?"

"Long enough," she says curtly.

"Why didn't you ever say anything before?"

My mother's face seems to empty of all expression. She stands looking at me, her arms hugged around her waist.

"It's only just now that I am sure," she answers. Her voice breaks and then there are tears in her eyes, streaming down her cheeks. I have never seen my mother cry. Not when Grandpa died. Not even when Bip died.

"Oh, Mama," I say, tears hot on my own face, "I'm so sorry."

"Don't feel sorry for me, missy. Nobody ever feels sorry for me. Grandpa used to say nobody ever thinks a big man needs help even when he's old and as frail as any little old man, nobody even thinks of it. Something in me, nobody ever feels sorry and that's just as well."

"Mama . . ." I say and the distance between us looms as she stands by the sink.

"So what will you do now?"

"I think I have to go away."

"Ach!"

"Not far. Listen, Mama, just over to Gatonsville maybe so I won't have so far to go to work. I could come to see you all the time. Every day if you want."

"No," she says. Her tears are dry but her chest heaves as she crosses her arms.

"Mama, you thought I would be leaving when I married David."

"It's not the same," she snaps and I feel my courage flag.

"What should I do, then, Mama?" My voice is so faint I think she won't even hear me. There is a long silence while Mama gazes out the window. Then her shoulders sag with a long sigh. "You should do what you think you should do," she says.

"Don't be sad, Mama, please," I say rising. We stand facing each other.

"How can I help it? This way I think you are going away when my work is only half done." She turns her head. "Just like Bip."

"Mama, I'm twenty-three," I say, and I feel the tears begin sliding from under my lids.

"Yes, I know you think that's very old, very grown-up. Here," she says handing me a handkerchief she has pulled from her apron pocket.

"It's your father," she says with a sigh as the hand-kerchief passes between us. "He'll miss you so much. You must promise to come often." She steps back and leans against the sink.

"I promise," I say wiping my eyes. The handkerchief is still warm from resting in Mama's pocket.

"Maybe on Wednesdays you could come for dinner and that silly show he likes on television."

"I will, Mama. On Wednesdays. I promise."

"Well, that's settled, then," she says briskly. "Will you tell your father today?"

"I want to."

"Will you tell him only about David? Leave your going away for another day. He's not like he used to be."

"All right," I say. I hear the swish of water in the sink as I turn to leave the kitchen.

In the living room the television casts blue patterns on the wall and plays to no one. My father sleeps in his chair.

"Daddy?" I say softly. He opens his eyes and smiles when he sees me.

310

"Hi, honey, I'm just resting my eyes for a minute." I laugh. It's an old joke between us.

"You didn't go to the store today?" I ask.

"No, I left Billy there. There won't be much business today with the snow."

"I guess not."

A silence falls in which he watches me expectantly. I sit down in a chair next to him and fold my hands. "Can we talk?" I say.

He yawns and pats his hair. "Of course, honey. You know you can always talk to your old dad." He is eager and sits forward in his chair. I think again how lonely he must be for Bip's company. On the television, three men on horses ride across the screen.

"Daddy, I don't want to marry David."

With a small fixed smile on his lips, he studies my face. "Have you told your mother?"

"Yes."

"Hmmm," he says nodding. He stares into space for a moment, then says, "I think what we have here is just a little case of cold feet. It happens to everybody. David is a wonderful young man."

"I've made up my mind, Daddy." And my father and I seem adrift in a boat that dips end to end with each thing we say.

"He's such a wonderful young man," Daddy repeats.

"I don't love him, Daddy."

"Then you mustn't marry him," he says as if he were thinking of something else. He stares down at the floor. On the television, a woman with a big painted mouth sings about hair tonic.

"Daddy?"

"Yes."

"I'm sorry."

He snaps to attention and turns. "Don't be sorry, Ellen. It's better to come to these things before marriage. It's much better that way."

He looks at me for a while and I'm frozen under his gaze, aching to comfort him. He reaches out and touches my cheek gently with his fingertips. "When you're young," he says, "you have the world by the tail, don't you?"

"I guess."

"Yes, I remember. Not knowing how your life will turn out, you think you might do anything . . . act on the stage, go to Egypt, anything."

"You still might do those things, Daddy."

"I don't guess so, honey," he says and drops his hand to the arm of the chair. "Can you see your mother in Egypt? She'd be dusting the pyramids." We laugh quietly together.

"Don't get me wrong. I wouldn't change my life . . . except for some things I said to Bip. But you know, I had Mama and you kids. I loved you and Bip the minute I saw you, you and the Bipper. Those were the best moments of my life, like I'd done something great, greater"—he lifts his hands—"greater than acting on television," he says and two men on the screen fight without losing their hats.

I can picture my father as a young man seeing Bip or me for the first time. I can see him full of his old bluster peering through the glass of the nursery and from all the tiny strangers there folded in on themselves like new leaves he would pick his own out. And it seems to me that Daddy's love for us began in some recognition of the best in himself rather than anything in Bip or me. He loved us at the beginning not knowing us and he still loved us the same way.

"You've never disappointed me, Ellen," he says, "and Bip, well, I always loved him. Do you think he knew?"

"I'm sure of it, Daddy," I say and he squeezes my hand.

The picture on the television begins to roll slowly. A man's head disappears at the bottom of the screen just as it reappears at the top. Daddy leans forward and adjusts the set. The talking face comes to rest as Daddy and I sit back in our chairs to wait for the movie to begin again.

312

"I wish you did love David," he says wistfully.

"I do too, Daddy," I say and we both smile ruefully. Then we turn to watch the television as a man on a horse crests a high hill.

I think of Bip. He is never still for me. In my mind, he rides joyous and strong on his motorcycle. He rides as fast as he ever dared to go, the wind cool as river water over his face. He rides and rides and rides free and fearless in some everlasting silent night. And that, it seems to me, is how it should be.

Oh, grief is like death in the heart and if we are to begin again, we lay our dead to rest in different ways. And if I could call upon the stars and touch the earth in prayer, I would wish for Darcy, now that he is gone, that it is warm and dark there in the ground and that the nearby river resounds like a heartbeat for only the dead to hear. And I would ask that Darcy in the secrecy of death might be given in that great pulsing a promise that he too would somehow begin again.

About the Author

Annie Greene lives in rural Maryland with her husband and three children and is at work on a second novel.